Edge Of Desire

A Novel

by
Zara Moné

ISBN: 979-8-9993059-1-6

Table Of Content

Chapter 1: Shattered Foundation   5

Chapter 2: Fractured Ties   9

Chapter 3: Resurfaced Pain   12

Chapter 4: The House on the Hill   17

Chapter 5: Choices and Consequences   21

Chapter 6: Family Shadows   25

Chapter 7: Buried Secrets   38

Chapter 8: What We Bury   48

Chapter 9: Collateral Damage   56

Chapter 10: Miami   66

Chapter 11: A Night to Remember   77

Chapter 12: The Man Behind the Mask   87

Chapter 13: Aftermath and Reflection   96

Chapter 14: Confronting Betrayal   105

Chapter 15: Curiosity and Temptation   116

Chapter 16: Uncharted Territory   125

Chapter 17: A Family Divided   133

Chapter 18: A Forbidden Triangle   142

Chapter 19: Unveiled Desires   150

Chapter 20: A Lazy Day   158

Chapter 21: Between Two Worlds   166

Chapter 22: The First Door   174

Chapter 23: The Upper Level   181

Chapter 24: Angel's Reckoning   188

Chapter 25: Shared Secrets   197

Chapter 26: Crossroads   204

Chapter 27: Entangled Passions   211

Chapter 28: Discovery   218

Chapter 29: The Reckoning   225

Chapter 30: Healing Begins   234
Chapter 31: Rebuilding Trust   241
Chapter 32: New Beginnings   247
Chapter 33: The Letter   254
Epilogue   261

Chapter 1: Shattered Foundation

April Jones adjusted her crimson blouse, the fabric hugging her slender frame as she turned to face the full-length mirror. At 5'9", her reflection displayed a hard-won confidence—not just in her appearance, but in the deliberate way she carried herself. Her long hair, still damp and silken, cascaded down her back. She reached for the dryer, setting it to cool, and after a moment of meticulous styling, she let her natural waves fall free. She was dabbing vanilla-scented lotion onto her hands to soothe her nerves when her phone buzzed on the dresser.

"Hey, baby," she answered, her tone instinctively playful.

"How about joining me at a party tonight?" The voice on the other end was deep and inviting.

"Hmm... what kind of party are we talking about?" she teased, already mentally scanning her closet.

"Make it sexy but classy," he replied with a chuckle. "You've got this. I'll pick you up at ten."

April grinned, setting the phone down just as the opening chords of Tupac's *"Dear Mama"* filled the room.

"Good morning, Mom," she said, her voice softening as she picked up a second, incoming call. Her mother's voice sounded warm but tired.

"Are you coming over for dinner tonight? Your dad and I miss you."

"Not tonight, but maybe tomorrow," April replied. "Love you, Mom."

She had barely hung up before a third call vibrated through. A vibrant, unmistakable voice shouted, "Hey, girl! What happened to you last night?"

April laughed. "Long story, but tonight I'm going to a party with Josh. I'll call you tomorrow to spill all the tea."

After silencing her phone, she sank onto the bed. The day stretched ahead of her, a volatile mix of anticipation and unease. A long nap and a shopping excursion later, she returned home with far more than she had intended: five dresses, three pairs of shoes, and a new purse that matched none of them. She slipped into a bath, the warm water easing the tension in her limbs. As the bubbles rose around her, her mind drifted back to her teenage years—that bittersweet knot of innocence and the decisions she could never take back.

At fifteen, April had been the envy of her high school. With her emerald-green eyes and a figure that turned heads, she had quickly learned the power her appearance held. But admiration invited malice. She had often found herself the target of girls like Rebecca, who masked their jealousy with sharp words and public taunts. April remembered one afternoon in particular when Rebecca had bumped into her in the hallway, scattering April's books across the floor.

"Watch where you're going, slut," Rebecca had sneered, her laughter echoing down the corridor.

April's emerald eyes had narrowed. "Touch me again, and you'll regret it," she had hissed, her voice low and dangerous, before walking away. She was not one to back down.

It was later that same day when Andre Ferguson, the school's golden boy, caught her off guard. With effortless charm and a smile that could light any room, he had slipped her a note asking her to the senior dance. It should have been a moment of pure joy, but the weight of her home life darkened the excitement. Her father, perpetually intoxicated and indifferent, made their house a battlefield. April spent her life avoiding his leering eyes and inappropriate remarks, seeking refuge in the few places that offered solace.

One of those places, however, had been an unexpected and troubling escape. Her memories drifted to her fateful encounters with Mr. Daley, the eccentric neighbor. What began as a chance meeting had turned into a secret arrangement that filled her pockets but left her drowning in shame. She hated herself for returning to his house, yet desperation and a longing to escape her circumstances drove her toward choices her young heart couldn't reconcile.

Snapping back to the present, April shivered in the now-cool bathwater. The clock read 8:45 PM.

"Damn," she muttered, rushing to dry off.

She chose a sleek, mid-thigh black dress and heels that accentuated the length of her legs. A hint of diamond jewelry completed the look. When Josh arrived at her door, looking effortlessly handsome in a tailored shirt and jeans, she smiled.

"Ready?" he asked, holding out a small blue box. Her breath caught as she opened it to reveal a Tiffany bracelet.

"It's beautiful," she whispered, leaning in to kiss him.

The party's opulence was overwhelming. The mansion, with its grand Victorian architecture and lush grounds, seemed a world away from the struggling neighborhood just across the street. Inside, the air was thick with the scent of roses and jasmine. Guests wandered through elaborately themed rooms: one resembling Mount Olympus, another the gates of heaven, and a third the depths of hell.

Josh led her toward the Greek-themed room, where actors dressed as gods offered them drinks and exotic fruits. April hesitated, then indulged, her nerves melting as she sipped the sweet nectar. The atmosphere was intoxicating—a blur of music, laughter, and whispered promises.

As the night unfolded, April found herself lost in the revelry. Couples and groups indulged their desires openly, the boundaries of societal norms dissolving within the mansion walls. When Josh disappeared into the crowd, leaving her to wander, her senses heightened. She found herself drawn to a striking figure—a man with broad shoulders and piercing eyes that seemed to see straight through her. Their brief exchange of glances ignited a primal connection she couldn't explain.

Eventually, April went looking for Josh, but the sight that greeted her shattered the night's illusion. He wasn't alone. The intimacy he shared with another left her breathless—not with desire, but with the cold sting of betrayal. Heart pounding, April fled the room, her heels echoing against the marble floors. The party's glamour blurred into a garish smear as she stumbled into the night air, grappling with the weight of what she had witnessed. The reality of her life, her choices, and her relationships crashed over her like a tidal wave.

Chapter 2: Fractured Ties

Josh caught sight of her as she reached the doorway and jogged over, his smile wide and seemingly oblivious to her fury. "Hey, beautiful! Sorry I slipped away. I had to take care of some business with a friend," he said, his voice warm as he leaned in for a kiss.

April stepped back, her stomach churning. "Don't touch me," she spat, her voice trembling with rage.

Confused, Josh tilted his head. "What's wrong? Did something—"

Before he could finish, her fist flew, landing squarely on his nose with a sickening crunch. The cartilage gave way, blood streaming down his face as he stumbled back, clutching the injury. The room seemed to pause, the whispers around them growing into a roar. April turned on her heel, the fire of betrayal burning in her chest as she stormed out. She didn't look back, not even as she heard Josh's muffled cries of pain.

Outside, the cool autumn air stung her face, but it did little to soothe her. "I can't believe him!" she hissed to herself, her breath coming in short, furious bursts. The suburban neighborhood blurred past as she walked, her thoughts spiraling into a toxic mix of anger and self-loathing. *How could I have been so stupid?*

Lost in the noise of her own mind, she crossed into unfamiliar territory. The neatly trimmed hedges and pristine sidewalks gave way to cracked pavement and dimly lit streets. A single, flickering streetlamp illuminated three hooded figures standing silently on the corner, their faces obscured. They stood perfectly still, watching.

April didn't notice them at first. But as the chilly wind teased a shiver from her spine, she looked up and froze. The men hadn't moved, but their presence sent a primal chill through her. Her instincts screamed at her to leave. She turned to retrace her steps, but when she glanced over her shoulder, the figures were following her.

Her heart raced. Their footsteps matched hers—slow and deliberate, each pace closing the distance. Panic set in. She quickened her speed, her heels clicking sharply against the concrete, the sound echoing like a countdown in the empty streets.

Suddenly, she collided with a solid frame. The impact halted her retreat, and her breath caught in her throat. "Sorry, I didn't mean—" she began, but the words died as she saw the hood obscuring his face. The other two men closed in behind her. Her breath came in short gasps; the cold air felt too thin to fill her lungs. Her hands trembled as she tried to think, but fear clouded her logic.

April made her move. Without a word, she broke into a sprint, pushing past the man in front of her. Her heels skidded on the pavement, but she kept running, her heart pounding against her ribs. She didn't dare look back.

After what felt like an eternity, she slowed, her lungs burning. She bent over, hands on her knees as she gasped for air, her legs trembling with exhaustion. But as she straightened, she realized she was even further from anything familiar. The streetlights were dimmer here, and the shadows stretched into long, grasping fingers.

Before she could catch her breath, a hand clamped around her waist, yanking her back. April screamed, but a palm slammed over her mouth, muffling the sound. She twisted and kicked, her fight instinct taking over, but her captor held her fast. Her eyes darted up, desperate to see his face. His hood slipped just enough for her to catch a glimpse of his features.

Her breath hitched. It was *him*—the man from the party. The one she had watched and fantasized about. His dark, piercing eyes bore into hers, and a smirk tugged at his lips. Her body went stone-cold. Fear and disbelief warred within her as the other two men appeared at his sides. Their lecherous grins were suffocating.

Adonis leaned in close, his breath warm against her ear. "Did you think you could run from me?" he whispered.

April struggled harder, but his grip only tightened. Before she could scream again, a cloth bag was pulled over her head. Darkness swallowed her as strong hands lifted her off the ground, carrying her away.

April awoke to a pounding headache. The air was cold and stale; her wrists and ankles ached. She tried to move, but rough ropes held her in place, cutting into her skin. Panic surged as she realized she was gagged, her voice silenced.

Footsteps echoed in the distance. Her heart thudded in time with the approaching sound. A door creaked open, and the faint, expensive scent of cologne filled her senses. She knew that scent. His presence was commanding, his steps deliberate as he entered the room. April strained against her restraints, her muffled cries filling the dark space.

"You've been quite the troublemaker," he said, his voice smooth yet menacing. "But don't worry—we'll teach you obedience."

She thrashed harder, her muffled screams growing louder, but Adonis only chuckled. "You can fight all you want, but it won't change anything." He crouched beside her, his fingers brushing slowly against her cheek. "Tonight, you're mine."

April's vision blurred as tears streamed down her face. She shook her head, silently pleading for mercy, but Adonis merely smiled. "You'll learn," he said, standing. His voice echoed as he gave his accomplices instructions, their laughter low and chilling.

Hours passed, or perhaps only minutes—it was impossible to tell. The darkness, the fear, and the suffocating sense of helplessness weighed on her like lead. Each time she tried to struggle, she was met with silence or a firm hand holding her still. When they finally left her alone, her body ached from the strain of resisting. Tears soaked the gag as she cried herself into exhaustion, her mind reeling.

She thought of her mother, of her friends, and of the choices that had led her here. *If only she had gone home tonight.*

Chapter 3: Resurfaced Pain

The warmth of the sun woke April, but the splitting headache and aching muscles immediately grounded her in a brutal reality. Every movement was a struggle against the stiffness in her limbs, but she managed to limp toward a crate near the warehouse door. A note was taped to its side, the words biting through her fragile state: *Good job last night. You are now free to become your true self.* Her hands shook as she crumpled the paper and threw it aside, forcing her focus onto the exit. When she pushed the heavy door open, the blinding sunlight hit her like a physical blow. She took one shaky step forward, the world spinning on its axis, before she collapsed onto the concrete sidewalk.

When she woke again, she was greeted by sterile white walls and the rhythmic, hollow beeping of a hospital monitor. A nurse's concerned face hovered above her. "You're awake," the woman said softly.

April didn't answer. She simply pulled the thin hospital covers tighter around her chin, the weight of a profound, suffocating shame pressing down on her chest.

Ignoring medical advice to rest, April signed herself out against orders and hailed a cab. The ride was a blur of silence, the city buzzing around her with an indifference that felt like mockery. The moment she stepped through her front door, she bolted for the bathroom and retched. Tears streamed down her face as she crouched over the tile, her body wracked with jagged, uncontrollable sobs.

She drew a bath, but the hot water felt like scalding needles against her skin. She welcomed the pain; it was a distraction from the images flashing behind her eyelids. Sinking into the tub, she stared blankly at the ceiling light, her mind a fragmented reel of the warehouse. Closing her eyes was out of the question—the fear of reliving those hours kept her awake until her eyes burned. Later, wrapped in a towel and clutching a bottle of sleeping pills, she sank into bed. The medication finally dulled the spiraling thoughts just enough to pull her into a fitful, heavy sleep.

***

April woke feeling more hollow than when she'd fallen asleep. The clock read past eleven. She was three hours late for work, but the office felt like a lifetime away—an impossibility. She pulled the duvet over her head, letting the twin waves of guilt and fear wash over her.

Her phone vibrated incessantly on the nightstand. Missy Elliott's "One Minute Man" alternated with Tupac's "Dear Mama," the contrasting vibes creating a maddening cacophony. She knew it was Angel and her mother calling, but she couldn't bring herself to answer. The weight of her choices—and the violations of the past twenty-four hours—felt too heavy to carry into a conversation.

When she finally emerged in the late afternoon, April began a frantic purging of her apartment. Everything tied to Josh—the silk shirts she'd bought him, the designer shoes, the tailored suits—went into a donation box. "At least the homeless will get some use out of his lies," she muttered, shoving the last of his belongings out of sight.

She put on *The Miseducation of Lauryn Hill*, hoping the soulful melodies would act as an anchor. Cleaning became her penance, each scrub of the tub or sweep of the floor an attempt to erase the lingering shadows of the warehouse. But her mind betrayed her, drifting back to the dark. A sudden shiver coursed through her, and she sank to the floor, clutching her knees until the tremors stopped.

Eventually, she powered on her phone to find fifteen voicemails. Josh's frantic apologies were deleted without a second thought. Her mother's reminder about the upcoming family barbecue brought a small, flickering warmth to her chest, but it was Angel's messages that pulled her back from the edge.

She called her mother first. "Hey, Mom," she said, her voice sounding thin and brittle.

"April? You don't sound right. What's going on?"

"I broke up with Josh," April lied, leaning into the convenient excuse. "I just... I need some time to process everything."

"Well, thank the Lord you're finally done with him. But don't you dare forget about the reunion this weekend! Bring the ribs and chicken, and don't worry about the rest. You know how the men in this family eat!"

April managed a weak, watery laugh. "I'll be there. Love you, Mom."

Angel picked up on the first ring. "Chica! I've been vibrating out of my skin! What happened at the party? Spill everything."

April hesitated, then the dam broke. She told Angel everything in halting, broken sentences. Her friend listened in a rare, heavy silence, her usual playful tone replaced by a somber, protective gravity.

"I'm coming over," Angel declared. Before April could protest, the line went dead.

Angel arrived like a whirlwind, pulling April into a tight, grounding embrace. "I'm here," she said firmly. They spent the evening in the trenches of trauma—talking, laughing through tears, and numbing the edges with wine and old movies.

As the night wore on, a strange, heavy warmth settled between them. When Angel leaned in to kiss her cheek, their eyes met, and something unspoken—something that had been simmering under the surface of their friendship—ignited. April's heart raced, but the timing felt like a betrayal of her own healing.

"We shouldn't," she whispered, breaking the gaze.

Angel nodded slowly, a soft, understanding smile touching her lips as she retreated to her side of the bed. "Good night, Chica."

The next morning, April was gone before the sun was fully up. She left a note on the counter: *I don't know what happened last night, but we shouldn't go there. Make yourself at home and lock the door when you leave. Love, April.* Angel stared at the note, the paper trembling in her hand. Their friendship felt like glass now—beautiful, but dangerously close to shattering.

April returned to work, desperate for the mundane to save her, but the office was suffocating. Charles, her most loathsome coworker, cornered her in the elevator. His leering smile made her skin crawl. When he leaned in with a crude comment, April didn't flinch. She looked him dead in the eye and delivered a flat lie: "I'm gay, Charles. Move."

His stunned silence lasted just long enough for her to escape. But the relief was short-lived. A plain manila envelope sat on her desk with no return address. Inside was a single disc.

Dread pooled in her stomach as she slid it into her computer. The screen flickered to life, and the nightmare from the warehouse began to play. It was high-definition, clinical, and devastating. She ejected the disc, her hands shaking so violently she nearly dropped it, and locked it in her desk drawer. Someone had been watching. Someone had recorded her soul breaking.

By lunch, she was meeting Angel at a secluded café. April shoved the envelope across the table. "I have to know what happened," she whispered, her voice hitching. "I was blindfolded. I don't know who they were, or why they did this..."

Angel looked visibly shaken but reached across the table to squeeze April's hand. "We'll find out. Together."

They left the café with more questions than answers. But as Angel walked back to her own apartment later that evening, the feeling of being hunted intensified. The shadows on the stairwell seemed to move. Before she could reach her door, strong arms wrapped around her. A cloth, sweet-smelling and chemical, was pressed over her mouth. As her vision faded, she looked up into a pair of deep brown eyes that felt hauntingly familiar.

April tried calling Angel hours later, but the calls went straight to voicemail. When someone finally answered, it wasn't Angel. It was a man, his voice a chilling, distorted rasp that froze the blood in April's veins.

"Lady Pain, your services are needed. Come back to the warehouse."

April didn't think; she moved on pure instinct. She sped through the city, the car engine roaring as she tore back to the site of her nightmare. Inside, the scene was gruesome. Angel was suspended from the rafters, a machine humming nearby, inflicting a methodical, mechanical torment.

April slammed the power switch, the silence that followed more deafening than the machine. She cut her friend down, catching Angel as her body collapsed—trembling, weak, and broken.

They drove in a haunting silence back to April's house. April bathed Angel with a tenderness that hurt, her mind looping the same questions: *Why us? Who is doing this?* As Angel finally drifted into a traumatized sleep, April sat by the bed, her eyes cold and her resolve hardening. Whatever was coming next, she wouldn't be the victim.

Chapter 4: The House on the Hill

April woke to the soft light of morning bleeding through the blinds. Beside her, Angel was still submerged in sleep, her breathing finally steady. Moving with practiced silence, April slid out of bed, careful not to disturb her friend's hard-won rest. After showering and dressing for the office, she left a note on the kitchen counter. Before heading out, she lingered for a moment, pressing a soft kiss to Angel's forehead—a gesture of protection and affection that felt heavier than usual.

Angel opened her eyes shortly after the front door clicked shut. She had been awake for the better part of the night, her thoughts a restless, swirling current of confusion. The events of the previous days replayed behind her eyelids like a haunting film reel—disjointed, vivid, and agonizingly real. She rubbed her temples, trying to massage away the lingering shadows. Her body was a map of dull aches, a physical receipt of the trauma she'd endured.

She eventually shuffled into the kitchen, the mundane task of making breakfast acting as an anchor. Her eyes snagged on the manila envelope April had left out. For a fleeting second, curiosity flared—a need to see the "Lady Pain" footage—but she quickly looked away.

"Not my place," she murmured to herself, her voice raspy. She poured a glass of orange juice and focused on the slow simmer of the grits, letting the domestic rhythm soothe her.

Once she'd eaten, the walls of the apartment felt like they were closing in. She needed to move. She scrawled a quick note for April, grabbed her jacket, and stepped out into the crisp, biting morning air.

At work, April was a ghost in a power suit. The weight of the warehouse pressed down on her, making every email and phone call feel like an impossible mountain to climb. Her secretary, Cynthia, handed her a stack of urgent messages, but

April merely set them aside. The corporate world felt like a charade she no longer knew how to play.

By midafternoon, she had barely touched her files. Her mind kept drifting back to the apartment—back to Angel. She had tried calling several times, but each attempt went to voicemail. As soon as the clock struck five, April packed her briefcase with work she knew she'd never open and practically ran to the parking garage.

When she pulled into her driveway and saw Angel's truck, the knot in her chest partially loosened. She hurried inside, her voice tight with suppressed panic. "Angel? You home?"

Silence. Her heart skipped a beat until she spotted the note on the counter: *Went for a walk to clear my head. Be back later.* April exhaled, a long, shuddering breath that drained the tension from her shoulders. She changed into sweatpants and began tidying the living room, using the mindless chore to quiet her nerves.

Angel's walk had taken her further than she'd intended. She found herself standing before a small neighborhood bar, its neon sign buzzing faintly in the twilight. A drink felt like a necessary escape—something to dull the sharp edges of her memory. Inside, the air was a familiar mix of old wood and stale cigarette smoke.

She slid onto a barstool, expertly ignoring the clumsy advances of a drunken regular. After a few sips of her drink, the physical tension in her neck began to melt. The low thrum of the music took hold of her, and before long, she was on the small dance floor, letting the rhythm dictate her movements.

As she swayed, she noticed a man watching her from the periphery. He was tall, carrying a quiet, grounded confidence that cut through the bar's hazy atmosphere. Their gazes locked, and for a heartbeat, the trauma of the past week seemed to recede. Encouraged by the heat in his eyes, Angel moved with more intent, letting the music ground her back in her own body.

When the song faded, he approached her with a slow, appreciative smile. "You've got some moves," he said, his voice a warm, low baritone.

Angel smiled back, a genuine spark of lightness fluttering in her chest. "I've had practice."

They found a quiet booth in the corner. His name was Malik. As the conversation flowed, Angel found herself doing something she thought she'd forgotten how to do: laughing. He was charming but maintained a respectful distance, a stark contrast to the lecherous men April usually dealt with or the monsters at the warehouse.

When he eventually leaned in, Angel hesitated for a split second before meeting him halfway. His lips were soft, his presence steadying. It was a brief kiss, but it left her feeling more "human" than she had in days.

"Let me walk you home," Malik offered as they stepped out into the cool night.

Angel nodded. They strolled through the quiet streets, the conversation remaining easy and unforced. At her doorstep, Malik paused. "Take care of yourself, Angel," he said, his tone carrying a weight of sincerity that moved her.

She watched him walk away before slipping inside. April was waiting in the living room, her expression a mix of relief and simmering frustration.

"I was worried about you," April said, her voice taut.

Angel gave her a sheepish, tired smile. "I just needed some air. Sorry I missed your calls."

They sat together on the couch, the silence between them thick with everything they weren't saying. Finally, Angel reached over. "Thank you, April. For everything. I don't know where I'd be right now without you."

April squeezed her hand, her thumb tracing Angel's knuckles. "You're my best friend. You're never going through this alone."

As the night deepened, they retreated into the safety of the past, swapping stories from high school and dreading the family barbecue April's mother was already planning. It was a fragile peace, but a peace nonetheless.

That night, as they lay in their separate beds, the nightmares stayed at bay. They didn't have the answers to the warehouse or the "Lady Pain" video yet, but for now, the simple fact of each other was enough.

Chapter 5: Choices and Consequences

The shrill ring of the phone shattered April's dreamless sleep. She fumbled for the receiver, the sunlight slicing through the blinds and stinging her eyes.

"Yes, Mother," she mumbled groggily.

Her mother's voice was loud and piercing, as always. "Don't forget the chicken and ribs, and be here on time. You're helping me cook." The line clicked dead before April could utter a word.

Sighing, she rolled out of bed. Her reflection in the bathroom mirror did little to improve her mood; dark circles clung to the hollows beneath her eyes, and her hair defied gravity in every direction. She splashed cold water on her face and grabbed her toothbrush, trying to scrub away the morning staleness along with the bitter memories of the day before.

Her mind drifted back—the sudden cold, the stranger's grip, the eerie silence that felt as if the world had paused. *Was it real?* It felt real. The dull throb in her arm where he had grabbed her was proof enough. She shook her head, forcing the thought away. Today was about family, not fear. She threw on a casual outfit and dialed Angel's number.

When it went straight to voicemail, irritation flared. "Angel, wake up. The barbecue is today, and I need you to come to the store with me," she snapped into the phone before hanging up.

Angel lay sprawled across her bed, ignoring the vibration of her phone. Her thoughts weren't on the barbecue or even April; they were on Charles. She could still feel the warmth of his hands and the velvet tone of his voice whispering in her ear. Her lips curled into a smile as she replayed the memory, savoring every detail.

But with the smile came a pang of guilt. *When did I start ignoring April's calls?* She buried her face in the pillow, ashamed.

April had always been her anchor, her constant. And yet, here she was, letting her best friend down for a man.

April maneuvered her cart through the grocery store, checking off items on her list. Her phone buzzed in her pocket, but when she saw a name other than Angel's on the screen, she silenced it. She couldn't handle small talk.

She reached for a package of chicken breasts in the frozen section just as another hand lunged for the same one. She looked up, startled. The man's expression was blank, almost detached, but his gaze locked onto hers with unnerving intensity. He wasn't unattractive—his sharp cheekbones and olive complexion were striking—but something about him felt fundamentally wrong.

"Um, excuse me," she said, summoning all the attitude she could muster. "I was reaching for that."

He didn't respond. He didn't even blink. He just stared. April's hand dropped from the chicken, her stomach tightening. "Okay, then. I'll just... grab another one."

She moved further down the aisle, but the man followed, his footsteps heavy and deliberate. Her breath quickened and her palms grew slick as she pushed her cart faster. By the time she reached the butcher's section, she was practically jogging. She ducked around a corner, hoping to lose him, but before she could react, a strong hand clamped around her arm.

The world spun as he yanked her backward into the butcher's walk-in freezer. The door slammed shut, the frigid air biting into her skin.

"What is your problem?" she screamed, her voice echoing off the stainless-steel walls.

The man didn't answer. His silence was more terrifying than any threat. Her eyes darted around the cramped space, landing on a rusty meat cleaver hanging from a wall rack. She lunged for it, gripping the handle tightly and thrusting it between them. "I swear, I'll use this!"

Still, he advanced. April swung wildly, the blade clanging harmlessly against the metal shelves. He stepped back, dodging her desperate arcs with an eerie, calculated calm that unnerved her further. Taking advantage of the gap, adrenaline surged; she bolted for the door and fumbled with the latch. Shoving it open, she stumbled out into the aisle, gasping for air.

A security guard stood nearby, eyeing her with suspicion. "Sir! Help! That man—" She spun around, pointing back toward the freezer, but the man was gone.

The guard sighed, unimpressed. "Ma'am, there's no one there. Maybe you should sit down—"

"I'm not crazy!" she snapped, tears stinging her eyes. But when she looked again, the freezer was exactly as she had left it. Empty.

Angel sat on her couch, nursing a cup of coffee and staring at her phone. April's voicemail echoed in her mind, but she still couldn't bring herself to call back. Guilt gnawed at her, yet she couldn't shake the memory of Charles. He was different—at least, she desperately wanted to believe he was.

Her phone buzzed again. This time, it was him. A wide grin spread across her face as she answered. "Hey, baby."

"Hey, mami," his voice dripped with charm. "How are you? I was thinking about you."

The way he spoke made her melt. She bit her lip, her earlier guilt evaporating instantly. "Just getting ready for a family barbecue. You?"

"Missing you already," he replied. "But I'll let you enjoy your day. Call me tonight?"

"You know I will," she whispered, hanging up with a contented sigh.

April parked outside her mother's house, her nerves still frayed from the morning. As she stepped out, she saw Angel pull up behind her.

"Nice of you to show up," April muttered under her breath.

Angel rolled down her window, her expression contrite. "I'm here now, Chica. What's wrong?"

April hesitated, then the floodgates opened. "I was attacked today, Angel. Some psycho at the store pulled me into a freezer. And you... you didn't answer your phone."

Angel's face paled. "Wait—what? Are you okay?" She scrambled out of the car, pulling April into a tight hug.

April wanted to stay angry, but Angel's warmth melted her resolve. "I'm fine. Just shaken. Let's go inside."

Inside, the house was a cacophony of laughter, music, and the rhythmic clatter of dominoes. Kids darted between legs, and the smoky aroma of barbecue wafted through the air. April's mother stood at the stove, directing traffic like a drill sergeant.

"April! Angel! Get in here and help!"

Angel grinned, rolling up her sleeves. "Yes, ma'am."

As they chopped vegetables and marinated meat, April leaned closer to her friend. "I'm serious, Angel. Something is wrong. I don't think this is over."

Angel nodded, her mind wandering back to Charles, but her gut finally began to settle on the same uneasy conclusion.

Chapter 6: Family Shadows

The familiar scent of barbecue wafted through the air as April stepped into her parents' backyard. Family members filled the space, animated by laughter, conversation, and the rhythmic clink of dominoes. Uncle John was already on his second—or fifth—drink, his boisterous laughter echoing across the yard. Danielle and Samantha, as always, perched on the edge of the group, batting their eyelashes and flipping their hair at every man who walked by, married or not. At the center of the chaos, the men dominated the dominoes table, slamming pieces down with theatrical flair and cursing with mock anger at every loss.

April scanned the crowd, trying to find her ease. It was hard to focus on the warmth of family when her mind was clouded by the incident at the grocery store. The memory of the silent man who had followed her into the butcher's freezer sent a fresh chill down her spine. She tried to push it away, but the unease clung to her like humidity.

"Hey, baby girl." Her father's voice cut through her thoughts as he pulled her into a firm hug. He smelled of Old Spice and wood smoke—a comforting scent that grounded her in a way only he could.

"Hey, Dad," she said, managing a small, weary smile.

"You doing okay?" His voice was gentle, but his sharp eyes searched hers, as if he could see the turmoil lurking behind her forced cheerfulness.

"I'm fine," she lied, holding onto him a beat longer than usual.

"Well, you know your mother and I are here for you if you ever need to talk," he said, releasing her with a soft pat on the back. His kindness was a balm to her frayed nerves. Yet, as she glanced over his shoulder, she caught sight of Angel standing on the patio. Nursing a glass of wine, Angel watched them with an intensity that felt almost accusatory.

Angel's grip on her glass tightened. It wasn't rational, and she knew it, but she couldn't suppress the flicker of jealousy flaring in her chest. April wasn't even their biological daughter, yet they showered her with a warmth Angel felt she had to beg for.

"It's stupid," she muttered to herself, shaking her head. She drained her glass and headed for the kitchen, determined to drown her bitterness in another drink.

As she passed through the living room, a rough hand caught her arm. "Come here, baby," Uncle John slurred, his breath reeking of cheap liquor. Before she could pull away, his free hand groped her backside.

The slap landed before she even realized she'd raised her hand. "Damn it, Uncle John! I'm your niece! Stop drinking that shit!"

The room fell silent for a heartbeat before the murmurs and laughter resumed. Uncle John stumbled back, rubbing his stinging cheek with a crooked grin. "Stuck-up tease," he muttered, staggering away.

Fuming, Angel stormed into the kitchen. She seized the nearest bottle of tequila, poured a generous shot, and downed it without hesitation. Her cheeks burned with embarrassment and rage. The liquor scorched her throat, but the rising haze of intoxication finally began to dull the sharp edges of her emotions.

Miles away, Charles paced his living room. The flowers and jewelry he'd bought for his wife lay untouched on the dining table—a silent, expensive reminder of his fractured marriage. His phone buzzed in his hand, Angel's name illuminating the screen.

"Hey, big daddy," her voice purred.

"Hey, beautiful," he replied smoothly, his frustration evaporating at the sound of her voice.

"You miss me?"

"You know I do," he teased.

"I wish you'd come with me to this boring family thing. It's dead here without you."

Charles chuckled, imagining her pout. "Why don't you come get me, then?"

"Give me five minutes," she said, her excitement clear.

After hanging up, Charles sighed and headed upstairs to shower. He needed to wash away the scent of guilt, as well as the lingering perfume of the other woman he'd spent the night with.

Back at the barbecue, April retreated to her childhood bedroom to escape the noise. The walls were still the same soft lavender, the shelves still lined with books and trophies from her school days. She sank onto the bed, pulling a pillow to her chest. The weight of the last few weeks pressed down on her: the party, the warehouse, the video, and now, the attack at the grocery store.

She squeezed her eyes shut, willing the tears to stay back, but they spilled over anyway. A soft knock on the door made her sit up. Her father stepped in, his face etched with concern.

"Hey," he said gently, sitting beside her. She leaned into him without a word, letting his steady presence anchor her.

"I'm so tired, Dad," she whispered.

"I know, baby girl," he said, stroking her hair. "But you're strong. You'll get through whatever this is."

She wanted to believe him, but the weight of her secrets felt too heavy to lift.

Angel pulled up outside Charles's house, her truck idling in the driveway. She tapped her fingers nervously against the steering wheel, glancing around the quiet neighborhood. It was almost eerily still, and a strange sense of unease crept over her.

When Charles stepped out, he looked impossibly handsome in a black shirt and jeans. She couldn't help the smile that spread across her face. "Hey, gorgeous," he said, pulling her into a hug that made her knees weak.

As he slid into the driver's seat and adjusted the mirrors, Angel noticed a car parked at the corner with its headlights on. She thought nothing of it until the car began to follow them, its high beams glaring in the rearview mirror.

Behind them, Tasha gripped the steering wheel until her knuckles turned white. She had followed her husband and his mistress from the moment they left the house. Each stolen glance and shared laugh stoked the fire of her fury. When Angel's head disappeared from view, Tasha's stomach churned with nausea. She didn't need to see the details to know exactly what was happening.

"This bastard," she hissed, her vision blurring with tears of rage. As they stopped at a red light, Tasha debated ramming her car into the back of their truck. Instead, she clenched her teeth and kept following, determined to see exactly where this road ended.

The barbecue was winding down by the time Angel and Charles arrived. Angel's mother greeted them with a forced warmth, while her father remained stiff and reserved. As Angel introduced Charles, April emerged from the house, her skin sallow and her expression haunted. She caught Angel's eye and frowned.

"Where were you?" April asked, her voice dropping to a low, accusatory whisper.

"Just picking someone up," Angel replied, her gaze darting toward the grass to avoid April's eyes.

The tension between them was thick enough to choke on, but before either could press further, a sharp commotion erupted near the back door. April's mother was shouting, her voice jagged with a raw, unbridled fury.

"John, you piece of shit!" she screamed. "Get out of my house! Now!"

The yard went still. Every head turned to see Uncle John stumbling across the threshold, his shirt half-buttoned and his face a deep, alcoholic flush. April's father followed a half-step behind him, his shoulders hunched and his fists white-knuckled.

"What happened?" Angel whispered, but her question was lost in the wind.

April stared at the scene, her mind suddenly racing at a terrifying speed. Fragmented memories from the night of the party began to click into place like jagged glass. Uncle John's heavy hands. The suffocating weight of his body. The sickening, sticky residue she had discovered on her skin when she woke up.

"No," she breathed, the word barely a puff of air. But the truth was a physical blow. Her knees buckled, and her father caught her before she hit the ground, his arms acting as a cage against the world.

"It's okay, baby," he choked out, holding her with a desperate strength. "We're here. We'll handle this."

For the first time in weeks, April let herself lean into that promise. Uncle John's undignified exit was met with a cacophony of gasps and frantic whispers. Older relatives moved to shield the children, trying to turn their eyes from the ugly fracture in the family foundation. April remained frozen, watching the loop of her trauma play out in real-time.

Her father's voice boomed, cutting through the collective shock. "John, you're done. You are no longer part of this family. If I see you within ten feet of her again, I'll make sure you don't walk away next time."

John staggered back, throwing his hands up in a mocking defensive gesture. "It ain't even like that! You're acting like she's some innocent—"

He didn't finish. April's father lunged, and it took two cousins throwing their weight against him to hold him back.

"You don't get to say her name!" he roared, his voice vibrating with a primal rage. "Get out before I forget we share blood!"

John stumbled into the darkness of the driveway, his muttered curses fading as he vanished. April's mother turned, tears carving tracks through her makeup. "Baby, I'm so sorry,"

she sobbed, pulling April into her arms. "I should've seen it...
I should've known..."

April stood rigid, her body refusing to respond to the
embrace. The heat of her mother's touch couldn't thaw the ice
that had settled deep in her marrow. "I'm fine," she said, her
voice sounding like it belonged to someone else. "I just need
some air."

She broke free and walked toward the edge of the yard.
The crowd parted for her like the Red Sea, their pitying stares
following her like a shroud.

Angel sat in stunned silence near the porch. Beside her,
Charles remained oblivious, his face illuminated by the blue
light of his phone as he scrolled through his feed. Her stomach
churned at the revelation. The audacity of Uncle John's
betrayal made her blood run cold, but what gnawed at her more
was the look April had given her—a devastating cocktail of
shock and perceived betrayal.

"She's blaming me," Angel muttered, her fingernails
digging into the wood of her chair.

"What?" Charles asked, finally tearing his eyes away from
the screen.

"April. She thinks I'm the one who told her mom," Angel
snapped, her voice sharp with defensive anxiety. "I didn't say a
word!"

Charles shrugged, slipping the phone into his pocket with
a bored sigh. "So what if you did? The guy's a predator; he
deserved to be outed. Why do you care what April thinks?"

Angel turned on him, her eyes narrowing into slits. "I care
because she's my best friend, Charles."

Charles smirked, leaning back with an arrogant tilt of his
head. "Well, it doesn't look like the feeling is mutual right now.
Don't stress it, baby. Come on, let's head back to your place
and leave all this drama behind."

The callousness of his words struck a nerve she didn't
know she had. Angel stood abruptly, the legs of her chair

screeching against the deck. "Maybe you should just go," she said, her voice low and dangerous.

"What?" Charles's smirk faltered.

"You heard me." She folded her arms, her gaze unwavering. "I need to be here for my family. For April. I don't need to be with you right now."

Charles's jaw tightened, his ego clearly bruised. He shook his head, muttering a dismissive "Suit yourself," before turning on his heel toward his car. Angel watched his taillights disappear, her anger slowly dissolving into a hollow mixture of guilt and confusion.

The cool night air nipped at April's skin as she sat on the patio steps, hugging her knees to her chest. The music and laughter had long since died, replaced by the hushed, mournful murmurs of relatives inside. She felt untethered, watching the aftermath of her own life as a distant spectator.

Footsteps crunched on the grass. She looked up to see her father approaching, a steaming mug held between his large hands. "Thought you could use this," he said softly, offering it to her.

She took it, letting the warmth of the ceramic seep into her palms. "Thanks, Dad."

He sat beside her, a solid, silent anchor. The silence lasted for a long time—heavy, but necessary. "I failed you," he said finally, his voice thick with a father's unique brand of grief.

April turned to him, startled. "What? No, you didn't."

"I should've protected you. I should've seen who he was..." He looked away, his profile etched with shame.

"You didn't know," April whispered, though the words felt like paper against the weight of the truth. They sat in the dark for a moment longer before April took a shaky breath. "Dad... I need to tell you everything. About what happened to me... before tonight."

His brow furrowed in concern, but he remained still, giving her the floor. And for the first time since the warehouse, the dam broke. April's voice trembled as she finally began to recount the events that had been haunting her every waking hour.

***

Across town, Tasha sat in her darkened car, her knuckles white against the steering wheel. The image of Charles with that girl—the way he looked at her—was a brand burned into her retinas. She had waited for hours, her rage simmering into something cold and calculated.

When her phone buzzed, she saw Josh's name. "Hey," she answered, her voice brittle.

"Are you okay?" he asked immediately, the genuine concern in his tone almost making her break.

"No," she admitted, the first tear finally falling. "Josh, he's cheating. With some... some girl who thinks she can just take what's mine."

"Where are you? I'm coming to pick you up."

Tasha hesitated, then rattled off her location. She didn't know what she wanted from him, but she knew she couldn't be alone with her thoughts. Not when those thoughts were spiraling toward revenge—toward making Charles feel every bit of the pain he had so casually handed her.

***

Angel found April alone on the patio, her shoulders slumped under the weight of the night. For a moment, Angel hesitated, hovering at the threshold. She wasn't sure if her presence would be a comfort or a reminder of the chaos. Finally, she stepped forward, her voice tentative. "Hey."

April glanced at her but said nothing.

"I didn't tell your mom," Angel blurted out, the words tumbling over each other in a rush. "I swear, April, I didn't say a word."

April stared at her for a long moment, searching her face, before finally nodding. "I know," she said quietly.

Relief washed over Angel, but it was short-lived. She could see the haunted distance in April's eyes—the visible construction of the walls she was putting up to survive. "I'm so sorry, April," Angel said, her voice cracking. "For everything."

April nodded again, but her gaze drifted to the dark horizon, her expression unreadable.

As the night wore on, the house settled into an uneasy quiet. April lay in her childhood bed, staring at the ceiling. The events of the day replayed in her mind, each memory sharper and more jagged than the last. Downstairs, Angel sat with April's mother, sipping tea in a moment of hushed solidarity.

Miles away, Charles sat alone in his car, the dashboard glowing in the dark. He hovered over Angel's name, debating whether to call her. But before he could decide, the screen changed. Another name appeared, flashing like a warning: Tasha.

In the quiet of the den, April sat with her parents, her hands trembling as she gripped the mug of tea her mother had prepared. The steam rising from the cup was a stark contrast to the cold dread settling in her chest.

Her father sat to her left, his jaw set so tight it looked like stone, his fists clenched on his thighs. Her mother was on her right, her face a mask of practiced calm, though her hands betrayed her, shaking slightly as she reached out to cover April's knee.

"Whatever it is, baby, we're here," her mother said gently. "You don't have to carry this by yourself anymore."

April took a deep breath, the words catching in her throat like shards of glass. "It's... it's not just what happened tonight," she began, her voice barely a whisper. "It's something else. Something much worse."

Her father's posture shifted; his fists unclenched as he leaned closer, his face softening with concern. "Go on, sweetheart."

And then the words came—halting and painful at first, then spilling out in a desperate torrent. She told them about the night of the party, the warehouse, the blindfold, the paralyzing fear, and the crushing confusion. She described the violation and the shame she'd carried like a shroud ever since. Her voice cracked, her tears flowing freely now. Her mother gasped, a hand flying to her mouth, while her father's face contorted with a mixture of visceral rage and pure anguish.

"Why didn't you tell us sooner?" he asked, his voice thick with unshed tears. "We could've helped you, April. We would have protected you."

"I didn't want to burden you," she whispered. "And... I was so scared."

Her mother pulled her into a fierce, protective hug. "Baby, you are never a burden. Never."

Her father stood abruptly, pacing the small room like a caged predator. "We'll find out who did this," he vowed, his voice low and dangerous. "I'll make sure they pay for every second of this."

April shook her head. "I don't want revenge, Dad. I just want... to move on. I want to feel whole again."

Her parents exchanged a look of shared pain and iron-clad determination. "Then we'll help you do that," her mother said. "Together."

For the first time in weeks, a flicker of hope sparked in April's chest. The secret was out. She wasn't alone in the dark anymore.

Angel couldn't stop thinking about Charles as she drove home. His touch, his voice, the way he made her feel like the center of the universe—it was intoxicating. But beneath the euphoria, a nagging doubt remained. He had left so abruptly, his demeanor shifting the moment the family drama intensified.

Needing reassurance, she called him the moment she stepped through her door. He picked up on the first ring, his voice smooth as silk. "Hey, beautiful. Miss me already?"

Angel smiled despite herself. "Maybe a little. Are you okay? You seemed... off earlier."

"I'm fine," Charles said quickly. "Just had a lot on my mind, you know?"

Angel hesitated, her hand tightening on the phone. "You'd tell me if something was wrong, right?"

"Of course," he replied, but she caught a slight edge to his tone. "Don't worry about me, babe. Just focus on how good we are together."

His words soothed her, but the relief was fleeting. As they said their goodnights, Angel couldn't shake the chilling thought that Charles was a man of many faces—and she was only beginning to see the cracks in the mask.

Tasha sat across from Josh in a dimly lit bar, her drink untouched. Josh listened intently, his expression unreadable in the shadows.

"He's been lying to me for months," Tasha said, her voice trembling with the effort to stay composed. "And tonight, I saw him with her. Some... girl in a truck."

Josh leaned back, his fingers drumming a slow rhythm on the table. "You're sure it was him?"

"Of course I'm sure," Tasha snapped. "I know my own husband, Josh."

Josh sighed, swirling the amber liquid in his glass. "What do you want to do?"

Tasha hesitated. "I don't know. Part of me wants to scream it in his face, to make him admit what he is. But another part of me..." She trailed off, her voice dropping to a dangerous whisper. "Another part of me wants to hurt him the way he's hurt me."

Josh's eyes darkened. "Tasha, be careful. You don't want to do something you'll regret."

"Regret?" Tasha laughed, a bitter, hollow sound. "I'm already living in regret. I'm done being the loyal wife while he plays me for a fool."

Josh reached across the table, placing his hand firmly over hers. "You're not alone in this. Whatever you decide, I'm with you."

Tasha looked at him, her resolve finally hardening into something cold and sharp. "Good. Because I have an idea."

Angel found April sitting alone on the back porch, her shoulders slumped and her face pale in the low light. She approached cautiously, measuring her steps, unsure if her presence would be welcome.

"Hey," Angel said softly.

April didn't look up. "Hey."

Angel sat beside her, the silence stretching thin and heavy between them. Finally, she blurted out, "I didn't tell your mom. I swear."

April turned then, her eyes red-rimmed but clear. "I know," she said quietly. "I was just... overwhelmed."

Angel let out a breath she hadn't realized she'd been holding. "I'm so sorry, April. For everything."

April nodded, her gaze drifting toward the tree line. "You didn't do anything wrong." The words were forgiving, but the tone remained distant. Angel felt the chasm between them widening, an ache she didn't know how to soothe. She wanted to say more—to reach across the gap—but the words wouldn't come. Instead, she stayed in the silence, hoping that simply being there would be enough.

As the night deepened, the players in this tangled web began to move into position.

Charles, back at home, watched his phone light up with a text from Angel: *I miss you already.* He smiled, his fingers hovering over the glass for a beat before he responded: *Me too, babe.* Tasha, fueled by a volatile mix of anger and Josh's encouragement, began laying the groundwork for her plan to expose Charles's infidelity.

And April, lying in bed, stared at the ceiling as her mind raced. She was done being a victim. It was time to take the architecture of her life into her own hands—to confront the choices of her past and reclaim a future that was actually hers.

The storm was building, and none of them would emerge unscathed.

Chapter 7: Buried Secrets

The bed between her parents smelled of lavender fabric softener and her father's Old Spice—a combination so specific it felt like a word she couldn't quite remember, familiar on her tongue but slipping away before she could speak it. April lay there in the dark, her eyes wide. Her mother's arm was draped over her ribs like a seatbelt; her father breathed steadily on her left. She could feel the rhythmic rise and fall of his chest. For now, he was still here. For now, that had to be enough.

She didn't sleep. She wasn't sure she was capable of sleep anymore. Instead, she stared at the water stain on the ceiling—the one shaped like the state of Florida—and let herself dissolve into the silence. Outside, a dog barked twice and went quiet. A car rolled past with its bass thumping, someone's Saturday night still going strong at an unknown hour. April pressed her palm flat against her sternum and breathed through the weight of it.

Her mother's voice came low, just above a whisper. "You still awake, baby?"

"Yeah."

A soft squeeze followed. "Okay. I'm here."

That was all. It was enough.

By the time the sun filtered through the curtains, April had made a decision. She wasn't going to cry anymore. Not today. She had cried until her sinuses felt like wet cement and her throat was stripped raw—in this bed, in the shower, and at the barbecue before she'd even found the vocabulary for what had happened. She was done. Grief could wait. Anger could wait. For now, she needed coffee, and she needed to determine how to walk back into the architecture of her own life.

She slipped out without waking them, padding down the hall in her socks. She stood at the bathroom sink for a long moment before turning on the light, the mirror catching her before she was ready.

She looked terrible: swollen eyelids, the particular hollowness around her cheekbones that followed neglect, the dull, glassy quality her eyes took on when running on fumes. But she made herself look. She gripped the edge of the sink with both hands and stared, the way she had forced herself to do since she was fifteen—practicing the belief that the only way through a thing was directly through it. She had stood in front of mirrors in worse shape than this. She had stood there after Mr. Daley. She had stood there the morning after the warehouse, when the face looking back had felt like a stranger wearing her skin.

This was not that. She was still here. She was still herself.

She washed her face with ice-cold water, dried it on a hand towel, and went downstairs to brew the coffee.

The weeks that followed moved the way grief always moves—not in a straight line, but in circles, covering the same ground from slightly different angles. April went back to school. She smiled at the right moments, said the right things, and folded every jagged feeling into a compartment she kept locked and labeled. She was good at that; she had been practicing since she was a little girl.

What she was not good at was watching her father get smaller.

The cancer had been there for a while before anyone named it. Her father was the kind of man who associated doctors with weakness and bad news with something best left unspoken. By the time the diagnosis came, it had settled deep—the kind of settled that meant treatment was about buying time rather than reclaiming it. April learned this in a hospital waiting room that smelled of antiseptic and burnt coffee, sitting between her parents on a row of bolted plastic chairs. She watched the doctor's mouth move, understanding the words before they had even finished landing.

She drove home that night with her hands at ten and two and the radio off. She did not cry until she was in the shower, the water hot enough to sting. She stood with her forehead against the tile while steam gathered around her, scrubbing her arms the way she always did when she didn't know what else to do with her hands—methodical, meditative, working from wrist to elbow until her skin was pink and the heat finally pulled something loose.

I cannot lose him, she thought. *I am going to lose him.* She turned the water up hotter and stayed until it ran cold.

His name for her changed as the illness progressed. For most of her life, she had been "April"—plain and clean, two syllables delivered without much warmth. But in the final months, somewhere after the second round of treatment and before the decision to stop, she became "baby girl." She wasn't sure he even realized he'd made the switch, and she wasn't going to tell him. She was going to let him call her that every single day they had left, filing each instance away like a pressed flower in the pages of a book she intended to keep forever.

He had not been an easy man. She had always known that, even when she was small enough to be lifted onto his shoulders and believed fathers were gods by definition. He possessed a temper that arrived without warning and a silence that was somehow worse—the kind that filled a space and pressed against the walls. She had learned to read his internal weather the way some children read the sky, watching for the tightening around his eyes, the set of his jaw, or a glass placed too carefully on the counter.

But illness changes a man; it sanded his edges down. The temper quieted into exhaustion, and the silence shifted, becoming less threatening—more like a man simply conserving his breath. He began asking her questions. *How was school? What did she want to do after graduation? Had she ever thought about leaving the city?* He stayed awake past his bedtime to watch whatever she put on television, and once—just once—he laughed at something she said. A full, real laugh that startled them both. They looked at each other across the kitchen table, and April thought: *There you are. There you finally are.*

She was not going to get enough time. She knew that. She filed it away, too.

Junior year arrived, and her father had become the kind of thin that frightened her—the skin loose at his neck, his hands papery, the particular smallness of a big man diminished. April began sleeping in four-hour increments, waking to check on him, sitting in the chair by his bed in the dark just to listen to his breath. Her mother had offered to take the overnight shifts, but April wouldn't give them up. She didn't know how to explain that this was the only thing she could do that felt like enough.

He passed on a Tuesday. It was early morning, just before 4:00 AM, when the sky was still fully dark and the neighborhood was silent. April was holding his hand. She had been reading to him from a book—something old her mother had left on the nightstand; she couldn't have named the title— and she felt the change before she saw it. A slackening. A stillness that was fundamentally different from sleep.

She set the book down. She kept holding his hand for a long time.

Then she got up, walked to the bathroom, and looked at herself in the mirror. Her face was composed. She did not understand why her face was so still. She ran cold water over her wrists and pressed her wet fingers against her eyes, standing there until she heard her mother's alarm go off down the hall. Then she went and knocked gently on the bedroom door.

"Mom," she said, very quietly. "Come."

The funeral was held on a Friday. Gray sky, sharp wind— the kind of day that committed fully to its own misery. April stood at the graveside in a black dress and her mother's pearls, which she had never worn before and likely never would again, and watched them lower her father into the ground.

Angel stood beside her. Angel had not left her side in three days—she had shown up the morning after and simply existed there. Making coffee. Fielding phone calls. Sitting next to April in silence when silence was what was required. For all the cracks that had formed between them, Angel knew how to be present in a crisis. April held onto that.

The Santos family arrived as a unit: Mr. and Mrs. Santos, Angel, and their son Marco, whom April had met twice at holidays and remembered as being quiet in a thoughtful way. They wore their grief like people who had actually known her father—who had loved her family in the easy, neighboring way of those who had watched a girl grow up from across the street. Mrs. Santos pressed both of April's hands in hers and said something in Spanish that April didn't catch, but understood completely in her chest.

It was after the burial, at the house, with paper plates balanced on knees and conversation doing what conversation does at funerals—filling space, circling the weight of the room's real subject—that Mr. Santos found a quiet moment beside April.

"April." His voice carried the gentleness of a man who chose his words carefully. "Elena and I have been talking. We want you to know—you don't have to figure out what comes next alone."

She looked at him. He had kind eyes—the kind that stayed kind even when delivering hard things.

"We'd like you to come stay with us," he said. "For as long as you need. You are family. That is not a small thing to us."

April opened her mouth and found nothing there. She looked across the room at her mother, who was surrounded by neighbors, holding herself together with the particular steel of a woman who had done hard things before and would do hard things again. April believed she would be okay. She needed to believe that.

She looked back at Mr. Santos. "I'll think about it," she said.

Angel materialized at her elbow the way she always did—radar calibrated to the exact frequency of April's distress. "You don't have to decide anything tonight, *Chica*," she said quietly.

"But just so you know—I already cleaned out the bottom half of my closet."

April looked at her. "Half?"

"I said what I said."

For the first time in days, April almost smiled.

She moved in on a Sunday, three weeks after the funeral, when the logistics had been settled and her mother had made her peace with it and April had run out of reasons to wait. Two suitcases and a cardboard box of things she couldn't leave behind—a photograph, a paperback, the small wooden cardinal her father had kept on his dresser for as long as she could remember. She didn't know where it had come from; she had never thought to ask. She wrapped it in a t-shirt, carried it into the Santos house, and put it on the windowsill of the room that was now hers.

The room was at the back of the house, overlooking the yard. It had a small window seat she immediately claimed. The closet, true to Angel's word, was half empty. The bed had been made up with clean linens that smelled like Mrs. Santos's detergent—a smell April associated with sleepovers and safety and childhood, a smell that made her throat close in a way that grief hadn't quite managed.

She unpacked methodically. She was good at that— converting an unfamiliar space into something that belonged to her through the careful placement of objects. Books on the shelf. Lotion on the dresser. Shoes lined up on the closet floor. She arranged her toiletries in the bathroom she would share with Angel, feeling the slight friction of negotiating shared space and the weight of belonging somewhere she had not grown up.

She was staring at herself in the mirror—a quick, involuntary check of her own architecture—when Angel appeared in the doorway behind her.

"Settling in okay?"

"Yeah. I think so."

Angel leaned against the doorframe, studying her with the particular attention she used when trying to determine what April wasn't saying. "You can tell me when it's weird. It's going to be weird sometimes."

"I know."

"I'm just saying. You don't have to perform 'fine' for me."

April met her eyes in the glass. Something complicated moved between them—the gravity of everything said badly, the arguments, the silences, and the love underneath it all that neither of them was entirely fluent in yet. "I know," she said again. "Thank you, Angel."

Angel nodded once and pushed off the doorframe. "Dinner's at seven. My mom made *arroz con pollo*." A pause. "She always makes extra when someone needs to be loved on."

April turned back to the mirror after she left. She stood there for a long moment. She looked like someone who was managing. She always looked like someone who was managing. She was going to have to figure out what she wanted instead of that.

The transition was, in the beginning, easier than she had expected and harder than she let on. Mrs. Santos had an instinct for care that manifested as sustenance; the table was always set, something warm always waiting on the stove. Mr. Santos was steady and quiet, leaving doors open without making a production of it, a specific and generous skill April recognized and valued. Marco visited on weekends, as easy to be around as she remembered.

And then there was Angel. Angel was complicated. April could see it the way you see something in your peripheral vision that vanishes when you look directly at it—the tight smile when her parents asked April about school, the slight withdrawal when April made her mother laugh. Angel had invited her here; April knew that. But knowing a thing and feeling it were not the same, and whatever Angel was feeling, she was working to contain. Which was to say, not entirely successfully.

April didn't push. She had enough of her own containers full.

He arrived on a Tuesday afternoon in March, four months after the move.

April had just come home from school. She had dropped her bag by the door and was standing at the kitchen sink eating a peach—an old habit, fruit eaten standing up, juice running down her wrist—when the doorbell rang. Mrs. Santos was at work. Angel had a late class. The house possessed that particular afternoon quiet April had come to love, the kind with a quality that felt chosen rather than empty.

She wiped her hand on a dish towel and went to the door.

The man standing on the porch was tall in the way of someone who had grown into their height gradually and didn't think much about it. He held a casserole dish with both hands, a kitchen towel folded over each side as a makeshift oven mitt. He was looking at her with brown eyes that were warm in a way that caught her off guard—warmth always caught her off guard when she wasn't braced for it.

"Hey," he said. His voice was smooth—not a practiced smooth, but naturally resonant. "I'm Angelo. Angelo Saxton. I live two doors down." He lifted the dish slightly. "I heard about your dad. Thought you could use a home-cooked meal."

April looked at him for a moment. She ran the quick inventory she always ran with men she didn't know—posture, eye contact, the quality of his stillness. He was standing easy, not pressing forward, giving her the full width of the doorway. His eyes remained on her face. The casserole smelled of garlic, savory and warm, and her stomach shifted in a way that reminded her she had eaten very little that day.

"That's really kind of you," she said. "Thank you."

"Mind if I come in? It'll stay hotter on the counter."

She hesitated for the half-second she always hesitated. Then she stepped back.

They sat at the kitchen table with the dish between them—chicken and rice, seasoned like a grandmother had made it—and talked. He asked about her father without drifting into the morbid. He mentioned his own mother without making it a competition in grief. He possessed a quick, dry humor that arrived without warning and vanished just as fast; twice, April laughed before she realized she was going to.

When he finally stood to go, the afternoon light had shifted into an early evening amber.

"I'm glad you're here," he said simply—meaning the Santos house, the neighborhood, and nothing more than exactly what he said. "You landed somewhere good."

"Yeah," April said. And she meant it.

She walked him to the door and watched him cross the porch and down the front path with his empty dish. She stood in the doorway for a moment after—the smell of garlic still in the air, the last of the sun warm on her face. Then she went back inside, put the leftovers in the fridge, and washed the casserole dish so it would be ready to return.

She didn't tell Angel about the visit. Not right away. She wasn't sure why—it wasn't deliberate, exactly, more like the instinct to hold something quiet for a little while before it became subject to interpretation. Angelo had been straightforward and kind, and she wasn't ready yet to watch that get examined.

But Angel had radar. And Angel, eventually, would be watching.

That night, April sat on the window seat in her room with her knees pulled up and the wooden cardinal in her lap—small and smooth from years of handling, painted red with a detail of black at the throat. She ran her thumb across its back. She thought about her father's hands. The way they had looked in the hospital. The way they had looked at the end. She thought about the way he had called her "baby girl."

She thought about a Tuesday afternoon and a casserole and a pair of warm brown eyes that had asked for nothing.

She set the cardinal on the windowsill. Outside, the street was settling into night, porch lights coming on one by one down the block. Two doors down, a light was on in a window she was already learning to locate without meaning to.

She was going to have to be careful, April thought. She wasn't sure if she was warning herself about Angelo Saxton, or about herself.

Probably both.

Chapter 8: What We Bury

The mirror in the Santos family bathroom was small, oval, and ringed with a gold-painted frame that had begun to peel at the bottom left corner. Angel had noticed that peeling the first day she moved in. Three years later, she still hadn't told anyone. Some things you just watched come undone.

She was thirty-one years old and staring at her own face as if she were meeting a stranger. The bathroom in her own apartment was nicer than this—newer fixtures, better lighting—but she'd come over to help April pack the last of her things from the childhood bedroom. Now, April was downstairs talking to Mama Rosa, and Angel was standing here with a towel in her hands that she didn't need, not going anywhere.

She knew this bathroom. She knew this mirror. And right now, both were showing her something she had spent sixteen years refusing to acknowledge.

***

She was fourteen the first time he noticed her.

Not the way boys at school noticed her—loud and clumsy, all elbows and bravado, "Aye, Angel, let me talk to you real quick." This was different. Quieter. It felt like being recognized rather than merely seen.

His name was Gerald Daley, and he lived three houses down from the Santos place in a brown-brick single-story with a garden he actually maintained. Rosebushes. A little birdbath. Wind chimes on the porch that Angel thought were corny until the sound of them came to mean something else entirely.

He was heavy-set, somewhere between forty and fifty, with thick-rimmed glasses and hands that looked too soft for a man his size. He wore short-sleeve button-downs even in October. He always had a glass of something—iced tea, he said, though Angel later wondered—and he sat on his porch in the evenings and watched the neighborhood happen around him like a man who had made his peace with stillness.

Angel had never made peace with anything.

She was the middle child in a family of five. Her older sister, Marisol, got the grades. Her younger brother, Tomás, got the illness—asthma, constant and demanding—and so he got the attention. Angel got the space between them. She learned early that performing was the only way to fill it: a loud laugh, a fast mouth, the first to arrive at any party and the last to admit she was tired.

Her parents were good people. This was important. They were not neglectful in the ways that showed. Her father worked construction and came home smelling of sawdust and heat; he sat at the dinner table and asked about her day, and she told him "fine" because it was easier than the truth—which was that she spent most of her days feeling transparent. Present. Visible. But never quite solid enough for anyone's hands to find purchase on.

Gerald Daley put his hands on her like she was made of something worth holding.

It started with a conversation.

She'd been sitting on the Santos front steps in August, school three weeks away, boredom sitting on her chest like a stone. He'd called over from his porch: "You look like a young woman with too many thoughts and nowhere to put them."

She'd looked up, squinting. "Excuse me?"

"Just an observation." He smiled. Slow. Like he had time for everything. "I'm Gerald. I've been watching you think for about forty-five minutes."

"Watching me?"

"Watching the neighborhood." He gestured at the street with his glass. "You happen to be in it. Come sit on the porch a minute if you want. I've got lemonade that's going to waste."

She should have gone inside. She knew that even then, in the abstract way a fourteen-year-old knows things— academically, without weight. She went and sat on his porch instead, because no one had told her she had too many thoughts in years, maybe ever, and the observation felt like a gift she hadn't known she was waiting for.

They talked for two hours. He asked about school, her family, and what she wanted to be when she was done with the life she was living now. He listened the way no one had taught the men in her life to listen—without looking at his phone, without waiting for his turn to speak, without making her feel like she was costing him something.

When she went home for dinner, the wind chimes followed her down the block.

The visits became a pattern through September and into October.

She told her mother she was going to the library. Her mother, managing Tomás's inhaler schedule and Marisol's college application essays, would nod and say, "Be back before dark," without looking up from the kitchen table. Angel would go to Gerald Daley's porch, drink his lemonade, and talk until the streetlights came on.

He was careful. She understood that now. But at fourteen, she experienced that carefulness as consideration—as proof that he was different from the boys at school who grabbed and said crude things and moved on. Gerald moved slowly, and the slowness felt like respect.

The first touch was her hand. They were talking about her father—about how she loved him but didn't know how to reach him, how they shared a house but not a language—and Gerald had reached across the space between their chairs and covered her hand with his.

"That kind of loneliness is real, Angel. Don't let anyone tell you it isn't."

The warmth of his hand, the sound of her name, and the fact that someone had finally called the thing inside her chest by its right name merged into something that felt dangerously close to love.

She was fourteen. She didn't know yet what love actually asked of people.

The touching escalated in the way these things do—slowly enough that she could construct a story around each increment. A hand on the shoulder. A hand on the knee. A conversation that drifted toward intimacy and stayed there. He called her his "bright one." His "girl with the fire in her." He said he'd never met a young woman with her particular combination of beauty and intelligence, and that most men her age wouldn't know what to do with her.

She heard: *You are exceptional. You are chosen. You are seen.*

She was fourteen. The distance between being chosen and being taken is not a distance a fourteen-year-old can measure.

When it happened—when the thing she would never name occurred—she filed it under love because the alternative was a category she didn't have the vocabulary for yet. He was careful. He was gentle. He said, "You're so special to me," and "I would never hurt you," and "This is our thing, just ours." She was fourteen and she believed every word, because wanting to believe made the believing easy.

She told no one.

Not because she was ashamed—not yet. She told no one because it was hers. The first thing that had ever been entirely hers, undivided by Marisol's grades or Tomás's illness or her parents' distracted love. This secret was a room only she had the key to, and she guarded it with a fierceness that confused anyone who didn't understand what it was like to spend a lifetime sharing everything.

She saw April for the first time on a Tuesday in November.

She hadn't known April existed until then. April wasn't in her grade, wasn't in her circle—she was one of the quiet, pretty girls Angel had catalogued and dismissed, the ones who moved through the hallways as if they were trying to take up less space than they occupied.

It was an accident of timing. Angel had been walking to Gerald's house later than usual, dusk already settling and her coat pulled tight against a wind that had arrived cold and unannounced. She had come around the side of his house—the back way she'd started using because it felt more private, more *theirs*—and stopped.

The kitchen light was on. The window shade was up three inches. And through those three inches, Angel saw April Jones pulling on her jacket at Gerald Daley's kitchen table while Gerald stood by the counter, counting bills into his hand.

One, two, three, four, five.

He folded them and held them out. April took them without looking at him, tucking them into her jacket pocket. Then she picked up her backpack.

Angel stood outside in the dark and watched, and she could not breathe.

She left before April came out the back door. She walked home, four blocks in the wrong direction—past a playground where two children were ignoring their mother's "time to go," past a corner store with a hand-lettered sign for boiled peanuts, past a woman walking a dog who said "evening." Angel did not respond because she was not there.

She was still in Gerald's kitchen, watching a transaction.

The thing that hit her was not outrage. She needed to be clear about that, even now, staring at herself in the Santos bathroom mirror. What hit her was not the "correct" thing. What hit her was—

Jealousy.

Burning, specific, irrational jealousy. Because if he was giving April money, then the thing between Gerald and Angel wasn't love. It wasn't special. It wasn't *chosen*. It was inventory. And if Angel was inventory, then the room she thought she alone had the key to had other doors she'd never been shown. Every single thing she'd filed under "love" needed to be refiled under something she didn't have a word for in either English or Spanish—something that sat in the chest like a swallowed stone.

She didn't blame Gerald. She knew that was wrong, even then. In the numb hours after, she understood on some level that a grown man had done something to both of them that they were too young to name. She understood it the way you understand a word in a foreign language—you know the shape of it, you can almost feel its meaning, but it doesn't land in the body. It doesn't become real.

What landed was April.

Pretty, quiet, effortless April, who apparently also had access to the thing Angel thought was only hers—except April had gotten money for it. That meant April had something Angel didn't. It meant Angel had given something away for free that had actual value. It meant—

She stopped thinking. The thoughts went somewhere she couldn't follow.

She never went back to Gerald's porch. She never told anyone what she'd seen, what she'd done, or what had been done to her. She deleted it all through a process she couldn't have named—not repression, exactly, but reclassification. She put it in a drawer labeled "the weird fall of eighth grade," pushed the drawer shut, and became someone else.

The "someone else" was loud.

Louder than she'd ever been—the girl at the center of every room, the first to arrive and the last to leave. She was the one who could read a man's desire from across a party and decide in five seconds whether she wanted to be *wanted* by him, or whether she would make him want her and then let him watch her walk away. She learned to control the space between being chosen and doing the choosing. The control felt like power, and the power felt, at certain angles and in certain lights, almost like safety.

She met April at fifteen through a mutual friend and recognized her immediately. That jawline, those green eyes, the quiet economy of her movements. Angel knew her. April didn't know Angel from anyone.

And something strange happened: Angel liked her.

Not at first. At first, it was complicated—every time April laughed or received a compliment, Angel felt that drawer in her chest rattle. But April was genuinely funny and genuinely kind.

She looked at Angel like Angel was worth looking at, not because Angel was performing, but because Angel was *there*. Eventually, the drawer stopped rattling so loudly and the liking took root.

They became sisters. That was the word they used because it was the truest one. April became Mama Rosa's honorary daughter, and Angel became the loudest presence in the Jones household. They shared everything: clothes, secrets, bad decisions, and good ones.

Almost everything.

The drawer stayed shut. Angel had decided this.

But a shut drawer still takes up space. And the thing inside it—the jealousy, the shame, the reclassified not-love, the night standing outside Gerald Daley's kitchen window—all of it had leaked out through the years in ways Angel could see clearly only now, at thirty-one.

It was every man she'd wanted who was already spoken for. It was every moment of April's happiness she'd felt as a personal dimming, even when she loved her, even when she was rooting for her. It was the way she'd circled Josh with questions at that first party, just to see. The way Charles's wedding ring had made her want him more, not less. The way she'd told herself she deserved the pieces of a man who was already someone else's whole.

She had spent sixteen years taking the wrong things from the wrong people and calling it desire. It wasn't desire. It was the drawer, rattling.

Downstairs, she could hear April and Mama Rosa laughing. April's laugh—that specific sound that started low and built before she could stop it—came through the floorboards, and Angel closed her eyes.

She loved April. This was not complicated. This was the one thing that had remained uncomplicated through everything.

She had also spent sixteen years competing with April for something she couldn't name, pursuing the men April loved or might love, sitting in the center of rooms where April sat too and silently taking measurements. And April had never known. April, who trusted completely and forgave reflexively, had never once looked at Angel and seen the drawer.

She would have to tell her.

Not today. Not while April was still raw from everything that had happened—Josh, the warehouse, her father's death. But someday. The Daley secret needed to stop being something Angel carried alone. It was getting too heavy. Secrets always did.

She looked at herself in the peeling gold mirror and tried to find the fourteen-year-old in the face looking back. She was there, somewhere—sitting on Gerald Daley's porch in the October dusk, convinced she was chosen, not knowing yet what that was going to cost her.

Angel reached up and touched the bottom left corner of the mirror's gold frame. The peeling paint flaked against her fingertip. She thought about telling Mama Rosa it needed fixing.

She thought: *I have to stop letting things come undone without saying anything.*

She picked up the towel. She folded it. She went downstairs to find her sister.

Chapter 9: Collateral Damage

Tasha had a system for being lied to. She had developed it over six years of marriage to a man who believed that charm was an acceptable substitute for honesty. The system was this: she did not confront until she had evidence; she did not gather evidence until she was calm; and she did not get calm until she had poured herself exactly one glass of Pinot Grigio, sat at her kitchen table alone in a quiet house, and decided what she actually knew versus what she merely felt.

What she felt: rage. The kind that sat low in her belly—not hot, but dense, like a stone that had been there long enough to become part of the landscape.

What she knew: Charles had come home after eleven three nights in the past two weeks. He had started showering before bed instead of in the morning. His phone now lived face-down on every surface it touched. And last Thursday, while looking out the front window for the mail carrier, she had seen a car she didn't recognize idling at the end of the block—a silver Honda, the driver's face turned away. Thirty minutes later, Charles had walked through the door claiming he'd been stuck in traffic on 285.

There was no traffic on 285 at nine-thirty on a Thursday night.

She had seen the woman once. Just a glimpse—pulling away from the curb in front of their house on a Sunday afternoon while Tasha was upstairs changing. Young. Dark hair. Something about the quickness of her exit felt practiced. It felt like someone who knew how to leave without being seen and had miscalculated the timing by thirty seconds.

Tasha sipped her wine, picked up her phone, and scrolled to Josh's name.

She didn't like Josh. She wanted to be clear about that, even to herself. Josh was a beautiful man with a boy's sense of accountability—the kind of man who treated his feelings as events that happened to him rather than choices he made. But Josh had known Charles since college and, more relevantly, Josh had known April. And the woman Tasha had glimpsed—the dark hair, the practiced exit—something about it nagged at her in the direction of April's name.

She hit "call" before she could talk herself out of it.

Josh answered on the third ring with the wariness of a man who had learned that late-night calls rarely brought good news.

"Tasha." Not a greeting. A statement. A *this-had-better-be-worth-it.*

"We need to talk." Her voice was the temperature of a February morning—not aggressive, just cold all the way through. "About Charles."

Josh set down the bottle of beer he'd been nursing in front of a game he wasn't watching. "I don't really do Charles's business."

"I think he's seeing someone." A beat. "I think it might be April."

The name landed the way she'd known it would. She could hear the shift in his breathing across the line—the small intake, the recalibration. Josh had never fully let April go. Tasha had figured that out the first time she'd been in the same room with him and heard April's name mentioned. His whole body changed temperature.

"What makes you think it's her?" he asked. Not a question, but a statement he was hoping she'd contradict.

"Young woman. Dark hair. Coming and going at odd hours." Tasha paused. "That describe anybody you know?"

"That describes half of Atlanta."

"Josh."

He was quiet for a moment. She could picture him exactly: standing in whatever apartment he was renting now, jaw tight, working through the arithmetic of his own wounded pride and deciding how much of it to let show. "What do you want me to do about it?"

"I want to know if it's her. And I want to know who I'm dealing with."

"Give me the address of wherever he's going to be tomorrow night."

Tasha looked down at her wine glass. Half empty. "He told me he's meeting clients for drinks at Monolith on Peachtree. Eight o'clock."

"I'll be there." Josh picked his beer back up. "But Tasha—if it's not April, I'm walking out the door. I'm not your private investigator."

"Fair enough," she said, and hung up before either of them could say something true.

Cynthia Reeves had worked for April Jones for four years and had learned to read her boss the way one reads weather—not by what was happening now, but by the patterns that predicted what was coming. The past few weeks had been low pressure across the board: April arriving late, leaving early, staring at her screen with the focus of a woman who was not reading what was on it. Distracted. Somewhere else.

Cynthia had been careful not to ask. April valued her privacy the way some people valued their credit score—obsessively, silently, as a measure of her own competence. Cynthia respected that.

But when her phone buzzed at seven-fifteen on a Thursday evening with a text from a number she didn't recognize—*Josh Coleman*—it changed things. *You know April's friend Angel? Seen her with a guy named Charles? I need to know what you know.*

Cynthia sat with it for twenty minutes, made a cup of chamomile she didn't drink, and then typed back: *Who is this and why should I tell you anything?*

His response was immediate: *Because something's about to blow up and April's going to be collateral damage if nobody's paying attention.*

Cynthia picked up her coat. She was, if nothing else, absolutely curious.

Monolith was the kind of bar that had strong opinions about itself. Exposed brick, Edison bulbs, and a cocktail menu that used the word "artisanal" without a hint of irony. The clientele on a Thursday night skewed toward young professionals unwinding from the week, their voices raised over a playlist that thought it was more interesting than it actually was.

Josh arrived first. He took a stool at the far end of the bar where he could see the door without being seen from it, ordered a bourbon neat, and waited. Cynthia arrived eight minutes later. She found him by process of elimination—the only man sitting alone who looked like he was conducting surveillance—and slid onto the adjacent stool without an invitation.

"You're the one who texted me," she said.

"You came," he replied. "So you know something."

"I know Angel Reyes has been spending time with a man named Charles who wears a wedding ring and doesn't mention it." She folded her hands on the bar. "I saw them together at April's family barbecue. I didn't say anything because it wasn't my business." She looked at him squarely. "Is it April's business?"

"It might be Charles's wife's business," Josh said. "She's on her way."

Cynthia absorbed this. "Lord." She flagged the bartender. "I'm going to need something with vodka in it."

Tasha arrived at eight-twelve in a cream blazer and slacks—the kind of outfit that said *I am not here to be seen; I am here to see.* She spotted Josh immediately, assessed Cynthia in one sweep, and took the stool on Josh's other side.

"She's not April," Cynthia said before anyone could ask. "The woman he's been seeing. I've seen them together, and it's not April Jones."

Tasha's expression didn't change. She had prepared for both outcomes and was not going to let either of them see her relief. "Then who is it?"

"Her name is Angel Reyes. She's April's best friend." Cynthia picked up her vodka tonic. "Or was."

The three of them sat with that for a moment. Outside, traffic moved. The playlist changed to something with more bass.

Josh stared at his bourbon. Angel. Of all people. He'd met Angel twice at April's gatherings—loud, beautiful, the kind of woman who walked into rooms as if she were already the most interesting thing in them. He'd found her exhausting and magnetic in equal measure. He thought of April finding out. His stomach turned.

"There they are," Tasha said quietly.

At a booth near the back, half-visible through the Thursday crowd, Charles and Angel sat close together. They weren't touching, but the quality of that not-touching—the deliberate inches between them, the way they both leaned slightly in—spoke volumes. Charles had his jacket off, his shirtsleeves rolled. Angel had her hair down and a glass of red wine, and she was smiling at something he'd said with the particular look of a woman who had decided, for at least this hour, to stop thinking about consequences.

Tasha stood up.

"Tasha—" Josh started.

"I'm not going to make a scene," she said. The flatness in her voice was more alarming than anger would have been.

She walked across the bar with the measured pace of someone who had rehearsed this walk in her imagination many times.

Charles saw her coming. Tasha watched the exact moment it happened—the way his face shifted from relaxed to calculating in under a second, his smooth social mask snapping into place. He had always been good at that. She used to admire it.

"Tasha." He said it as both a question and a greeting, his tone calibrated to suggest her presence was a pleasant surprise rather than the end of something. "What are you—"

"Having fun?" She stopped at the edge of the booth but didn't sit. The height advantage was intentional. She looked at Angel the way one looks at a math problem already solved. "I'm Tasha. Charles's wife."

Angel's composure held for perhaps two seconds. Then, she set her wine glass down too carefully on the table, sat up straighter, and said, "I know who you are." It was either brave or foolish—possibly both.

"Funny," Tasha said. "He never mentioned that you two were so close."

Charles stood. He had six inches and forty pounds on everyone in the conversation, yet he used none of it; Tasha's stillness made the very concept of physical presence irrelevant. "This isn't the place," he said, his voice low.

"You picked the place." She tilted her head slightly. "I just showed up."

Josh materialized at Tasha's shoulder, with Cynthia a half-step behind him. The booth had become a theater. At the adjacent table, a couple had stopped pretending not to listen.

"You don't know what you're talking about," Charles said. His voice was shifting now—still controlled, but with an edge underneath. It was the sound of a man who did not enjoy losing the narrative.

"I know what I saw." Josh stepped forward. His voice carried the blunt-instrument quality of wounded pride made righteous. "And I know who Angel is to April. So maybe somebody wants to explain to me how this happened."

Angel looked at Josh, and something flickered across her face—recognition, followed by a shame she refused to perform for this audience. She stood. She was not a small woman, and she did not make herself small. "This is not your business, Josh. You and April have been done for months."

"April is my business when someone who's supposed to be her best friend is—"

"Her best friend." Angel's voice dropped to something quieter and more dangerous. "You want to talk about what a best friend does? Or do you want to talk about what a boyfriend does? Because I remember what you did at that party. April told me everything."

The silence that followed had weight. Josh's jaw worked. He was the first to look away.

Cynthia set her glass on the nearest surface and quietly inserted herself between Josh and the table. "Okay," she said, with the calm of a woman who had managed difficult personalities for four years and was intimidated by none of them. "I think we've established that everyone here has done something they're not proud of." She looked at Tasha. "You got what you came for. You know who it is." Then to Charles: "And you need to figure out what you're going to do about your marriage, and that conversation does not happen in a bar." Finally, to Angel: "And you need to decide what April means to you before she finds out from someone other than you."

No one spoke.

"I'm going home," Cynthia announced, picking up her bag. "And I suggest the rest of you do the same."

Angel left first. She walked through the front door without looking at Charles, her heels sharp against the hardwood and her back straight. Her face was arranged into an expression that would not give the room the satisfaction of watching her break.

She made it to the parking lot before her hands started shaking. She sat in her car for six minutes before starting the engine.

The anger came first—at Charles, for putting her in this position; at Tasha, for a look that was sadder than it was furious and therefore harder to defend against; at Josh, for invoking April's name like a weapon; and at Cynthia, for being right about everything in the most infuriating way possible.

Then, beneath the anger, was the thing she didn't want to face: shame. Not a performed shame, nor the strategic lowering of eyes she deployed when a situation called for it, but real shame—the kind that sat in the sternum and radiated outward. She had been sitting in that booth smiling at a married man, telling herself it was complicated. And it was. But it was also simple: she had known Tasha existed, and she had shown up anyway.

Her phone buzzed. Charles. She let it go to voicemail. It buzzed again. She declined it. The third time, she picked up. "Don't," she said.

"Angel, just let me explain—"

"There's nothing to explain." Her voice surprised her with its steadiness. "I knew what this was. I let it be what it was. That's on me." She stared at the parking lot through the windshield—at the cars, the lampposts, and a couple walking out of the bar laughing, unburdened. "But I'm done, Charles. I told you that before, and I meant it. I mean it now."

"You don't have to—"

"Go home to your wife." She said it without heat, which was worse than if she'd said it with any. "Figure out what you want. But don't call me while you're figuring it out."

She ended the call. She found his name in her contacts and deleted it. She knew the number by heart—she always would—but knowing a number and having it saved were different things. One was a memory she couldn't control; the other was a door she could finally close.

She drove home through the Atlanta night, the city lights blurring past her windows. The air coming through the cracked glass smelled of warm asphalt and honeysuckle—the particular sweetness of a Southern summer night that always felt, to Angel, like a promise the city made without explaining what it was promising.

She was tired. Not sleepy, but bone-tired—the kind of exhaustion that comes from carrying something too long in the wrong position. She thought about April, and the conversation she would have to have someday, in a form she couldn't yet picture. She pressed the thought flat and drove.

Charles sat alone in the booth for eleven minutes after the others had left. The bartender came by twice; Charles waved him off both times. His jacket remained on the seat beside him, folded neatly. He looked at it the way one looks at a version of oneself no longer recognized.

He was good at stories. This was the trait people mistook for charm—he wasn't charming, exactly; he was narrative. Every situation had a frame, and he was skilled at building them: the frame in which Tasha was distant and the marriage had drifted through mutual neglect; the frame in which Angel had pursued him; the frame in which what he felt for Angel was something real and separate from the obligations of his other life.

All of those frames lay shattered on the bar floor.

He recalled Tasha's face when she walked up to the table. He had watched her process it—not the discovery, for he could see she had already done that, but the confirmation. The thing about confirmation is that it removes hope. Suspicion holds hope, however small. Confirmation does not.

He thought about Tasha at twenty-three, dancing at his roommate's birthday party with her eyes closed and her arms above her head, completely unconcerned with who was watching. He had watched. He had thought: *That one. That specific one.*

He picked up his jacket. He left two twenties on the table—too much, but he didn't have the patience for change.

Outside, the Atlanta night was warm, the air carrying the faint sweetness of jasmine from down the block. He sat in his car and did not call Angel back. He did not text Tasha. He drove home through streets known by habit, parked in his own driveway, and sat there listening to the engine tick as it cooled.

The porch light was on. Tasha always left it on when she knew he was coming home. He didn't know if she would leave it on after tonight. He thought she probably would, because Tasha was the kind of woman who maintained the architecture of a life even while deciding whether to stay in it, and the porch light was part of that architecture. But he couldn't be sure. And that uncertainty was the first honest thing he had felt in a long time.

He went inside. The house smelled of the lavender candle Tasha burned on Thursdays. His dinner sat wrapped in foil on the counter.

He stood in his own kitchen and understood, clearly and without the buffer of a frame, that he had been a fool. The understanding didn't fix anything, but it was real. And after months of carefully constructed unreality, reality felt like something he could finally stand on.

Chapter 10: Miami

She booked the flight at eleven-forty-three on a Tuesday night. April sat cross-legged on her bathroom floor in a T-shirt and underwear, her back against the tub and her laptop balanced on her knees. She'd been in there for forty minutes, originally intending to run a bath she never turned on. The tile felt cold through the thin cotton of her clothes, but she didn't move.

The search had started as a distraction—the way one scrolls through flights when not actually going anywhere, using the possibility of *elsewhere* as a crutch to get through the *here*. Atlanta to anywhere. Nonstop preferred. Departing Friday.

Miami appeared first. Round trip, reasonable fare, a direct shot south. April stared at the screen.

She thought about her father—the way he used to say that when life got too loud, you had to find somewhere it couldn't follow. He'd usually meant church, or the back porch with a glass of sweet tea and the sound of the neighborhood settling into the evening. But he'd also taken her to the beach once when she was nine—a long weekend at Tybee Island that cost more than he could afford and about which he'd never complained. She had stood at the edge of the Atlantic for the first time and felt a release in her chest—a breath she hadn't known she was holding.

She needed to find somewhere it couldn't follow.

She clicked "purchase" before her practical self could form a counterargument.

The confirmation email landed in her inbox with a small, satisfying chime. April closed the laptop and sat in the cold bathroom for a few more minutes, listening to the quiet of her apartment. For the first time in weeks, she felt something akin to anticipation.

Miami International hit her before she was ready—the humidity finding her the moment she stepped through the terminal doors. It was warm and dense, smelling of salt, jet fuel, and a floral scent she couldn't quite identify—some blossoming thing growing in the median that had no business being so extravagant in an airport pickup zone. The air had weight here. In Atlanta, the summer heat was aggressive; in Miami, it was generous, enveloping—the kind of heat that asked nothing of you except that you slow down.

She slowed down.

The cab ride to South Beach was forty minutes of gradual recalibration. The driver had the radio on—something with congas and a horn section that April didn't recognize, but it felt correct for the palm trees sliding past the window and the flat, blue expanse of Biscayne Bay appearing between exits. The city assembled itself around her: the causeways stretching over turquoise water, the Art Deco pastels of South Beach arriving in blocks of coral and seafoam, and the ocean presenting itself at the end of Ocean Drive like a reward for the journey.

Her hotel was small and deliberate. Terrazzo floors, a ceiling fan in the lobby turning as slow as a thought, and a young woman at the desk who handed over the key and said, "You're going to love it here," with the conviction of someone who meant it. April's room faced the beach. She dropped her suitcase, stepped onto the narrow balcony, and stood with both hands on the railing while the Atlantic arranged itself below her in long, unhurried lines of surf.

She exhaled.

The sound was not quite a sigh and not quite a word; it was the sound of something held too tight finally being released. She stood there until her shoulders dropped, her jaw unclenched, and the particular frequency of tension she'd carried for weeks began, slowly, to demodulate.

Below her, a man walked a dog along the packed wet sand. Two women in matching sun hats took pictures of each other against the water. A pelican coasted past at eye level, utterly indifferent, ancient and serene.

April went inside and unpacked her suitcase with more care than usual—hanging items she normally would have left folded and arranging her toiletries on the bathroom shelf in a neat row. She had three days. She was going to use them correctly.

On the first morning, she walked to Little Havana before the heat peaked.

The neighborhood woke up slowly and completely, like a person who doesn't do anything halfway. By nine o'clock, Calle Ocho was already in motion. The smell of Cuban coffee threaded through the open doors of every café—thick, dark, and slightly sweet. It was the kind of coffee that made one understand why people arranged their entire mornings around it. April stopped at a *ventanita* and ordered a *colada*. The man behind the counter handed her a small styrofoam cup of espresso so concentrated it was almost syrup. She drank it standing on the sidewalk and felt it move through her like something purposeful.

She walked through Máximo Gómez Park and watched old men play dominoes at stone tables with the focused ease of a ten-thousandth repetition. The sound of the tiles—a sharp click, then a deliberate placement—mixed with the low murmur of Spanish and the occasional triumphant laugh. April sat on a nearby bench and watched, feeling less like a tourist and more like a guest visiting a ritual, grateful for the invitation.

A vendor near the park entrance was rolling cigars by hand at a small wooden table, working with the efficiency of hands that knew the task without instruction. April stopped to watch. The cigars were dark and fat, the leaves pulled tight with a practiced twist.

"You smoke?" the man asked without looking up.

"No," April said. "But I'd like one anyway."

He looked up then, assessing her briefly the way people do when a request doesn't quite make sense but isn't worth interrogating. "For someone else?"

April thought about her father—about the way he'd smelled faintly of pipe tobacco in the winters, the particular warmth of that scent on a cold Sunday morning when she was small enough to climb into his lap. She thought about him staying awake through the coughing at the end, holding her hand without squeezing, trying to make the moment last.

"For a memory," she said.

The man nodded once, accepting this as a reasonable answer, and held out a cigar. She paid him and tucked it carefully into the side pocket of her bag, wrapped in a small paper sleeve. She would not smoke it. She would carry it home and put it somewhere she could see it—an object that did the work a photograph cannot. It wasn't a record of something lost, but proof that the thing had been real.

She walked back to the hotel through Wynwood, where warehouses had been transformed into a street museum that spanned for blocks—murals stacked against one another like arguments in a conversation about what art was allowed to be. A ten-foot woman with jaguar eyes peered down from a corner wall. A swirling abstract piece in indigo and copper occupied an entire building face. A young painter perched on a ladder caught her eye and raised his brush in a loose salute, a drop of chrome yellow falling from the tip and hitting the sidewalk like punctuation.

April raised her hand in return and kept walking. For the first time in a long while, she felt like herself—not the self she performed for work, nor the one she assembled for other people's comfort, but the interior self. This was the woman who had always moved through the world with more curiosity than she usually dared to show.

Coconut Grove in the afternoon was a different Miami entirely—quieter, shadier, its streets canopied by old banyan trees whose roots had cracked the sidewalks and who seemed to feel no remorse for it. April found a small restaurant with ceiling fans and a chalkboard menu. She ordered *ropa vieja* that arrived in a deep bowl over white rice—the beef pulled soft and savory, tasting of cumin, tomato, and slow time.

She ate alone at a table by the window and did not look at her phone.

She hadn't checked it in three hours, and the abstinence felt first like an itch she was refusing to scratch and then, gradually, like a profound relief. There was nothing on that device she needed. Josh was not going to say anything worth reading. Angel's silence was better than Angel's words right now. Work would manage itself for seventy-two hours.

A jazz quartet was setting up in the corner, unhurried, adjusting stands and tuning instruments with the comfortable non-urgency of those who knew the music would be ready when it was ready. The bassist plucked a low note that resonated in April's sternum. She ordered a glass of white wine she didn't strictly need and sat with it while they played. The afternoon stretched around her like a space she had almost forgotten how to inhabit.

This, she thought. *This is what normal feels like.*

It wasn't happiness, exactly—she wasn't ready to call it that. But it was normalcy: the ordinary beauty of a meal eaten slowly, a glass of wine in the afternoon, music played in a room for no reason other than that music deserved to be heard. She had spent so long surviving that she'd forgotten survival was supposed to be a means to an end.

She dressed for the evening with the same deliberateness she'd applied to her unpacking. She chose the black silk dress she'd packed on impulse—she had stood in front of her closet in Atlanta at midnight holding it, certain she'd never wear it, yet packing it anyway. Now, she was grateful for that midnight instinct. She applied her makeup slowly, watching herself in the bathroom mirror with an attention that differed from her usual scrutiny. She wasn't searching for flaws; she was just looking. She was learning the face that had gotten her through the last several months and deciding it was sufficient.

She stepped out onto Ocean Drive at nine o'clock, and the night received her.

The neon was fully deployed—pink, blue, and coral light washing the Art Deco facades. The bass from three different venues overlapped on the sidewalk into a unique, thrumming composition. The crowd moved with a particular Miami Friday energy that April could only describe as intentional pleasure—people who had decided they were going to have a good time with the same seriousness they brought to any other commitment. Convertibles crawled down the strip. A group of women in matching gold dresses passed her like a constellation.

April walked into Mango's Tropical Café and was immediately absorbed by the sound and light. The live band was mid-set, playing salsa at a tempo that made the floor feel like it was breathing. Dancers moved through a cleared center space with the fluid precision of those who had been doing this since before they could articulate why it felt necessary. April ordered a mojito at the bar—mint, lime, and rum over ice, the mint bruised just enough—and stood at the edge of the dance floor, watching the way bodies communicated without language.

A man in a white linen shirt appeared at her elbow. Cuban, she guessed, mid-forties, possessing the kind of handsome that had made peace with age rather than fighting it.

"You're watching like someone who wants to but thinks she shouldn't," he said. His accented English turned the observation into something almost musical.

April looked at him. "Is it that obvious?"

"Only to someone who has looked the same way." He extended his hand. "I am Marco. I promise I dance better than I look."

She laughed—genuinely and unexpectedly, a laugh that started low and built before she could stop it. "That's a strange selling point."

"But honest."

She took his hand.

He was right. He danced the way people do when the body has performed the steps long enough that the mind can let go. His lead was gentle and clear, his frame solid but not controlling. April found the rhythm in thirty seconds and then stopped thinking about whether she had it; she just moved. The band was playing something she didn't know the name of and didn't need to. The mojito was cold in her hand, and then it wasn't in her hand at all—it was on the bar, and she was fully inside the music. For four minutes, she was not April Jones with the weight of her own history; she was just a woman in a black silk dress dancing on a Friday night in Miami because the night had offered an invitation and she had said yes.

When the song ended, she laughed again. Marco bowed with theatrical sincerity, and she thanked him—and meant it.

Later, she moved through the night as if she were getting away with something. She found a club down the block where the DJ played something dark and electronic that suited the late hour. At one in the morning, she walked along the water's edge, heels in hand, the wet sand cold against her feet and the Atlantic black and enormous beside her.

She stopped at the shoreline and let the water come to her—cool, insistent, retreating and returning in its ancient, biological rhythm. The city hummed behind her. Ahead was nothing but open water and the faint suggestion of a horizon where the ocean met a sky thick with clouds.

She thought about her father standing at the edge of Tybee Island. She remembered the way he'd draped his arm around her nine-year-old shoulders and said, "All that water, baby, and it still knows to come back to shore."

She hadn't understood what he meant then. She was beginning to now.

She stood there until the cold water had reached her ankles three times and retreated three times, and then she turned to walk back up the beach. The city welcomed her with its noise and neon, and its absolute refusal to be anything other than exactly what it was.

On the second day, she slept late.

This was its own small miracle. April Jones did not sleep late. She was a woman who woke at six-fifteen regardless of when she'd gone to bed, her body having internalized the rigid schedule of a life that required her to be ready before anyone else arrived. But the Miami morning filtered golden and unhurried through the curtains, and her body whispered *not yet*. For once, she listened. She didn't open her eyes until nine-twenty; the sensation of having slept until mid-morning at thirty-one years old felt like a gift she'd given herself without knowing she'd needed it.

Room service arrived: fresh papaya and mango, croissants with cold butter, and a small pot of Cuban coffee. She ate on the balcony in her hotel robe while the beach assembled itself below—the umbrella rental man setting up his uniform rows, the first joggers appearing on the packed sand, and a child dragging a plastic bucket toward the water with the focused ambition of someone with significant construction plans.

She called her mother.

"Miami?" Her mother's voice carried that particular blend of mild alarm and forced casualness she deployed whenever April did something spontaneous. "You didn't tell me."

"I didn't know until Tuesday night."

A pause stretched between them. "You okay, baby?"

April looked at the ocean. The morning light was doing something specific to the water—turning it translucent green near the shore, then sapphire, then a deep teal further out, the colors stacked in vibrant bands. "Yeah, Mama. I'm okay. I just needed to go somewhere."

Her mother was quiet for a moment, the kind of silence that suggested she understood more than she intended to voice. "Your father used to do that," she said finally. "Just go. Said some problems needed air they couldn't get at home."

April felt her throat tighten. "I know."

"You eat something?"

"I'm eating right now."

"Good." A beat. "Call me when you get home."

"I will."

She sat with the phone in her lap for a while after they hung up, watching the child at the waterline fill the bucket and carry it with enormous seriousness toward the dry sand. The bucket was far larger than the logic of the task required. April found this quality admirable.

The afternoon was a blur of the Pérez Art Museum, the Wynwood Walls, and a boat tour of Biscayne Bay she had almost declined. She was glad she hadn't. The guide pointed out the mansions along the water—absurd and magnificent structures with names she half-recognized. The Miami skyline, viewed from the water, was its own argument for the audacity of creation—the human need to place something tall against the sky and say: *Here. We were here.*

She bought herself a drink at the hotel bar that evening and sat alone at a corner stool. She made no effort to be approachable, which paradoxically made her feel more at ease in her own company than she had in months. She was not lonely. This realization surprised her. She had been afraid, when booking the ticket, that solitude would feel like punishment—a continuation of the isolation that had pressed down on her since Josh, since the warehouse, since the long unwinding of everything she'd once counted on.

Instead, it felt like ownership. She was the sole architect of this trip. Every choice—where to walk, what to eat, how long to stand at the edge of the tide—had been entirely hers. There was no one to perform for, no one to manage, and no one for whom she had to hold herself together.

She could just be.

She was still figuring out who that was, exactly. But Miami was a good place to do the work.

On the final night, she found the jazz club by accident.

She'd been walking back from dinner, taking a longer route through a quieter pocket of the neighborhood, when she heard it—not the recorded approximation of jazz that most bars piped through speakers, but the real thing. It was the particular breathing of live instruments finding one another in a room. She followed the sound to a door marked only with a small placard, the kind of place that relied on the loyalty of those who already knew it existed.

The interior was dim and intimate: a dozen tables, candles flickering in glass jars, and a low stage where a quartet played to an audience that had come specifically to listen. No one talked over the music or used it as a backdrop for business. They simply listened. April stood in the doorway for a moment, adjusting to the shadows.

A woman was singing. Her voice was low and round—the kind that didn't need to reach for notes because the notes were already where she was. She sang without theatrics, devoid of the performance of *performance*; it was just the song, moving through her, finding its way into the room. April didn't recognize the melody, but it didn't matter.

She found a small table near the back and ordered a glass of red wine, sipping it slowly. The quartet played through three more songs—the bassist anchoring the room with resonant pulses, the pianist adding splashes of color, and the drummer keeping time so lightly it was felt rather than heard. The singer moved between numbers without announcement or patter, letting the music speak with a confidence that had nothing to prove.

April sat in the half-dark and felt something in her chest open that she hadn't known was closed.

It wasn't dramatic—not a breakdown or a sudden revelation. It was a quiet unlocking, like finding a door in a wall she'd stopped thinking of as a wall. She thought about her father and the barbecue, about Angel and Charles and Josh, the warehouse and the disk and the fallout of it all. She let herself think about it without flinching. It was still painful, but the pain was manageable now because she was here, in a dim room in Miami, listening to a woman sing, and nothing that had happened had prevented this moment.

She had arrived anyway.

She stayed until the last song faded. She left a generous tip, walked back to the hotel through the warm night with the music still humming in her blood, and she slept deeply and without dreams. In the morning, she packed her suitcase, checked out, and took a cab to the airport.

On the flight back to Atlanta, she held the cigar in its paper sleeve on her lap. The woman in the adjacent seat glanced at it once but said nothing.

April looked out the window as Florida disappeared beneath a shelf of clouds. She did not know what was waiting for her in Atlanta, but she knew what she was bringing back to it.

Herself. More or less whole. A little sanded down, a little lighter.

That would have to be enough. She was starting to believe it was.

Chapter 11: A Night to Remember

The club did not announce itself. There was no marquee, no velvet-rope theater, no promotional signage competing with the neon of the strip. Just a door on a side street off Collins Avenue, a bouncer who looked like a former tight end, and a line that moved with unusual efficiency—as if the people inside valued their time too much to make those outside wait unnecessarily. April had found it the way one finds things in a city not their own: by following music she could feel in her chest before she could hear it with her ears.

She'd been walking after dinner—full and unhurried, following no particular route—when the bass reached her through the warm night air. It wasn't aggressive; it was a suggestion. A low, cycling pulse that her body registered before her mind made the decision to follow. She turned a corner, found the door, and joined the line without overthinking it.

This was the version of herself she was practicing: the one who followed the music.

Inside, the club opened up wider than the exterior suggested. High ceilings and a lighting design moved through the room in slow waves—deep amber to violet to a haunting shade of blue. The colors shifted too gradually to be jarring, just present enough to feel intentional. The DJ booth was elevated at the far end, and the DJ himself was unhurried, letting tracks breathe before building upon them, rewarding the crowd for paying attention. The floor was packed but not oppressive. People moved with the music the way they do when the rhythm is good enough to make movement feel inevitable rather than performed.

April ordered a rum and ginger at the bar. The bartender had island roots, she guessed, by the way he built the drink without measuring and handed it over with the confidence of a man who had made ten thousand of them. She found a spot at the edge of the floor where she could feel the bass through the soles of her sandals and watch the room calibrate itself around the sound.

She was not looking for anyone. She wanted to be clear about that, even to herself. She was out alone on her last full night in Miami, wearing a silk dress she'd packed on impulse, and she was there for the music, the rum, and the particular freedom of being in a city where no one knew her name.

She was not looking.

He was at the bar when she went back for her second drink, leaning against it with the ease of a man comfortable being still in a moving room. Tall—she noticed that first, the way height presents itself as a fact before anything else. Caramel skin, close-cropped hair, and a jawline that looked as if it had been drawn with intention. He was dressed simply— dark shirt, dark jeans, no jewelry—possessing the kind of understated style that doesn't try to be noticed and therefore is. He was watching the dance floor with an expression neither bored nor eager, just present—the same quality of attention she'd been practicing herself.

He glanced over when she stepped up to the bar. She glanced back.

These things have a grammar. April had spent enough of her life reading rooms to know when a glance was punctuation and when it was the beginning of a sentence. This one was a beginning.

"You've been standing at that edge for forty-five minutes," he said. His voice had a Southern roundness to it— not thick, just warm at the edges, the vowels taking their time. "Watching like you're deciding something."

"Maybe I am."

"What are you deciding?"

April looked at him steadily. "Whether the music is worth getting closer to."

He considered this. "What's the verdict?"

"Still deliberating."

The corner of his mouth moved in a way that wasn't quite a smile but was adjacent to one. He turned to the bartender, ordered, and then looked at her again with the direct, unhurried attention of a man who wasn't performing interest but actually felt it. "I'm Jason."

"April."

He extended his hand. She shook it, his grip firm without making a point of it. When he released her, she was aware of the absence of his touch before she was aware she'd even noticed it.

"The music's worth it," he said. "In my experience."

"Then lead the way," she said, picking up her drink.

He danced the way he stood—unhurried, with a sense of rhythm that required no external validation. He wasn't showy; he wasn't the kind of man who used the dance floor as an audition. He moved with her rather than at her, which was rarer than it should have been. April found herself relaxing into the motion the way one relaxes into a chair that is exactly the right height—less a decision than a recognition.

The music shifted under the DJ's hands, the tempo dropping slightly as the bass line became more deliberate. The crowd around them adjusted. April adjusted. Jason's hand moved to her waist—light, asking rather than taking—and she let it stay. They found the kind of proximity the music makes logical, close enough that she was aware of his warmth and the faint, clean scent of his skin: cedar with something warmer underneath.

She was aware of her own body in a way she hadn't been in months.

It wasn't the guarded, armored awareness she'd carried since the warehouse—that constant monitoring of entrances and exits, the hypervigilance that had settled into her nervous system like weather that wouldn't move. This was different. This was the awareness of a body that was choosing. Present-tense, active, hers.

She thought, briefly, of the warehouse. Of the way it had stripped choice from her—not just physically, but in the deeper sense of existing in her own skin without fear as the undercurrent. She had not felt safe in her body since that night. She had felt managed. Functional. Defended.

Standing here in this dim room with Jason's hand at her waist, the bass thrumming through the floor, and Miami three stories below going about its luminous Friday business, she felt something else. It wasn't the absence of fear, exactly. It was the discovery that fear was no longer the only thing available.

She chose to stay.

They moved from the dance floor to a booth when her feet demanded a break. The conversation that followed had the particular quality of late-night talk in a room where the music is too good to waste but quiet enough in the corner to be heard—shorthand and directness, the way strangers talk when both understand that time is finite and small talk is a tax neither is willing to pay.

He was originally from the outskirts of Savannah, he told her, and had moved to Miami three years ago for work. He said "work" without elaboration, and she didn't push. She registered that he guarded certain things just as she did, and she found it easier to trust him for it. When he asked what had brought her to Miami, she said she needed air that Atlanta couldn't provide. He nodded as if that were a complete answer.

"You get what you came for?" he asked.

She thought about the cigar in her bag. The jazz club. The wet sand at one in the morning. Her mother's voice on the phone. "Mostly," she said.

"What's the part you're still looking for?"

The question was direct enough to feel presumptuous, but it wasn't—his attention had the quality of genuine curiosity rather than strategy. He wasn't building toward a goal; he simply wanted to know.

April looked at him across the small table, the candle between them throwing unsteady light. "I'm still figuring out the question," she said. "It's hard to find something when you don't know what it looks like."

"That's honest."

"I'm working on it."

"Honest, or the other thing?"

"Both," she said. He smiled—fully this time, not the adjacent version—and it transformed his face in a way that made her understand why people wrote entire novels about the power of a smile arriving when you'd stopped expecting one.

The choice, when it came, was hers in every particular.

She wanted to be precise about this, even later, even when turning it over in the quiet of the next morning: it had been hers. It wasn't something that happened to her, not something she had drifted into, and not the consequence of rum or the late hour. She had looked at this man across a small table in a Miami club and decided, with the full deliberate weight of her own wanting, that she wanted to be close to him. Not because he was beautiful, though he was. Not because the night was running out. It was because he had listened to her the way people rarely did, neither trying to fix what she shared nor redirecting it toward himself. His hands were steady as he held his glass—and she wanted to know what those hands felt like making a choice of their own.

She leaned forward. "We could leave," she said.

He looked at her with that level attention that held nothing of the predatory. "We could," he said. "Where do you want to go?"

"Somewhere quieter."

He nodded. He left money on the table—enough, but not performatively so. He held the door. These were small things. They were not nothing.

His hotel was four blocks away, which felt to April like the city being generous.

The room was clean and simply furnished, featuring a window that faced the water. The ocean was visible as a dark expanse beyond the glow of the strip. He left the curtains open. April appreciated this—the sense of the world still existing outside, the darkness and the distant movement of the tide, a reminder that they were inside something chosen rather than something hidden.

He turned on the lamp, choosing the lowest setting, and the room turned warm and amber.

"Tell me what you want," he said. It wasn't a performance; it was a genuine question offered with the same directness he'd brought to everything else. The request was an act of respect so specific and unexpected that April felt her chest respond before her words could.

In the months since the warehouse, she had not told anyone what she wanted. She had told people she was fine. She had told people not to worry. She had managed their concern with the smooth competence she brought to everything requiring distance. No one had asked her what she wanted. She wasn't sure when anyone last had.

"This," she said. "I want this."

He crossed the room, and she met him halfway. The equal distance felt important—both of them moving toward the same thing at the same pace. When he kissed her, it was unhurried and thorough, possessing the quality of someone who understood that this was not a step toward something else, but its own complete entity, deserving of attention.

She kissed him back with her whole self. Not the managed, performed self. The interior one.

His hands were steady, just as she'd imagined. He moved with attention and without urgency, and she understood within minutes that he was the kind of man who listened with his body the same way he listened in conversation—orienting toward her, responsive, adjusting when she shifted or stilled or moved closer. She had never been touched like this. Not as if she were someone whose specific responses truly mattered.

The window stayed open. The Miami night remained outside, patient and illuminated. The ocean continued its ancient work.

April stayed in her own body the entire time. She noticed this later—the absence of the dissociation she had feared. A part of her had worried she might go somewhere else, slipping out of herself the way she'd learned to in the warehouse, the way she'd learned years before that in a wood-paneled den filled with cigar smoke and the drone of the television. But she hadn't gone anywhere. She had stayed. Present, choosing, hers.

Afterward, she lay on her back in the amber light and felt the specific quality of her heartbeat slowing—not the racing return-to-earth of panic or shame, but the gradual quieting of something that had been working hard and was now, briefly, at rest.

Jason lay beside her, not touching. He had read the room with the same generous accuracy he'd shown all evening. After a moment, he turned his head to look at her.

"You okay?"

"Yeah," she said. And then, because honesty was what she was practicing: "Better than okay."

He nodded and looked at the ceiling. The quiet between them was comfortable—two people who had shared something real and felt no need to paper over it with conversation.

They found a diner three blocks away at two in the morning. It was the kind of place with laminated menus and a counter where the cook worked in full view. The coffee came automatically; it wasn't good, but it was hot. April ordered eggs and toast with the appetite of someone who had, without realizing it, burned through dinner hours ago. Jason ordered the same. They sat in a window booth while the city moved past them—Miami still humming at two a.m. with the certainty of a place that understood the night as its own territory.

They talked. Not about what had just happened—neither needed to narrate it. They spoke of other things: cities they'd lived in and those they'd dreamed of, a book she'd read twice and couldn't fully explain, and the particular grief of watching a parent age. They discussed the strange way that losing someone rearranges one's sense of time. He spoke of his mother in a way that revealed the loss was not recent, yet not resolved—the wound healed over but still there beneath the surface, sensitive to the touch.

She talked about her father more than she had to anyone since the funeral. Not about the sickness or the end, but the earlier parts—the Sunday mornings, the Tybee Island weekend, and the way he could make a room feel settled just by being in it. Jason listened the way he did everything: fully, without redirecting the narrative.

"He sounds like someone worth missing," he said when she stopped.

"He is," she said. Present tense. She hadn't used the present tense before, but it felt true.

Haulover Beach at five in the morning was a different planet from the Miami she had been inhabiting.

Jason had suggested it with the casualness of someone who had watched sunrises there before and knew what they were worth. They drove up the coast with the windows down, the pre-dawn air finally cool enough to feel like relief, the city thinning out around them as they moved north. The beach parking lot was empty. The sand was pale and wide, and the Atlantic was doing its thing—eternal, indifferent, and magnificent in the way things are when they operate entirely outside of human concern.

They walked to the water's edge and stood there while the sky performed its pre-dawn ritual—no longer dark, not yet light, a deep blue at the horizon already beginning to separate from the water. The first barely-there gradations of color appeared at the seam where sea met sky.

April stood with her sandals in her hand and the sand cold and fine between her toes, watching the horizon. Beside her, Jason was quiet. He seemed to understand that this was not a moment for words; the sky was doing something that required no commentary, and the best thing two people could do was simply be present for it.

I came here not knowing what I was looking for, she thought.

The sky was turning now—the deep blue bleeding into something softer, the first pale gold appearing at the line where the Atlantic met the morning. A pelican came from nowhere and sailed past them, low over the water, riding something invisible and utterly sure of itself.

I think I found some of it, she thought.

The sun breached the horizon in stages—a glow first, diffuse and promising, then the edge of the disc itself, copper and enormous, pulling itself from the water with the patience of something that has been doing this since before anything watching it existed. The light hit the ocean, and the ocean caught it and threw it back in a thousand different directions. The beach around them went from gray to gold in the span of thirty seconds, and April felt her eyes sting in a way that had nothing to do with the light.

She did not cry. But she was close to it, and she let herself be close, which was its own kind of progress.

Jason reached over, unhurried, and took her hand. He just held it. He didn't say anything. The sun kept coming.

They stood there until the gold had normalized into morning light and the beach woke around them—a jogger appearing at the far end, a man with a metal detector moving methodically through the dry sand above the tide line. The world was resuming its business.

"Thank you," April said.

"For the sunrise?" Jason said. "That wasn't me."

"For the night." She looked at him. "For listening."

He squeezed her hand once and released it. "Thank you for trusting me with it."

He dropped her at her hotel as the morning fully arrived, golden and already warming. They stood on the sidewalk in front of the Art Deco facade with its terrazzo steps and the ceiling fan visible through the glass lobby door. He looked at her with that steady attention she had spent a whole night learning to trust.

"I'd like to see you again," he said. Simple. Direct. Not a line, but a statement offered with the willingness to hear "no" as an answer.

April looked at him in the morning light and thought about Atlanta—about the life she was going back to and everything that waited there: the unresolved, the painful, and the ongoing work of becoming someone who could stand in her own story without flinching.

"I live in Atlanta," she said.

"I know." He reached into his pocket and held out a card. It was plain, with just a name and a number: *Jason Mercer.* "So does this."

She took it. She looked at the card for a moment, then back at him. "I'll call you," she said.

"I'll be here."

She went inside. She rode the elevator up and stood in her room for a moment before doing anything else—just stood in the quiet with the morning light filtering through the curtains and the Atlantic churning below the balcony. She held the card in her hand and breathed.

She had the strangest feeling—quiet, tentative, and unused to the light—that something was beginning. She wasn't sure she was ready, but she wasn't sure readiness was the relevant question.

She set the card on the nightstand, exactly where she would see it first thing when she woke; then she lay down on top of the covers in the clothes she'd worn all night. She slept, deeply and without apology, into the Miami morning.

Chapter 12: The Man Behind the Mask

She slept on her side, one hand tucked under her cheek, breathing with the complete surrender of someone who had finally allowed herself to rest. Jason sat in the chair by the window in the early morning light and watched her. He didn't touch her; he didn't want to wake her. For the first time since he'd known her, she looked entirely unguarded.

He'd been awake for an hour. This was not unusual—he was a light sleeper by long habit, the kind of man who surfaced at four a.m. without urgency. He would lie in the quiet, performing the mental accounting that daylight hours were too full to permit. Usually, the ledger was professional: deals in progress, decisions pending—the inventory of a life organized around execution. This morning, the ledger held April.

He thought of the question he'd been carrying since Miami, from the moment he watched her walk into his hotel lobby three months ago. She'd arrived with her suitcase, her careful poise, and something vibrating beneath that composure—something he had recognized immediately, even if he hadn't yet found the words for it.

He had the words now. It had taken three months to find them.

She was someone who had been through something. She had learned—the way one only learns through specific, difficult experience—that the world was not reliably safe. She knew that the self was something you had to protect actively, rather than assume was shielded. He recognized this particular knowledge because he possessed it himself, written in different circumstances but in the same fundamental script.

Watching her breathe, he felt the specific tenderness of recognizing a person—not the surface version, not the beautiful woman in the silk dress who'd followed the music into a club, but the interior soul who had stayed in her own body all night like it was an act of will. Because it was.

He was afraid of losing her. He wanted to name this clearly; he had a history of failing to name things, only to be surprised when the unnamed thing caused damage. He was afraid of losing her, and he did not entirely know how to *not* lose people.

This was the part he hadn't figured out yet.

He'd grown up in Millen, Georgia—the kind of small town that appeared on maps but rarely in conversation. It was a place people passed through on the way to somewhere with more reasons to stop. Population three thousand and declining, one traffic light, and a Dollar General that had replaced the hardware store his grandfather remembered. A Baptist church sat on every other corner, each serving a slightly different interpretation of the same fundamental argument.

His mother, Diane Mercer, was the kind of woman Millen produced occasionally but could never quite keep—too sharp for the available opportunities, too principled for the available compromises, and too tired by forty to be anything but extraordinary. She worked the morning shift at the county hospital for twenty-two years as a CNA—the job that involved everything the nurses were too busy to do and received approximately none of the credit. She would come home smelling of antiseptic and, underneath it, the cocoa butter she applied every morning to her elbows and knees. It was a ritual she maintained with the consistency of someone who had decided that one small luxury was non-negotiable, regardless of what the budget dictated.

Jason had grown up measuring safety by that smell. Antiseptic and cocoa butter meant his mother was home, the day was closed, and the night was manageable.

His father had left when Jason was six. It wasn't dramatic— no argument Jason could recall, no door slammed with the force of a defining moment. It was a gradual subtraction: the truck in the driveway appeared less frequently, then not at all; the spot at the dinner table sat empty, then was set for two. Over the months, his father's name shifted in his mother's mouth from a noun to a silence. By seven, Jason understood that some people left. He learned that understanding this was not the same as being okay with it, but that being okay with it was not actually required. You could carry a weight and still move.

His mother never spoke badly of his father. He only understood later, as an adult, that this was a deliberate choice made at a great personal cost. She simply didn't speak of him much at all, leaving Jason to construct the story himself. He filled the absence with narrative, making meaning out of the shape of what wasn't there.

He'd been a quiet kid. This often surprised those who met him as an adult, who read his stillness as confidence—the composure of a man who knew his own weight. The stillness was real, but its origin was humbler than confidence: he'd learned early that rooms were easier to read from the edges. The boy who watched carefully made fewer mistakes than the loud boys. Knowledge was a form of protection when you were small and the world was large and indifferent.

He read. The school library in Millen was modest, but Jason worked through it with the systematic hunger of someone for whom books were oxygen rather than entertainment. History, science, whatever novels were available—he read without discrimination, filing it all away to build an interior world larger and more navigable than the exterior one. His mother watched this and rarely commented, except for the occasional night she found him at the kitchen table at eleven p.m. with a book and a glass of milk.

"Baby," she'd say, "the words will still be there tomorrow."

He always said okay. He rarely stopped.

She died when he was twenty-one. A heart attack, the doctor said. That was the medical fact, but the fuller truth was that she had worked double shifts for twenty-two years to put him through school and never once complained about the cost. Her heart had eventually submitted to the arithmetic of that sacrifice. She was fifty-two years old. She had not yet seen him graduate.

He graduated three months after the funeral. He walked across the stage at Morehouse College with her face in his chest—not just the photograph tucked in his jacket pocket, but the actual memory of her. He carried the specific geography of her features and the way her eyes crinkled when she was proud but trying not to make a scene. As he stood at the podium to receive his diploma, he was more alone than he had ever been in his life.

He was also entirely clear about what he was going to do with the life she had worked so hard to give him.

Miami had been strategic. He had built his career in Atlanta first—finance, the kind of work that rewarded the qualities his childhood had ingrained in him: patience, the careful reading of a room, and the willingness to remain at the periphery until it was time to move. He was good at it. He was good at most things when he applied that specific, unwavering attention. The professional world possessed a legible logic that he found navigable, if not exactly comforting. You did the work. You read the people. You made fewer mistakes than those who were louder and less careful. The outcomes followed.

What did not follow with the same reliability were the personal ones.

There had been women. He was no monk and had never pretended to be. But a pattern had emerged in his relationships—one he only identified in retrospect, after enough of them had ended in the same haunting way. He was present, attentive, and dependable, yet he held back. Not out of coldness—he was not a cold man. But there was a room inside him he did not show, a depth of interior life he had learned to manage privately back in Millen. He was open up to a point. That point was where the real things lived.

Her name had been Vanessa. Three years—his longest. She was a corporate attorney, precise and warm in equal measure. She was the kind of woman who noticed everything, said only what mattered, and possessed the patience for a long game. She had loved him. He had loved her, or had felt the thing so close to love that the distinction required more philosophy than he had to give.

She left on a Tuesday. She sat across from him at the kitchen table in his Atlanta apartment and said, with the composure of someone who had rehearsed the words but was bleeding through them anyway: "I love you, Jason. I have loved you for three years. But I can't keep loving someone who won't let me in."

He had listened. He had recognized the truth in it. He had said, "I hear you."

She had waited—the way one waits when they've said something that deserves more than a mere acknowledgment. She was waiting for him to argue, to reach for her, to say something that proved she mattered enough to fight for. He had said none of those things. Not because he didn't feel them, but because the room where those words lived was the one he never opened. By the time he realized Vanessa was asking to be let in rather than told to wait outside, she was already reaching for her coat.

He let her walk out without asking her to stay. He stood in his kitchen for a long time afterward, enveloped by the specific silence of a space that had recently held someone who was no longer there. He understood, with a clarity that felt almost clinical, that he had made a mistake he couldn't unmake.

He moved to Miami six months later. It wasn't a retreat— he was precise about that, even with himself. Running implied urgency, and Jason moved only with deliberation. Miami was a strategic recalibration: a new office, a new context, new rooms to master. He had hoped that in learning new spaces, the interior one might finally become easier to unlock.

As he sat in the chair by the window, he admitted he had been wrong. The room hadn't become easier to open; he had simply become better at ignoring the door.

He had seen April before she saw him. It was a habit of his—arriving early to orient himself before a space filled. He'd been at the bar for twenty minutes when she appeared at the edge of the dance floor. She wore a black silk dress and the posture of someone who had decided to be present, even though presence cost her something. He noticed the cost first—

the deliberateness of her stance, the focused attention of a person deciding something vital.

He'd thought: *That one knows what it's like to carry a weight.*

The recognition was immediate and, at first, non-romantic. It was the identification of a familiar frequency, like hearing a song in a dialect he hadn't realized he spoke. He stayed where he was; he wasn't the type to approach women at bars. But when she returned to the bar for her second drink and their eyes met, the recognition shifted. It took on a specific, undeniable weight.

He talked to her. The rest followed with the inevitable logic of things meant to happen: the dance floor, the booth, the diner at two in the morning, and eventually Haulover Beach at dawn. Her hand had felt small and certain in his as the sun rose. He had listened to her talk about her father and heard, beneath her words, the same story he carried about his mother—the irreplaceable person, the loss that rearranged the very architecture of time. He had wanted to tell her he understood. Instead, he had simply held out his card. She took it with an expression that tried not to hope, and failed.

She had called him six days later. He had answered on the first ring.

April stirred in the bed. She didn't wake, but her breathing shifted for a moment before settling. Her hand moved from beneath her cheek to the pillow beside her.

Jason watched her and thought about the pattern—the one Vanessa had named and he had confirmed by letting her go. He thought of the way he held back, treating his private interior world as a form of protection rather than a form of isolation.

He remembered his mother coming home smelling of cocoa butter and antiseptic, hanging her keys on the hook, and asking how his day was. He thought of his standard answers— "Fine," "Good," "Okay"—and the truths he had withheld. He hadn't told her the actual interior weather of an eleven-year-old managing more than a child should. She had accepted the surface answers not because she didn't care, but because she was tired, and the surface was all she had the capacity for. He had loved her enough not to add to her load.

He had learned to manage his life alone to protect the people he loved from the weight of it. It was a reasonable adaptation for a boy in Millen, Georgia.

It was a failure of an adaptation for a thirty-four-year-old man who wanted to be known.

April shifted again. Her eyes opened—not with a start, but with the slow grace of someone returning from a deep sleep. She looked at the ceiling for a moment, then turned her head and found him in the chair.

"How long have you been sitting there?" she asked, her voice rough with sleep.

"A while."

"Watching me sleep is a little intense, Jason."

"I was thinking," he said. "You just happened to be in the same room."

She looked at him. The morning light did something specific to her face—the emerald in her eyes catching the glow, highlighting the soft architecture of a woman who had let her guard down enough to rest. "What were you thinking about?"

He considered the available answers—the managed ones, the surface-level ones. He thought about the door to his interior room. He thought about Vanessa at the kitchen table with her coat already on.

"You," he said. "And whether I know how to do this right."

She was quiet for a moment. Then, "Me too."

"What are you afraid of?" he asked.

She looked at the ceiling. The question deserved a real answer, and she was weighing whether to give one. He waited the way he had learned to wait—not with impatience disguised as patience, but with a genuine willingness to give her whatever time the answer required.

"Disappearing into someone," she finally said. "I've done it before. I get close to a person and I start managing them instead of being with them. I lose the thread of myself." She turned her head to look at him. "You?"

"Not letting people in," he said. "I love people from a certain distance and then act surprised when the distance becomes the relationship."

She absorbed this. "We're a mess," she said.

"Probably," he said. "But at least we know where the landmines are."

She almost smiled. "Is that supposed to be reassuring?"

"It's supposed to be honest."

She sat up against the headboard and pulled the sheet around her, watching him in the chair by the window with the morning light at his back. He looked back at her, and what passed between them was not exactly a promise—they were both too careful for promises made at this hour—but something in the category of intention. It was a decision to try, and an acknowledgment that trying would require things from both of them that were not yet easy.

"I'm not going to disappear on you," he said. "I want you to know that. Whatever happens, I'm not the kind of man who just goes quiet."

She searched his face for a long moment. "Okay," she said softly, as if filing the words somewhere vital.

He nodded. He made a private vow in the language of a man who had spent his life managing his interior world alone: he was going to let her in. Not all at once—he wasn't built for that, and neither was she. "All at once" was usually a performance rather than a truth. He would do it incrementally. Door by door. He would open the room that had been closed for a long time—carefully, letting the air in slowly, giving his eyes time to adjust.

He was going to let her in.

He did not know yet what it would cost him when the fear grew loud or when old habits reasserted themselves. He didn't know how he would react when Angel appeared at the wrong moment with that particular vulnerability that only loneliness makes possible. He did not yet know the shape of his own worst mistake.

He only knew his intention. And for now, in the morning light, with April watching him with her careful, searching eyes, intention felt like a foundation he could build on.

He got up from the chair and moved to the bed. He sat on the edge of it, and she made room. The morning spilled through the window and the day began in the ordinary way that days do—which was all either of them was asking for.

Chapter 13: Aftermath and Reflection

The flight home was forty-seven minutes shorter than the flight down, which felt inherently wrong. Going to Miami had taken forever—each mile of altitude a deliberate separation from the life she was leaving behind. The city below had shrunk until it was a grid of lights, then a mere glow, and finally, nothing. Coming back, Atlanta assembled itself too quickly outside the window. The red clay was visible even through the cloud cover, the sprawl of the interstate threaded between suburbs, and the skyline arrived ahead of schedule—like someone who didn't know how to give you a moment to prepare.

April pressed her forehead against the cool plastic of the window and watched it come.

She had Jason's card in the interior pocket of her carry-on, the one reserved for things she couldn't afford to lose. She hadn't moved it since the hotel room, where she'd set it on the nightstand and then, while packing, held it for a long beat before tucking it away. She was aware of it the way one is aware of a specific weight—not heavy, just present. It was a fact about her life that hadn't existed a week ago.

She thought about Haulover Beach. The sun ascending in stages. His hand. The way the morning had arrived around them as if it were in no hurry at all.

Then she thought about everything waiting at baggage claim: Angel's unanswered calls, the mountain of deferred work, and the specific silence of an apartment she'd left in a haste—dishes in the sink and feelings she hadn't finished having. She had not solved anything by going to Miami. She had simply granted herself three days in which the problems weren't actively happening. The distance had done what distance does: it made the shape of things clearer without making the things themselves any smaller.

The wheels touched down. The cabin pressure shifted. Someone two rows back muttered "finally" to nobody in particular.

April straightened her spine, rolled her shoulders, and made a decision on the runway that she carried through the terminal, into the cab, and all the way to her front door: she was not going to pretend the Miami version of herself had been temporary. That woman—the one who followed music down side streets, who danced with strangers, who stood at the edge of the Atlantic at one in the morning and let the cold tide find her feet—that woman was available. She had always been available. She'd just been buried under the management of other people's emergencies for so long that she'd forgotten to look for her.

She was not going to rebury her.

____

The apartment smelled like the candle she'd left burning too long before her departure—bergamot and cedar, the scent now faded to a faint suggestion. She stood in the doorway with her suitcase and took it in: the couch with the throw she'd straightened, the kitchen counter holding a mug she hadn't washed, the particular stillness of a space that was only now remembering it was supposed to house a person.

She left the suitcase by the door and washed the mug. She stood at the sink, running warm water over her hands longer than the task required, watching the soap spiral down the drain. She thought about nothing specific for ninety seconds—its own form of luxury.

Then she picked up her phone.

Fourteen missed calls from Angel. Three from her mother—already accounted for and returned from Miami. Two from an unrecognized number that turned out to be a work vendor. And one, at the bottom of the list, timestamped two days ago, from Josh.

She looked at Josh's name for a moment. She did not call him back. Instead, she moved Angel's name to the top and pressed call.

It rang once.

"Where the hell have you been?" It wasn't a question; it was an accusation delivered by someone whose worry had curdled into something sharper.

"Miami," April said. "I told you I needed space."

"You told me you needed space, not that you were leaving the state. There's a difference, April. I called fourteen times."

"I know. I'm sorry." She moved to the couch, sat down, and pulled her knees to her chest. "I needed to be unreachable for a few days. I needed the break to actually work."

A beat of silence followed. She could hear Angel's breathing—the specific quality that meant she was deciding whether to stay angry or let it go. "You could've texted me that you were alive."

"You're right. I should have."

The anger shifted, recalibrating. "Are you okay?"

"Better," April said. "Genuinely. Miami was... it was what I needed."

"Good." A pause followed, heavy with unspoken things. "I need to talk to you. Not on the phone."

April registered the shift in Angel's voice—the drop from sharp to something more guarded, more interior. "Come over," she said. "I just got home. Give me an hour."

"I'll be there in two."

She showered first. The Miami residue—not unpleasant, just the accumulated sensory facts of a city that leaves its mark—rinsed away in a stream of water she let run hotter than usual. It wasn't punishing, just deliberate. She stood in the steam and performed the mental accounting she'd started on the plane: what she knew, what she suspected, and what she was going to have to address.

She knew Angel had been involved with Charles. The barbecue had made it plain enough, though April hadn't asked direct questions—a choice made with the vague awareness that some truths are better confirmed on one's own schedule. She suspected the situation had grown complicated in her absence.

Angel's voicemails had started urgent and gone quiet as the days passed, which usually meant an acute crisis had settled into something chronic.

She stood in the steam and took her own temperature honestly.

Hurt, yes. Not the burning kind, but the dull, persistent ache that comes from watching someone you love make choices whose cost you can see clearly from the outside. She felt worried for Angel and angry on Tasha's behalf, even though Tasha was not her responsibility.

Yet, it wasn't exactly betrayal. There was something beneath the hurt she'd been trying to look at directly since the bar confrontation—a thought she hadn't finished having.

She turned off the water. She dressed in things that were comfortable and entirely hers—no Miami silk, just a soft sweater, jeans, and bare feet. It was the uniform of a woman who was no longer performing.

Angel arrived with a bottle of red wine, which she set on the counter without asking, and a face that was doing a lot of work to appear composed. She looked tired in a specific way—not sleep-deprived, but the kind of tired that comes from carrying something for too many consecutive days without being able to set it down.

April poured two glasses without being asked. They sat on the couch the way they always did—April tucked into the corner, Angel crosswise with her feet on the cushion, the configuration of two people who had been having conversations in this position for years, their bodies knowing the choreography.

"Tell me," April said.

Angel told her. Not everything—April would understand this later, when the fuller picture emerged—but enough. The bar. Tasha. Josh showing up. Cynthia's speech. The parking lot afterward, her hands shaking. Deleting Charles's number.

April listened without interrupting. This was a skill she'd developed specifically for Angel, who needed the space to say a thing all the way through before she could hear a response.

"I'm not going to pretend I didn't know something was happening," April said when Angel finished. "I saw you with him at the barbecue."

Angel's eyes came up. "I know you did."

"I didn't ask because—" April stopped. Why hadn't she asked? She'd told herself it wasn't the right moment, that Angel would come to her. But the more honest reason was that asking would have required her to have a feeling about it that she wasn't ready to have. "I wasn't ready to know," she said. "That's on me."

Angel shook her head. "It's on me. All of it. I made choices." She looked at the wine in her glass. "I always make the same choices, April. I just never saw it clearly before."

There was something in the way she said it—the weight of it, the specific quality of a person recognizing a pattern they've been living inside—that made April want to ask more, to press into what Angel meant by the same choices, by always. But Angel's face had closed slightly, the way it did when she'd gone as far as she was going to go for the night, and April knew better than to push through that particular door.

"You deleted his number," April said instead.

"I know it by heart," Angel said. "But yeah."

"That matters."

Angel looked at her. "Does it?"

"It means you chose yourself," April said. "Even a little bit. Even imperfectly. That matters."

Angel was quiet for a moment. Then something in her face shifted—not quite breaking, more like releasing, the way a held breath releases when you finally stop needing to hold it. She leaned her head back against the couch cushion and looked at the ceiling.

"I'm tired, April."

"I know."

"Not like sleepy tired."

"I know," April said again. "Me too."

They sat in the quiet of it for a while, the wine between them, the apartment settling around them. Outside, Atlanta went about its evening—traffic on the boulevard, someone's music carrying up from the street, the particular urban hum of a city that doesn't stop for your specific pain.

April refilled both glasses and changed the subject to something lighter, and Angel let her. They talked until ten-thirty, and when Angel left, she hugged April in the doorway longer than usual, both of them holding on without making a thing of it.

After the door closed, April stood in her quiet apartment and thought about what Angel had said: *I always make the same choices.* She'd heard something in it she hadn't fully absorbed yet. She filed it in the part of her mind where things went to finish being understood.

She went to see Tasha the next afternoon.

This wasn't something she'd planned when she woke up. The impulse arrived after her second cup of coffee, with the clarity of something that had been decided below the level of conscious thought and was only now surfacing: this needed to happen in person, and it needed to happen now. Leaving it any longer would mean she was avoiding it rather than timing it, and she was done with avoidance as a strategy.

Tasha opened the door in work clothes—still dressed at five p.m., which said something about the kind of day she was having. She stepped back without a word, and April walked into a house that smelled of the lavender candle April would later learn Tasha burned every Thursday, though on this day it was a Tuesday.

"I heard what happened at the bar," April said before Tasha could arrange whatever she was planning to say. "I'm sorry I wasn't here. I'm sorry you had to find out that way."

Tasha crossed her arms. Not defensively—more like holding herself together from the outside.

"Were you surprised," she asked, "when you found out it was Angel?"

April considered the honest answer. "Not completely," she said. "I saw something at the barbecue. I didn't put it together until later."

Tasha nodded, the slow nod of someone processing information that is painful but not surprising.

"Charles and I are in therapy," she said. The announcement was flat and precise, offered without the emotional wrapper that would invite sympathy. She was not asking for sympathy. She was offering a fact. "We started this week. I don't know what's going to happen with the marriage. But I'm not making any decisions from inside the wound."

"That's—" April paused. She'd been about to say *smart*. What she meant was: *that's braver than it sounds*. "That's the right call."

"I know."

Tasha looked at her steadily. The assessing quality again—the woman who read everything and said only what mattered.

"You don't have to come here and apologize for what Angel did, April," she said. "You didn't do it."

"I know. I came because it felt like the right thing to do." April held her gaze. "And because I think you're someone worth knowing under better circumstances."

Something shifted slightly in Tasha's expression. Not warmth exactly—it was too early for warmth. But recognition. Two women looking at each other across the wreckage of other people's choices and finding themselves, unexpectedly, standing on solid ground.

"Under better circumstances," Tasha said. "I'd like that."

Cynthia's face when April walked into the office the next morning was a masterclass in professional restraint.

"Welcome back," she said, her tone carefully calibrated— the voice of a woman who had opinions and was making a conscious choice not to voice them.

"I know," April said. "Don't."

"I wasn't going to say anything."

"You were about to say everything."

Cynthia set a coffee on April's desk—the good kind from the cafe two blocks down, not the swill from the office machine—and allowed herself one small, knowing smirk. "You've got everyone on edge, you know. But I'm glad you're back. The Hendricks account almost caught fire without you."

"How close is 'almost'?"

"Fire-adjacent. I contained it. You're welcome."

"Thank you, Cynthia." April meant it. "Genuinely."

Cynthia nodded once, accepting the gratitude with the grace of someone who is exceptional at their job and requires only a single acknowledgment to feel seen. She turned to leave, then paused. "For what it's worth—whatever you were looking for in Miami, I hope you found some of it."

April looked at her. "More than some."

"Good." Cynthia straightened a folder on the desk that didn't need straightening. "Now, the Hendricks people want a call at two, so—"

"Set it up."

She was back.

Josh called at seven-fifteen that evening, while she was eating leftover rice and watching nothing in particular on television. She looked at his name on the screen and felt—not the old, familiar ache, and not the reflexive spike of anger— but something quieter. It felt like finality. It was the sensation of a door you've decided to close, watching it swing shut slowly and without drama.

She answered. She would give him the courtesy of one final conversation.

"April." His voice had the carefully assembled quality of a man who had rehearsed his opening line. "I just... I needed to hear your voice."

"I'm here," she said. She wasn't warm, but she wasn't cold. She was simply a witness: *I'm here, I'm listening, and this is all you get.*

"I messed up," he said. "I know I messed up. I've been— " He stopped. She could hear him mentally shuffling through his script and realizing it wasn't going to land. "I still care about you. That's real."

"I believe you," she said. And she did. The caring was real; she had never doubted that. Caring had never been Josh's problem. "But caring about someone isn't the same as being what they need. And Josh—" She paused, finally finding the words she'd been searching for over the last few months. "I need you to stop calling. Not because I'm angry, but because I'm trying to build something new. I can't do that with one hand still reaching back."

Silence stretched over the line.

"He means something to you," Josh said. It wasn't an accusation; it was the quiet observation of a man finally reading the subtext. "The Miami thing."

April thought about Jason's card in her carry-on. The sunrise. His hand. "Yeah," she said. "He does."

Josh was quiet for a long moment. She let him sit in it.

"Okay," he finally said. The word carried the specific weight of a man setting down a burden he'd been carrying for far too long. He wasn't happy, but he was finished. "Okay, April."

"Take care of yourself, Josh."

"You too."

She ended the call and sat with the phone in her hand. Outside, the boulevard traffic moved in its evening rhythm, the city indifferent and ongoing. She replayed her own words: *I'm trying to build something and I can't do it with one hand still reaching back.*

She thought: *That's true. That's actually true.*

She set the phone down and picked up her bowl of rice. She watched the flickering screen and let the evening settle around her. For the first time since she'd landed in Atlanta, she felt something that wasn't hope exactly, but was certainly in the neighborhood. It was the specific quality of a life that had finally cleared some space and was deciding, slowly and intentionally, what to put there next.

Chapter 14: Confronting Betrayal

The networking event had been someone else's idea. Angel remembered this clearly, the way one remembers the small decisions that yield massive consequences. A colleague had double-booked and needed coverage; Angel had said yes because she was good at rooms. She knew how to work them—how to find the most useful person in a crowd and make them feel discovered. It was a skill she'd developed young and refined into professional fluency. She was never not aware of it operating.

Charles had been across the room, in the cluster near the drinks table, laughing with the full-body ease of a man who enjoyed his own company and expected others to do the same. He was well-dressed without being precious about it—the tailored-suit kind of handsome that suggested he'd made money legitimately and hadn't forgotten the hustle that got him there. Angel had clocked him the way she clocked every man in a room: quickly, involuntarily, with an efficient assessment she rarely turned off.

She'd clocked him. She'd moved on. She'd worked the room.

He found her twenty minutes later near the appetizer table. She was standing with a plate she wasn't eating from and a conversation she was already wrapping up. He introduced himself simply—first name, a brief handshake, no business card deployed like a weapon—and asked what she'd thought of the speaker, whose talk had been aggressively mediocre. She said exactly that. He laughed in a way that signaled genuine agreement rather than a performance of it, and the conversation opened.

It lasted forty minutes. She knew because she'd checked her watch at the start and again when she finally walked away; the gap surprised her.

He hadn't been wearing a ring. She looked for rings. She looked habitually, automatically, the way she looked for exits, power dynamics, or the small tells that let her read a room before it read her. No ring. Nothing in his conversation suggested a wife, a partner, or a life already claimed. She had believed what was in front of her because she had been careful, and what was in front of her had been meticulously constructed to look like the truth.

This was the realization she had to keep returning to in the months that followed, whenever she felt the temptation to cast herself as the fool of the story: she had been careful. She had looked. She had read the room. Charles had simply been exceptional at rooms himself—good enough to deceive someone who was not easily deceived.

He called three days later. She'd given him her card because the conversation had been worth it. She answered because she was curious, and she was allowed to be curious. They went to dinner at a restaurant she suggested—her choice, her turf, her terms. The evening was easy in the way evenings are when two people are genuinely interested in each other and neither is performing. She laughed more than she expected to. She talked about things she didn't usually reveal during first meetings: her mother, her ambitions, and the gap between the life she'd imagined at twenty and the one she'd built by thirty-one.

He listened well. She remembered thinking: *He listens like he means it.*

She found out about Tasha eight weeks in.

It wasn't from Charles. It was from LinkedIn, of all things—a mutual connection's post that tagged him, and a comment below it from someone who signed off as Tasha Merriweather-Cole. The woman wrote with the dry precision of someone very smart and slightly exhausted. Her profile listed her as married to Charles Merriweather Cole. Angel had sat with her phone in her hand in the darkness of her office parking garage for six minutes. Then she'd driven home. Then she'd called Charles and said, "Tell me something you haven't told me."

His silence was the answer before his words ever arrived.

"I should have told you sooner," he said. It was a non-apology apology—the kind of acknowledgment that sits in the structure of contrition without actually being it.

"Yes," she said. "You should have."

She should have ended it there. She knew that. She had always known that. She ended it there in her head—in the clean version of the story she told herself in the following days. In that version, she discovered the truth and walked away with her dignity intact and her choices unimpeachable. That wasn't the version where she continued, for another four months, to see a married man who had lied by omission and then, when confronted, made her feel like the discovery was a complication in their love story rather than the end of it.

The truth was messier. The truth was that he had said, in the same quiet voice that had been telling her exactly what she wanted to hear for eight weeks: *I didn't plan this. I didn't plan you.* The thing she hated most was how much she'd heard in that sentence—the same thing she'd heard from other unavailable people in other chapters of her life. It was the siren song that whispered: *You are the exception. You are the one worth complicating everything for. You are chosen.*

She had been hearing that sentence her whole life, from different mouths. She still didn't know how to stop needing it.

Tasha had known something was wrong before she knew what it was. This was the part that would take her the longest to work through in therapy—not the discovery or the confrontation, but the months prior, when she had known and had chosen, repeatedly, not to know.

She and Charles had been good once. She held onto this not as a comfort, but as a fact; she was a woman who required facts even when they complicated her narrative. They had been good. It wasn't just chemistry—though that was real—it was the kind of "good" that came from two people who shared an understanding of what mattered and a willingness to work for it. She had fallen in love with his laugh first. Then his mind. Then the specific way he showed up in a crisis—not loudly, not with the demonstrative heroics some men performed as a substitute for steadiness, but quietly and completely. He was the load-bearing wall that held the house without announcing its presence.

She had become a doctor, and the career had required everything. She was honest with herself about that. The residency years had been a kind of disappearance. She had been present in her marriage the way a person is present when they're also somewhere else—her body at the dinner table while her mind catalogued patients, decisions, and the specific weight of being responsible for lives that had nothing to do with her own. Charles had been patient. She had told herself this was the shape of their partnership: she gave everything to the work for a season, he held the structure of their life, and then the season would end and she would return.

The season had not ended. It had simply changed its name.

Tasha had noticed the phone first. It wasn't the behavior itself—the face-down screen or the subtle shift of his body when a message arrived—but her own reaction to it: the total absence of suspicion. She should have been suspicious. She knew, with the part of her brain that dealt in evidence and differential diagnosis, that the pattern was consistent with concealment. But something in her had decided, without consulting the facts, that the secrecy was likely work-related. She told herself Charles was managing a professional crisis he hadn't mentioned yet—that the explanation was benign and would reveal itself when the timing was right.

She had wanted it to be work.

The text she eventually found was not dramatic, nor was it explicit. It was simply intimate in the specific way that messages between people who share interior lives are intimate. It was the shorthand, the effortless reference to a shared memory, the small joke that meant nothing to an outsider but everything to the two people who had built the language for it. Tasha had read it while standing in the kitchen with Charles in the next room, and her first emotion was not rage, but recognition. It was the cold, clarifying recognition of a scientist whose hypothesis had just been confirmed by data she'd never wanted to collect.

She had asked him. He had told her.

In the weeks that followed, what surprised her most was not the grief. She had expected the grief; she'd even identified its stages with the diagnostic precision of someone who treats patients in crisis and recognizes the architecture of trauma from the inside. What surprised her was the anger she felt toward herself. It wasn't directed at Angel—Angel was a stranger who had made unconscionable choices, but she hadn't taken a vow. The anger at herself was specific: she had known something was wrong. She had looked at the evidence and diagnosed it as something else because the correct diagnosis was one she didn't want to live inside.

"That's not failure," her therapist had said when Tasha finally named it. "That's hope. You were hoping. That's human."

"I'm a doctor," Tasha replied. "I don't misread evidence."

"You misread evidence about your own life all the time. Everyone does. That isn't a character flaw; it's a feature of loving something."

She had sat with that thought for several sessions before she could find a use for it.

The apartment Charles rented after Tasha asked for space was a furnished one-bedroom in Midtown that smelled of other people's lives—the faint ghost of someone else's cooking, a detergent he didn't use, the sterile neutrality of a space maintained for temporary occupancy. He unpacked his suitcase and stood in the bedroom, staring at the queen-sized bed with its white duvet and hotel-grade pillows. It was then he understood, with sudden, jarring clarity, that he had made a category of mistakes.

These weren't mistakes in the sense of miscalculations. They were choices that had been visible to him, and he had made them anyway because his internal ledger had excluded certain variables. Variables like: what it would feel like to stand in a temporary bedroom and realize he had taken a woman who loved him completely and turned her love into a liability she had to manage alone. Variables like: the cost a person pays to discover the life they thought they were building had a room in it they never knew existed.

He thought about Tasha at twenty-three, dancing at a roommate's party with her eyes closed. He remembered the exact moment he decided she was the one he'd been looking for. He hadn't been wrong about that. He had simply, in the years since, let that decision calcify into an assumption—as if choosing her once meant he could stop the work of being someone she would want to stay with.

He thought about Angel. He considered the frame he'd built around their situation for the duration of the affair: the marriage was drifting; he and Tasha were merely roommates who respected each other's schedules; what he felt for Angel was real and not just an escape. He had believed in that frame with the conviction of an architect who had built it himself, never noticing how load-bearing it was until the walls came down.

What he felt for Angel had been real. He wasn't going to unmake that truth just because it was now inconvenient. But *real* was not the same as *right*. And the quiet pain of losing her— not the drama of the bar or the parking lot, but the realization that she had finally meant it when she said she was done—was inseparable from the way he had used her feelings as raw material for a story about himself he wanted to believe.

He called his father from the apartment that first week. His father, married to his mother for forty-one years, possessed the moral authority of a man who had done the work rather than just theorized about it. He listened without interruption. Finally, he asked, "Did you tell her the truth when she asked you?"

"Yes," Charles said.

"Then you start there," his father replied. "Everything else is secondary."

It wasn't the absolution Charles had been half-hoping for. It was better. It was direction.

Charles arrived at Angel's door on a Thursday evening, three weeks after the confrontation at the bar. She'd known he would—not out of arrogance, but from knowing the shape of his persistence when he believed something could still be salvaged. When she heard his knock, she stood in her kitchen for a moment with her hands flat on the counter and centered herself.

She opened the door. He looked like a man who hadn't slept, a fact she registered and refused to let soften her.

"Angel—"

"I'm going to say something, and I need you to let me finish before you respond." Her voice was level. She had rehearsed the steadiness of it—the tone of a woman reporting a decision rather than performing one. "What we had was real. I'm not going to pretend otherwise. But it was built on a foundation I didn't consent to. You chose what to tell me and what to leave out. I made choices based on incomplete information. That means the entire relationship was compromised from the start, regardless of whether our feelings were true."

Charles opened his mouth to speak. She held up a hand.

"You love the idea of me," she said. "You love who you are when you're with me. That's not the same thing as loving *me*." She paused. The words felt like something she'd known for a long time but was only now brave enough to voice. "I've been accepting that from people my whole life. I'm done with it."

She saw it land—not the rejection, which he'd expected, but the clinical diagnosis of their dynamic, which he hadn't.

"Angel," he said, his voice dropping. "I hear you. I do. But what I felt for you—"

"Was real," she finished for him. "I know. So was everything you did. Both things are true."

He stood in the hallway, working through it. She watched him attempt to build a new frame around her words, only to find that the structure wouldn't hold.

"I'm sorry," he said finally. It wasn't the non-apology this time. It was the real thing, offered with the exhausted directness of a man who had run out of options and found the truth at the bottom of the pile.

"I know," she said. "Take care of yourself, Charles."

She closed the door. For a moment, she stood with her back against the wood, listening to his footsteps recede down the hall. Then she went to the kitchen, made a cup of tea, and stood by the window to watch the street below. It was an ordinary Atlanta evening—people moving through the humid air on their own errands, the city churning on without knowledge of or interest in the quiet ending that had just occurred in her apartment. Beneath the grief and the bone-deep fatigue, she felt the specific relief of dropping a weight that had never been hers to carry.

She did not call April that night. She wanted to—the reflex was a physical pull toward her best friend's voice, the comfort of the couch, and the safety of being known. But there was something she needed to do first, something that had nothing to do with Charles.

She needed to sit with what she'd said to him at the door. About accepting scraps from people her whole life. About being done.

The sentence had surprised her when it left her mouth; it had arrived with a clarity that suggested it had been building in the dark for years. She didn't yet know the full shape of what it meant, only that it pointed toward a destination she was finally ready to reach.

She sat with the thought until her tea went cold. The city continued its business outside the window, and Angel remained still until she could feel the edges of her new reality, the way one feels the dimensions of a room they cannot yet see.

The therapy was Tasha's idea. She had suggested it to Charles and herself in the same week, applying the same clinical detachment she used for difficult diagnoses: *this is the treatment, these are the steps, this is the work.*

What she hadn't anticipated was how much harder the work would be from the inside. She was accustomed to being the one in the room with perspective, the one who could hold complexity without being dismantled by it. Sitting across from Dr. Okafor—a woman with the composure of someone who had heard everything and found all of it fascinating—Tasha discovered that the skills that made her excellent at managing other people's pain were not transferable to her own.

"You keep explaining it," Dr. Okafor said during their third session.

"Isn't that what I'm supposed to do?"

"You're supposed to feel it. You keep getting to the edge of the emotion and then explaining it away."

Tasha looked at her. "I'm a diagnostician. Explanation is my process."

"You're also a woman whose husband of six years fell in love with her best friend's best friend. Explanation might not be sufficient for that."

The silence that followed had several distinct layers. Tasha sat with them, peeling them back one by one.

"What did she have that I didn't?" she asked finally. It wasn't accusatory; it was a genuine request for data—the question she'd been circling for weeks.

"That's the wrong question," Dr. Okafor said. "This isn't about what she had. It's about what Charles was afraid to ask for from you."

Tasha turned toward the window. Outside, a tree was dancing in a slight wind, its branches moving with that precarious grace that only happens when the air is just barely enough to sustain the motion. "He never told me he was unhappy."

"Did you tell him?"

The question arrived quietly but sat in the room with absolute mass.

Tasha thought about the residency years. The dinner-table absences. The way she had come home so depleted that care had to be rationed—and Charles had been the one she'd rationed it from. She had trusted him to understand; she'd *needed* him to understand. Asking for his silent endurance had been easier than examining whether that endurance was enough to sustain them.

"No," she said. "I didn't."

Dr. Okafor nodded. "So you both had needs you weren't voicing. That isn't an excuse for his choices, but it is the fuller picture."

The fuller picture. Tasha had spent her career obsessed with the fuller picture—the patient in front of her was never just the presenting symptom. You treated the system; you looked at the environment; you held the complexity. Yet she had failed to apply this to her own marriage. She had treated the symptoms—the distance, the disconnection—without ever looking at the system itself.

She was looking now.

Two weeks after she closed the door on Charles, Angel called April.

She didn't call to report or to ask for a favor. She called just to say: *I miss you. I've been in my own head and I want to come over and sit on your couch and eat bad takeout and not talk about anything that matters for a few hours.*

April's response was immediate: "Yes. Obviously, yes. What are you in the mood for?"

They ordered Thai food and settled into the particular configuration they had perfected over the years. They didn't talk about Charles or Josh or Tasha. Instead, they talked about a documentary Angel had watched regarding deep-sea creatures with no eyes—creatures that lived where there was no light. April found it fascinating and unsettling in equal measure. They debated whether Atlanta had peaked or was still becoming something new. They talked until midnight, when Angel fell asleep mid-sentence. April gently draped a blanket over her and turned off the lamp.

She stood in the darkened living room, looking at her best friend. This was the woman she had known since they were nineteen, who carried her burdens in ways April was only beginning to decipher. She felt something complicated move in her chest: love, worry, and the faint outline of a question she didn't yet know how to ask.

She went to bed. The question waited.

It would wait as long as necessary. Some things required time to ripen before they could be said aloud; both women knew it, and neither pushed. This was the particular grammar of a friendship that had lasted long enough to develop its own patience.

The fuller picture was still assembling itself. Not everything was visible yet, but the shape of it—the silhouette in the dark—was becoming something both women could almost name.

Chapter 15: Curiosity and Temptation

She woke on the living room floor with her trench coat still on, rain drumming against the windows, and the particular disorientation of surfacing from a depth she hadn't fully charted. For a moment, she didn't move. She lay with her cheek against the area rug and took inventory the way one does after a seismic event: body, mind, and the room around her gradually assembling into the familiar geometry of her apartment.

The note from the coat pocket lay on the floor beside her, unfolded. She looked at it without picking it up. The handwriting was clean and economical—a practical message, devoid of embellishment. She had read it six times last night and had not fully processed it; she wasn't sure she was ready to process it now.

She stood up, moving toward the bathroom with the careful pace of someone whose limbs had strong opinions about the previous night. The cold tile under her bare feet was clarifying. At the sink, she let the water run warm, washed her hands, and finally looked into the mirror.

The woman looking back was familiar and yet not. Same face, same architecture, but her eyes held something she was still learning to read—not shame, and not the morning-after flinch she'd half-expected. It was something more complex. The marks on her wrists were already fading, shallow impressions in skin that healed quickly. She touched one of them with two fingers, not to catalog the injury, but to verify the memory: *Yes. That happened. You were there, it was real, and you did not dissociate. You chose it.*

The question she grappled with was not whether she regretted it. She was honest enough to know she didn't—at least not in the traditional sense. The true question was what it meant that she felt no regret. She wondered what it revealed about the interior map she'd been living by, and whether that map contained rooms she hadn't known to look for.

She showered and made coffee. Sitting on the couch in the gray Atlanta morning, watching the rain work its way down the glass, she thought about the house on the hill. She didn't dwell on the specific room, but the quality of the place—the way it held space for versions of desire that the rest of the world required one to manage quietly, if at all. She remembered what it felt like to be in that space: present, deliberate, and unafraid of her own wanting.

She thought about Jason's card in her nightstand drawer.

She had called him from Miami, and he had answered on the first ring. In the months since, they had been building something—careful, layered, the kind of bond forged by two people who had every reason to move slowly and who both understood exactly what the slowness was for. Atlanta, she had learned, was where Jason lived too. He had been there for three years. The discovery had arrived not as a coincidence, but as an inevitability: the city deciding for them what they had been circling toward on their own.

She had not told him about the house. Not yet. She wasn't sure what the telling would require of her—what it would mean to show him this part of the map she was still drawing. But she thought of him the way you think of the first person you want to tell when something significant happens.

She picked up her phone, then put it down. She watched the rain. By evening, the pull had become an impulse she was done arguing with.

She dressed differently this time. She avoided the armor of her first visit—the professional presentation and the clothes that declared, *I am in control of how I am perceived.* She chose something simpler and more honest: a wrap dress the color of deep wine, heels that were elegant rather than imposing, and her hair worn down. She was not dressing to be seen; she was dressing to see.

The drive to the house took on a different quality. The first time, it had been curiosity with a jagged edge of trepidation—the feeling of approaching a game without knowing the rules. Now, the rules were partially known. The trepidation remained, but it had changed character. It was the anxiety of someone returning to a place that had shown her something real, rather than the fear of the unknown.

The parking attendant recognized her, offering a small, professionally neutral nod. She walked through the front door and the house received her as it did everyone: with low light, the central fountain casting a slow rainbow across the ceiling, and a hum that was part music, part atmosphere—the acoustic quality of a space designed for a particular kind of attention.

She stood for a moment to let her eyes adjust, letting the city fall away. It wasn't denied or disappeared; it was simply set aside in favor of what the house offered instead.

"You came back."

She knew the voice before she turned. It had that particular Southern roundness, an unhurried quality. Jason stood near the fountain, dressed in dark clothes. His expression wasn't one of surprise, but something adjacent to pleasure—the look of someone whose expectations had been confirmed and who found confirmation far more interesting than shock.

April looked at him for a moment without speaking. The "coincidence" of his presence was no coincidence at all, she realized now, in the same way Miami hadn't been. The city was small in the ways that mattered, and the house was smaller still—the overlap of two people moving in orbits that tended toward intersection.

"You know this place," she said. It wasn't an accusation, merely a naming of the obvious.

"I do." He didn't elaborate, which was an answer in itself. He looked at her with the level attention she had spent months learning to trust. "You okay?"

"Better than okay," she said.

Her own words, echoed back from the morning after Miami. He recognized them; she could see the acknowledgment in the slight shift of his expression, a softening at the corners of his eyes.

"Are you here for something specific?" he asked.

She thought about the corridor, the doors, and the rooms she had bypassed versus the one she had finally entered. "I'm here to understand something," she said. "About myself. About what I want."

He considered this with his characteristic gravity. "Can I come with you?"

She looked at him for a long moment. The question was deceptively simple. He was asking for entry into a space she was still mapping herself. She thought of their conversation in Chapter 13—his vow to open the rooms he kept closed, door by door, slowly. She thought of her own: her refusal to disappear into another person, yet her burgeoning desire not to lock them out either.

"Yes," she said. "Stay close."

They moved through the house the way she had learned to move through it—without haste, without the performance of casualness, simply present in the space. The corridor off the main hall received them with its particular density of atmosphere: warm, slightly close, the sound and light managed with a precision that made the outside world feel like a distant memory.

The doors remained as she remembered them. Jason walked beside her, his hands loose at his sides, his attention distributed evenly between the space and her. He didn't pepper her with questions or perform a forced fascination. He simply looked, and occasionally their eyes met. Something passed between them in those moments that had the quality of recognition—the silent realization of two people discovering they spoke the same dialect.

At one door, she stopped. She had passed it the first time without looking; an instinct had pulled her past, whispering *not yet.* Now, she looked. Behind the glass, the scene was unhurried and deliberate—two people in complete communication, nothing withheld. April watched for a moment and felt something in her chest that wasn't voyeurism, but witnessing. It was the difference between watching a performance and watching a truth.

"What do you see?" Jason asked quietly.

She took a moment to find the honest answer. "Two people who know what they want," she said. "And who trust each other enough to want it out loud."

He was quiet for a beat. "That's a hard thing to find."

"I know." She moved on, and he followed.

They reached the far end of the corridor where the staircase ascended to the upper level—the forbidden zone, the sign that had called to her during her first visit, which she had not yet dared to follow. She stood at the foot of the stairs and looked up into the shadows.

"Not tonight," she said. It wasn't fear; it was timing. She understood the distinction now.

"Okay," Jason said simply. No push, no negotiation.

She turned to look at him in the low light of the hall—this man she had been building something with for months, who had been moving in these same circles all along. He had watched the same sunrise and asked the same questions, and now he was standing beside her in a place she had never shown anyone else. She felt the vertigo of it—not the sickening kind, but the thrill of a beautiful view that confirms the height is real.

"I want to show you something," she said.

She had found it during her second pass of the main level on her first visit—a room off the east corridor she had glimpsed and then fled because she hadn't been ready for its contents. It was a room of mirrors.

This was not the ordinary arrangement of a dressing room or a dance studio; the space was built for the act of looking. Every surface was mirrored at angles that multiplied a reflection into something that felt less like vanity and more like archaeology. You could see the back of your own head, the slope of your shoulder, the way your face changed when you believed you were unobserved. You could see yourself seeing yourself.

She led Jason inside. He stopped just past the threshold and took it in without comment, which was the only correct response.

April walked to the center of the room. In the mirrors, she became infinite—every angle accounted for, no version of herself hidden from her own gaze. She looked.

The woman in the reflections looked back with that same complexity she had seen in her bathroom mirror that morning—neither shame nor triumph, but something more patient than either. A woman in the middle of a process. A woman who had survived experiences that tried to reduce her to a fixed, manageable version of herself, and who had finally declined the reduction.

She thought about the warehouse. She thought about Mr. Daley's den before that—the memory she had not yet fully allowed herself to touch. She thought of the fourteen-year-old girl in the mirror who had learned to leave her own body as a form of protection. She realized how long she had operated from that learned distance—the way she had managed Josh rather than loved him, the way she had organized the surface of her life while the interior remained a fortress.

Then she thought about Miami. About staying in her own body. About choosing.

In the mirror behind her, she could see Jason. He stood near the door, watching her with the specific intensity of someone who understands they have been granted access to something sacred and is holding that trust carefully. His face wore the expression she had learned to read over the months: present, attentive, and entirely unperformed.

"What do you see?" he asked, throwing her own question back to her.

She took her time. "Someone still figuring out who she is," she said, "when she's not busy managing everyone else's version of her."

Jason moved away from the door. He walked to her side and stopped, and in the mirrors, they became infinite together—two people standing close in a room built for scrutiny. He looked at her reflection rather than her face, which felt, somehow, more intimate than direct eye contact. It was like seeing her without the mediation of a presentation.

"I like her," he said. "The one who's still figuring it out."

April looked at his reflection. "She's not as put together as the other version."

"The other version doesn't need anyone," he said. "This one might. I find that much more interesting."

She felt the words land somewhere real. Not in the performative way, not the way words land when you're cataloging them for later use—but the way they land when they arrive in the right place at the right time and do something that can't be undone. She turned from the mirror to look at him directly.

He was already looking at her.

She kissed him first. This was important to her—not symbolically, not as a statement, but as the simple fact of who moved first, who chose it. She kissed him, and he kissed her back with the unhurried completeness she had come to associate with everything he did. The mirrors held the whole thing in infinite patience, every angle accounted for, nothing hidden.

Later, they sat in the main room near the fountain, the water catching the low light in its slow rotation of color. She held a glass of something amber and lightly sweet that the bartender had prepared without being asked, as if the house had a way of knowing what a person needed at a particular hour. Jason sat close but not touching—the comfortable nearness of two people who didn't require physical contact to maintain a connection.

"How long have you been coming here?" she asked.

He considered. "Three years. Since I moved to Atlanta." He paused. "A colleague told me about it. I was skeptical."

"And then?"

"And then I came once and understood what it was for." He looked at the fountain. "It's not about the rooms. Or not only. It's about the permission. The idea that you can know something about yourself and not have to manage the knowing alone."

April absorbed this. It was exactly what she had felt on her first visit, expressed in the language she hadn't yet found for it. "I thought it was about desire," she said.

"It is," he said. "Desire and honesty are closer than people think. You can't have one without the other—not the real versions."

She thought about this. She thought about the long gap between what she had wanted in her life and what she had allowed herself to name. About Josh, and the way she had shaped herself into what he needed without asking what she required in return. About the warehouse, and the horrific inversion of desire into something weaponized and stripped of choice. About Miami, and choosing. About the mirror room, and finally being seen.

"I haven't been honest about what I want," she said. "For a long time."

"I know," he said. It wasn't an accusation—just the simple acknowledgment of someone who had been paying attention. "I'm patient."

She looked at him. "Don't be *too* patient. I need some pressure, or I'll manage the feeling instead of experiencing it."

He looked at her with something that was very close to a smile. "Noted."

The fountain turned. The house went on around them, doing what it did—holding space, offering permission, being quietly and consistently itself in a world that required most people to be something else most of the time. April sat in the atmosphere and felt the specific rightness of a place that did not ask her to be smaller than she was.

She finished her drink. She thought about the upper level—the sign, the stairs, the thing she had said "not tonight" to. She thought about timing. About readiness. About the fine line between delay and patience.

She was not ready for the upper level. She knew what was up there—not the specific contents, but the category of it, the depth of it, the particular kind of attention it would require from her. She would need to be very sure of herself before she climbed those stairs. Very sure of what she wanted and why.

She was getting there. She could feel the process—the gradual accumulation of honesty that was starting to feel less like exposure and more like an arrival.

She set her glass down. She looked at Jason beside her—steady, present, not pushing, but not performing patience either. He was just genuinely there, the way he was genuinely everywhere he went.

She took his hand. He let her.

Outside, Atlanta moved through its evening, indifferent and ongoing, lit up under a sky that had cleared after the rain. The stars did their work above a city that rarely looked up long enough to notice them. But in here, the house held its particular silence, and two people sat beside a fountain that never stopped moving, and for once, neither of them was anywhere else.

Chapter 16: Uncharted Territory

She was in the bath when it happened.

It wasn't a slow realization—the kind that builds through layers of accumulating evidence until it arrives with the politeness of something that has been patient. This was the other kind. The bolt-of-lightning kind. The kind that makes the body respond before the mind has finished processing.

She sat up so fast that water sloshed over the rim of the tub and hit the tile with a sound like punctuation.

"Jason."

She said it out loud to the steam of her own bathroom, because vocalizing it was the only way to verify the thought was real—not a trick of hot water or the dreamlike quality of a long day finally ending. She said it, and she felt the two images snap together with the finality of pieces that had always belonged to each other: the man in the dark shirt in the Miami club, his hand at her waist, the Haulover Beach sunrise—and the man from the house on the hill, steady and unhurried, who had stood beside her in the mirror room and said, "I find that much more interesting."

The same mouth. The same Southern-edged patience. The same quality of attention she had spent months learning to trust. She had trusted him in two different cities without knowing she was trusting the same man.

She sat in the cooling water and did the arithmetic. Miami to Atlanta. A direct flight, just under two hours. He'd told her he moved to Atlanta three years ago. He'd been at the house for three years. She had met him in Miami—his city, she'd thought—and he had given her his card. She had called him six days later, he had answered on the first ring, and the conversation had found its footing so naturally that she hadn't thought to ask certain questions. When she returned to Atlanta and they began building whatever this was, she had taken the city's smallness as a pleasant coincidence—fate with a sense of humor.

It wasn't coincidence. It was geography. He had always been here.

She got out of the tub and wrapped herself in a towel. Standing on the bath mat, she scrutinized what she was actually feeling, which took a moment to identify because it arrived in a tangle. Surprise, obviously. Something close to vertigo. And underneath those—the part she had to sit with—was a feeling that shared territory with both relief and fear. It was the recognition that she had built trust with this man twice, in different contexts and with different information, and had arrived at the same place both times. It wasn't a fluke. It was evidence.

She stood in the steam until the mirror cleared itself.

She paced. This was atypical for her; April's version of processing usually involved stillness, cleaning, or the deliberate physical organization of her environment as a substitute for interior order. Pacing was something her body did when it had more energy than the situation had instructions for.

She paced and thought about what it meant that he'd known. He had recognized her in the parking lot—that much was now clear. The pause she'd registered, the quality of his attention... he had chosen to say nothing, waiting to see if she would connect the dots herself. She turned this over, examining it from every angle. She could read it as manipulation—the deliberate withholding of information to manage her discovery on his own timeline. Or, she could read it as what he'd said during their original conversation at the coffee shop months ago: *I didn't want to push. I figured if you remembered, you'd bring it up.*

She picked up her phone, then set it down. She went to the kitchen and stood in front of the open refrigerator for thirty seconds without removing a thing, then closed it.

She needed to talk to him. But first, she needed to know what she was going to say.

What was she going to say? She rehearsed several versions. The accusatory one: *You knew and you let me figure it out alone.* The deflective one: *I've been thinking about Miami.* The honest one, which was harder to script because honest things rarely arrive pre-packaged.

She went to bed without calling. She lay in the dark with the ceiling fan turning above her and thought about the night they met in Miami—the club, the dance floor, the diner at two in the morning, the way he'd listened to her talk about her father and received it without redirecting. She thought about every conversation since, in Atlanta, building the same structure she'd started in Miami without knowing the foundation was the same. In the quiet, a truth finally emerged: she had not been wrong about him. Either time. Both times, she had read something true.

The vertigo settled. What remained was simpler than she'd expected. She wanted to see him.

She didn't plan to run into him the next morning. She went to the coffee shop two blocks from her apartment because it was her Saturday morning ritual—a place to set down the weight of the week. It offered good coffee, outdoor seating, and the specific quality of a neighborhood unhurrying itself. She took her usual table with her usual order, her phone face-down, and the book she'd been carrying in her bag for two weeks.

She opened it. She read two pages. She was not reading.

"April."

She looked up. He was at the adjacent table—or had just arrived; she hadn't seen him come—with a book of his own and a coffee already half-finished, as if he'd been there long enough for the morning to settle around him. He looked at her with an expression that was neither surprised nor unsurprised. It was the expression of someone who had also been doing the math.

"Jason," she said.

A beat passed, heavy with subtext.

"Sit with me," she said. It was a statement rather than an invitation—an accurate reflection of the moment.

He moved to her table. He set his book down—she clocked the title, something on organizational behavior, which felt perfectly characteristic—and placed his coffee beside it. He looked at her with the same level attention that had been consistent across two cities and multiple months. It was consistent now.

"You figured it out," he said.

"Last night. In the bath." She watched his expression closely. "You knew. At the house—the parking lot—you recognized me."

"Yes."

"Why didn't you say anything?"

He was quiet for a moment in that characteristic way of his—not evasively, but actually processing. "Because I wasn't sure what I was to you in Miami," he said. "Whether it had been significant or just one good night in a city that wasn't yours. I didn't want to show up in your Atlanta life as the person who'd decided our night meant something when, for you, it might have been... complete in itself."

April looked at him. "So you waited."

"I let you lead." He picked up his coffee. "You called me. You came back to the house. You showed me the mirror room." He met her gaze steadily. "I figured you were building toward something. I didn't need to name it before you did."

She sat with that. She had a gift for identifying when she was being managed, and this wasn't that—the explanation had the texture of something he had actually reasoned through rather than a script constructed for her benefit. He had been consistent. Both times. He had let her lead, and then he'd been there when she arrived.

"You could have told me," she said. It wasn't an accusation; it was just a fact.

"Yes," he said. "I could have. I thought about it. But I decided the telling was yours to do, not mine." He paused. "Was I wrong?"

She thought about the bath. The bolt of recognition. The pacing. She thought about the way the arithmetic had resolved, in the quiet of her own process, into something she could trust. She wondered if having him tell her would have changed the resolution—if the arrival would have felt different had it been handed to her rather than found.

"No," she said. "You weren't wrong."

He nodded. It wasn't relief—he wasn't a man who required validation to feel secure in his choices—it was just acknowledgment. An update to the shared record of what stood between them.

They sat for two hours. The Saturday morning assembled itself around them—the neighborhood waking up, a dog being walked by a man who was, in turn, being walked by the dog. The coffee shop filled and thinned and filled again with the weekend rhythm of a street that knew exactly what Saturdays were for.

They talked about Miami in a way they hadn't before— as a shared memory rather than a private one. It was the difference between looking at the same photograph separately and looking at it together. He had been in Miami for a three-day conference, he told her. He didn't get there often and had only been at the club because a colleague had suggested it. He had gone with the same openness he brought to most things. He had seen her at the edge of the dance floor, watching the room with the particular attention of someone deciding something, and he had thought: *I want to know what she decides.*

She told him about booking the flight at midnight. The cigar in Little Havana. The jazz club. The way the city had given her back something she hadn't known she'd lost.

"What did you lose?" he asked.

"Myself," she said. "The interior version. The one that's curious and reckless and follows music down side streets." She looked toward the street. "I'd been managing her for a long time. Miami was the first time in years I let her out without a plan."

"She's the one I met in the club," he said.

"Yes."

"I thought so." He was quiet for a moment. "She's the one I've been getting to know in Atlanta, too. You're not as good at keeping her managed as you think."

April looked at him. "Is that a compliment or a criticism?"

"It's an observation," he said. "With warmth."

She almost laughed. "You're very precise."

"I try to be." He looked at her over his coffee cup. "Imprecision in language costs more than people think."

She thought about the imprecision she'd spent years deploying as a form of protection—the *fine*, the *okay*, the *I'm managing*—all the words that maintained the surface without saying anything true. She was learning a different vocabulary now. It was slower and more exposed, and she wasn't always sure she was using it correctly, but she was using it.

"Jason," she said.

"Yeah."

"I want to do this right. Whatever this is." She looked at him directly. "I don't have a clean track record with that. I've been in relationships and not actually been *in* them—present in body, absent in the ways that matter. I don't want to do that with you."

He set his cup down. He gave her statement the weight it deserved—not jumping to reassure her, not deflecting, just receiving it. "What would doing it right look like for you?"

"Saying what I mean." She paused to think. "Asking for what I need instead of managing around it. Trusting you with the actual version of me instead of the put-together one." She hesitated. "And you doing the same."

"I'm working on the same thing," he said. "In case that's not already obvious."

"It's getting obvious," she said. "Slowly."

"I'll take slowly."

She walked home through the neighborhood in the late morning, the weekend air warm and unhurried. She thought about the recognition—not the bolt of it in the bath, but the slower recognition underneath that had been building for months. This man was not an accident. He was not a coincidence or a cosmic joke. He was someone she had moved toward twice, in different cities, with different information, and she had arrived at the same conclusion both times.

That was not nothing. It was, in fact, the kind of data point that her practical self—the one that dealt in evidence and differential diagnosis, the one she shared with Tasha—could not rationally dismiss.

She thought about what she'd said at the table: *I want to do this right*. She held the sentence and found it was true without qualification. Not *I'll try*, or *I want to want to*. Just: *I want to*. Present tense, active, hers.

She thought about the house on the hill—the upper level, the stairs she had not yet climbed. She thought about the mirror room. She thought about the interior version of herself that Miami had recovered and Atlanta was slowly learning to keep.

There was so much uncharted territory here. It wasn't frightening; it was the kind of uncharted that is new because it is genuinely unmapped, waiting for two people who are both, slowly, learning to be honest about what they need.

She had once been afraid of disappearing into it. She was also, for the first time in a long time, more curious than afraid. Curious was enough to begin with.

She had always been good at following music she could feel before she could hear. This felt like that—a frequency her body registered before her mind had the words. She had followed it to a door on a side street in Miami and found Jason on the other side. She was going to keep walking toward it.

She turned the corner onto her street. Her apartment building waited at the end of the block, ordinary and familiar. The morning was warm, she was in it, and she was no longer performing or standing at the edge, deciding whether to enter.

She was inside it. All the way inside.

That was new. It was also, she was starting to believe, permanent.

Chapter 17: A Family Divided

She had overpacked, and she knew it. The suitcase on her bed contained enough clothing for a week despite the trip only lasting four days. But the logic of overpacking wasn't about fashion—it was about control. It was the illusion of preparing for every contingency when the actual contingency—meeting the family of the man she was becoming serious about—had no wardrobe solution.

"You don't need four pairs of shoes," she told herself. Then she left all four in the suitcase.

The trip had been Jason's idea, offered two months ago with the same direct simplicity he brought to everything: *I go home for Thanksgiving every year; I want you to come this year.* She had said yes with the part of her that had committed to experiencing things rather than managing them. The rest of her had spent the subsequent weeks in a low-grade negotiation between that commitment and the old habit of self-protection. That habit kept whispering that meeting a family was a significant threshold, and significant thresholds had historically not gone well for her.

She folded a dress she'd already folded. She set it on top of the others.

Jason had grown up outside Savannah—a small town with a close-knit family. It was the kind of geography that shaped people in specific ways, giving them either deep roots or a desperate reason to leave, and sometimes both. His mother was gone. He had an aunt who had effectively stepped into that space, a cousin he was close to, and an assortment of others. The picture he'd painted over months of careful conversation was warm but not uncomplicated—a family defined by love and the fault lines that loss creates. They were people who had gathered around an absence and learned to hold each other across the gap.

She zipped the suitcase before she could second-guess it further.

Her phone buzzed. *Jason: Flight's at 9. I'll pick you up at 6:30.*

She texted back: *I'm ready.* It was approximately sixty percent true.

The airport at six-thirty in the morning had the specific character of a place where everyone is in transit and no one is fully awake. The coffee lines were long and patient, the gates filling with the particular holiday mix: families with children who had already lost their shoes, solo business travelers projecting studied indifference, and couples arranged in the comfortable proximity of people who had negotiated their shared space long ago.

Jason arrived at her door at six-twenty-eight, a punctuality she appreciated. He was dressed simply—dark jeans and a charcoal sweater she hadn't seen before—possessing that same understated quality he brought to everything. He looked at her suitcase, then at her.

"Four days," he noted.

"I know," she said. "Don't."

He picked up the suitcase without further comment, which was the correct response.

The flight was two hours long, and they were late enough in the boarding sequence for the process to feel unhurried. They settled into their seats, the plane taxied and lifted, and Atlanta disappeared below them into the pre-dawn haze. April watched it go with a feeling she couldn't quite name—not a goodbye, nothing so heavy. It was more like a pause. The week set aside; the city agreeing to wait.

Jason was reading within five minutes of reaching altitude. This was something she had come to know about him: he moved easily between conversation and quiet, between presence and interiority, without the transitional anxiety most people experienced. He didn't need to fill the silence. He was comfortable in it the way people are comfortable in their own homes—the silence was a room he lived in and was glad to share.

She watched him read for a while without pretending to do anything else.

"What?" he asked, without looking up.

"Nothing. You just make reading look intentional."

He glanced over. "As opposed to accidental?"

"As opposed to performative. Most people read in public like they want to be seen reading. You read like the book is the only thing actually happening."

He considered this. "It *is* what's actually happening."

"I know. That's what I mean."

He looked at her for a moment with that expression she'd cataloged over the months—the one that meant he found her interesting in a way that was genuine rather than polite. Then he went back to his book. She felt, unexpectedly, entirely at ease. The nerves were still there—present, noted, but not debilitating. Underneath them was something steadier. She was with someone she trusted, going somewhere she'd been invited. That was sufficient. She didn't need more certainty than that.

She opened her own book. She actually read it.

The Georgia coast in late November had a quality she hadn't expected—not the bare-limbed austerity of an inland autumn, nor the muted palette she associated with the season. The live oaks kept their leaves, heavy and dark green, while Spanish moss hung from them in silver-gray curtains that swayed in the salt-edged wind. The light was low and golden, the way winter light is on the coast when the sun takes its time going down. It smelled of salt, pine, and something faintly smoky—a fireplace or a woodpile—the particular warmth of a house preparing for company.

Jason drove with the ease of a man who knew these roads by feel. The turns came before the signs suggested them, shortcuts taken with the confidence of someone who had navigated them in the dark. April looked out the window, letting the landscape assemble around her, and thought about him at fifteen, at twenty, moving through these streets with his entire future still ahead of him.

"Tell me about your aunt," she said.

He glanced over. "Aunt Renee. My mother's younger sister. She's... direct. She has opinions and shares them without much preamble." He paused. "She's also the most genuinely warm person I know. It coexists with the directness in a way that takes getting used to, but eventually, you can't imagine her any other way."

"She sounds like someone I'd like."

"She'll like you," he said. "She'll also have questions. She asks the questions she wants answers to. Just know that going in."

"What kind of questions?"

"The real kind." He turned onto a residential street lined with ancient oaks. "She'll want to know who you are under the presentation. She won't ask it that way, but that's what she's assessing."

April thought about the mirror room. She thought about what she'd seen there—who she was under the presentation—a question she'd been working on for some time. "I can handle real questions," she said.

Jason pulled into a driveway in front of a house that was exactly what the approach had suggested: old and well-maintained, with a wide front porch and two rocking chairs. The warm orange light from the windows spilled into the November evening. A woman was already standing, descending the porch steps with the forward momentum of someone who doesn't wait when she can walk toward you.

"That's Renee," Jason said.

Renee Mercer was sixty-one and looked it in the way women do when they've decided age is not a problem to be solved. She possessed Jason's bone structure—the strong jaw, the unwavering directness in the eyes—along with a quality entirely her own: she was a person who had long ago decided what mattered, organized her life accordingly, and remained at peace with the result. She hugged Jason first—the embrace of someone who had been doing it for thirty years and still meant it—and then she turned to April.

"So, you're the one," she said. Not unkindly; just with clinical precision.

"I suppose I am," April replied.

Renee scrutinized her with the direct assessment Jason had described. She found something satisfactory, apparently, because her expression shifted from measuring to warm in the span of three seconds. She took April's hand in both of hers. "Come inside. You look like someone who needs a real meal and a glass of something decent."

Inside, the house smelled of everything a Thanksgiving home is supposed to: roasting meat, warm bread, and the sweet-spicy top note of a pie still in the oven—cinnamon layered over something earthier. The kitchen was the heart of the operation—large, comfortably cluttered, and centered around a woman April's age stirring a pot at the stove. She looked up and smiled with Jason's eyes.

"My cousin Dani," Jason said. "April."

Dani wiped her hands on her apron and stepped forward, shaking April's hand with the uncomplicated friendliness of someone prepared to believe the best. "He talked about you," she told April, casting the sort of sidelong glance at Jason that only cousins can deploy.

"Don't," Jason warned.

"I'm just saying." Dani retreated to the stove. "He talked about her," she repeated to Renee—quietly, but not quietly enough.

Renee handed April a glass of red wine with the efficient hospitality of a woman who had been making people comfortable in this house for decades. "Ignore them both," she said. "Sit. Tell me about yourself."

April sat at the kitchen table, the undisputed center of the home—the place where everything was decided, resolved, eaten, and felt. She held her glass and watched Renee, thinking:

This woman loved his mother. She is holding the space his mother left. April thought of her own mother and father, and the particular shape of the family that had gathered around her adoptive identity—the love that had been real regardless of biology.

"What do you want to know?" April asked.

Renee smiled. "I want to know if you're someone who says what she means."

"I'm learning to be," April said. "I'm better at it than I was a year ago."

Renee considered this. "That's the honest answer. I'll take it."

Dinner on Thanksgiving Eve was an informal affair: the kitchen table extended by a folding addition, seven people in various states of dress, and a conversation running on several tracks at once. Jason's uncle, Gerald, occupied the far end of the table with the presence of a man who considered himself the patriarch and was mostly right. He was a large man in his fifties, fond of his opinions and generous with them. His wife, Claudette, wore the expression of someone who had been married to Gerald for twenty-eight years and had developed the selective hearing necessary to love a man while surviving a dinner party.

April watched the family from her position beside Jason, reading the room as she did all rooms—mapping alliances and frictions, noting who deferred and where the love had calcified. Gerald asked Jason about work twice, using the tone of a man who had opinions about Jason's career and was choosing this forum to air them tangentially. Jason answered both times with the measured patience of someone who had forged very specific tools for this exact conversation.

"You should have stayed in Atlanta finance," Gerald remarked over the sweet potatoes, clearly not for the first time. "That consulting business—"

"Is doing well," Jason said pleasantly. The pleasantness was load-bearing.

"I'm just saying. Your mother—" Gerald stopped. The table fell quiet in the way rooms do when a name is invoked that carries its own weather. "Your mother worked hard to give you options."

"I know she did," Jason said. "I use them."

The conversation moved on. Beneath the table, April felt Jason's hand find hers. He wasn't gripping or performing comfort; he was just present. She turned her hand over and held his, feeling the specific warmth and steadiness that had been consistent since Miami. She understood then something she hadn't quite articulated: this man had been navigating this geography—the love, the expectation, the loss, and the ghost of his mother—for a long time. The room he kept closed wasn't empty; it was full.

Renee caught April's eye across the table. An acknowledgment passed between them—the silent language of two women who are paying attention. Renee nodded, fractionally. April nodded back.

After dinner, they retreated to the back porch as the house settled into its post-meal lull—the clatter of dishes, muffled voices, and the hum of the television Gerald had claimed in the living room. The backyard was a dark expanse beyond the porch light, the oaks visible only as silhouettes against a slightly lighter sky. The air was crisp, cold enough to be felt but not enough to drive them indoors.

April wore a borrowed sweater from Dani and held a glass of bourbon she was more interested in holding than drinking. She felt the specific relief of having survived a nervous threshold and finding it more nourishing than frightening.

"Your aunt is exactly what you said she was," April noted.

"She usually is."

"She loved your mother a lot."

He was quiet for a moment. The oaks shifted in a salt-edged wind coming off the water. "Yes," he said. "They were very close. After my dad left, it was basically the three of us—

my mother, Renee, and me. Renee lived ten minutes away. She was there every Sunday and most Thursdays."

"She kept showing up."

"She kept showing up," he agreed. "Without being asked. Without making a production of it. She just... arranged her life so that being present for us was part of the structure."

April thought about the architecture of that kind of love—not grand or announced, but the consistent choice to be present, woven into the ordinary fabric of days. She thought of her own parents, especially her adoptive mother, who had done the same: shown up, stayed, and made presence structural.

"She looked at me differently when I said I was learning to be honest," April said. "Like I'd passed a test."

"You did," Jason said. "The thing Renee has no patience for is people who pretend they're already finished. She figures if you think you're finished, you've stopped being interesting."

"Smart woman."

"She raised me for about five years after my mother died, in everything but name," Jason said. "I think that earns the 'smart' label."

April turned to look at him. He was looking at the dark yard, his profile defined by the porch light, the quality of his stillness that she'd come to associate with the moments when he was actually present rather than managing a presentation of presence. The distinction was one she'd learned to read.

"What was she like?" April said. "Your mother."

He was quiet long enough that she thought he might not answer, and she was prepared for that—there were rooms you didn't push, thresholds where you simply waited to be invited across.

Then he spoke. "She was the most capable person I've ever known. Not in a showy sense, but in the way of someone who looked at what needed doing and did it without needing anyone to notice." He paused, his gaze fixed on the dark tree line. "She smelled of cocoa butter and antiseptic. She worked the morning shift at the county hospital for twenty-two years."

Another beat. "I measured safety by the sound of her coming home."

April felt something shift in her chest. She thought about her own father—the specific scent of his presence, the tectonic safety of a Sunday morning. She realized then that grief doesn't diminish a person's presence; it only changes its address.

"She sounds like someone worth missing," she said, her own words from the Miami diner echoing back to her.

He turned his head. Recognition sparked in his expression—he remembered. "She is," he said. Present tense. For both of them, now.

They sat in the cold and the dark, enveloped in the particular intimacy of two people who have shared the right things at the right time and find themselves, unexpectedly, in exactly the right place. Inside the house, the television murmured. Renee's laugh carried through the kitchen window—full and unguarded, the laugh of a woman who was truly home. The oaks shifted in the salt-heavy wind blowing in from the sea.

April leaned her head against Jason's shoulder. He put his arm around her without ceremony.

I could love him, she thought.

She did not say it. It was too new, too real, and the night was doing fine without the weight of the words. But she held the thought, and for once, she did not try to manage it into something smaller. She let it be exactly what it was.

Chapter 18: A Forbidden Triangle

The guest room in Renee's house featured a quilt that smelled of cedar and something older—not musty, just deep, the scent of fabric that had lived with a family for generations. April sat on the edge of the mattress after Dani had shown her upstairs, tracing the stitching. Someone had made this. Someone had cared enough about the people who would sleep under it to craft something meant to last.

She could hear the house settling into the night—the television fading downstairs, the low, rhythmic conversation of two women in the kitchen performing the post-dinner accounting that kitchens require, a solitary footstep on the stairs. Through the window, the oaks were dark silhouettes against a sky lighter than she'd expected; the coastal overcast held the day's warmth like a blanket.

A soft knock at the door. Jason.

He entered and sat beside her on the edge of the bed. He looked around the room with the expression of someone revisiting a familiar haunt—not with nostalgia, exactly, but with the specific attention one pays to a place that has changed in small ways. He was cataloging the differences.

"You good?" he asked.

"Better than good." She meant it. The dinner had sparked a realization she hadn't anticipated: it made her want things she hadn't known she was allowed to claim. The kitchen table, the borrowed sweater, Renee's laugh, Jason's hand under the table. A life could be assembled from those things.

"Renee pulled me aside after dessert," he said.

"What did she say?"

He was quiet for a moment. "She said, 'Don't mess this one up.' Those exact words." He looked at April with a ghost of a smile. "She doesn't usually editorialize."

"So this is a special occasion."

"Apparently."

April looked at him. In the low lamplight of the guest room, with the cedar scent of the quilt and the evening settling in, she felt the quality of a moment that was both ordinary and seismic—the kind you only recognize as a turning point later, when looking back at the sequence of events. She was aware of its weight in real time.

"Your uncle Gerald," she said. "The comment about your mother."

"He does that." The flatness in Jason's voice wasn't anger; it was the practiced neutrality of someone who had developed specific tools for managing a specific pressure. "He has opinions about what her sacrifice meant and what I owe it. He's not wrong, exactly. He's just not right in the way he thinks he is."

"What *do* you owe it?"

He looked at her. "To do something real with it. Not something legible—something real." He paused. "She worked double shifts so I could choose. Gerald thinks choosing means maximizing. I think choosing means doing something that actually matters to you. We disagree on the definition."

April thought about her own father. About the Tybee Island weekend that had cost more than he could afford and about which he'd never complained. About the specific kind of love that says: *I want you to have more than I had.* Not more money, but more world.

"Your mother sounds like she would have agreed with you," she said.

Jason was quiet, holding the thought without immediately responding. "Yeah," he said finally. "I think she would have."

He reached over and turned off the lamp. The room plunged into darkness before resolving into the softer charcoal of a clouded coastal night, the window pale against the trees. He lay back on the quilt, and she lay beside him. They looked at the ceiling and listened to the house. The intimacy didn't require anything but presence—just two people in the same room, in the same dark, breathing together.

After a while he turned toward her. She was already looking at him.

What happened next was slow and deliberate and entirely unhurried, the way it was when both people are present rather than performing presence—no urgency, no audience, nothing to prove to anyone including themselves. The cedar smell of the quilt and the coastal dark outside the window and the distant sound of Renee's television doing something low and companionable one floor below. April kept her eyes open. She had been keeping her eyes open, every time, since Miami—the choice to stay in her own body, to see what was happening rather than manage it from behind glass.

She saw him. All of him. The steadiness and the room he kept closed that was slowly, incrementally opening—she could feel it opening in the way he touched her, the quality of attention that was not performance but genuine presence, as if she were something he had decided to pay attention to with his whole self rather than the portion he kept available for most things.

She thought, in the middle of it, with the particular clarity that the middle of such things sometimes produces: *I am in exactly the right place.*

She did not manage the thought. She let it be true.

She woke to the smell of coffee and something baking— corn bread, she thought, the sweetness of it reaching her before consciousness fully had. Gray light through the window. The cedar quilt tucked around her, Jason already gone, the slight compression in the mattress where he'd been the only evidence.

She lay still for a moment and took inventory: body, mind, the room. The body was content in the specific way of someone who has slept deeply and woken into warmth. The mind was quieter than it had been in months. The room was exactly the same as the night before, the quilt still smelling of cedar, the window still pale with coastal overcast.

She got up. She borrowed the bathroom across the hall, moving quietly through a house that was still in its early morning state—the sounds beginning to accumulate: a cabinet closing downstairs, a murmured conversation, the specific creak of the second stair from the bottom that she'd noticed on the way up.

When she came down, the kitchen was already occupied by three people and the entire collective project of Thanksgiving. Renee stood at the stove with the authority of someone who had commanded this space for thirty years and expected the room to cooperate—which it did. Dani was at the counter, her movements precise and slightly competitive as she worked a pie crust. Jason sat at the kitchen table with his coffee and a book, maintaining the comfortable disposition of a man who had learned exactly where to position himself to be visible and available, yet never underfoot.

He looked up when she appeared in the doorway. "Morning."

"Morning." She stepped inside, and the kitchen received her. Renee handed her a mug without being asked; Dani offered a look that suggested a preliminary assessment had been confirmed. April accepted the coffee and stood for a moment, letting the warm industry of the room settle around her—the smells, the rhythmic sounds, the shared purpose. She thought: *This is what it feels like to be in a family.* Not the performed version, but the actual thing—imperfect, warm, and simply going about its business.

"Can I help?" she asked.

"Can you make biscuits?" Renee countered.

"I can make biscuits."

"Then get in here."

By noon, the house had expanded. Gerald and Claudette arrived first—Gerald bearing a bottle of bourbon and several opinions about the football matchup. Dani's partner, Marcus, arrived with the kind of reliable, easy energy that smoothes over large gatherings without calling attention to itself. Two of

Renee's neighbors—older women who had been coming to this table for as long as anyone could remember—arrived with a sweet potato casserole that smelled of brown sugar and immediately earned its place.

There were fourteen people in a house built for comfort rather than capacity. Conversation ran at several pitches simultaneously: the football contingent in the living room; the kitchen, where the final dishes were being managed with the precision of a small military operation; and the dining room, where the table had been extended to its full length and set with the particular care that signaled: *This matters. We are doing this correctly.*

April moved through the crowd and found, to her own surprise, that she wasn't "managing" the experience. She wasn't performing ease or monitoring herself for signs of social exhaustion that would need recovering later in private. She was simply *there*. She talked to Claudette and found her perspective sharper and more interesting than her quiet dinner presence the night before had suggested. She fell into an easy rhythm helping Dani, two women of different styles but identical underlying competence finding a natural collaboration. Across the room, she watched Jason handle Gerald with the same measured patience she'd witnessed previously, feeling that specific tenderness for a man who had forged such specialized tools for navigating the places that shaped him.

The meal itself was what a Thanksgiving dinner is supposed to be and rarely is: actually good. The turkey wasn't dry. The gravy was rendered from actual drippings. The biscuits April had made under Renee's supervision sat in a cloth-lined basket and vanished within the first ten minutes.

"She made those," Dani announced to the table at large.

"My grandmother's recipe," Renee added. "I just supervised."

April felt the heat rise in her cheeks and was grateful for the secondary currents of conversation that kept anyone from making a spectacle of it.

Jason caught her eye from across the table. He wore the expression she had learned to read as his version of happiness—not demonstrative or announced, but a specific quality of stillness that meant he was exactly where he wanted to be. She held his gaze and felt a surge of something she recognized now as love—actual love, the kind that had been building in increments since a Miami club at midnight and was now present enough to name without flinching.

She didn't say it. The table wasn't the place. But she held it.

The dishes took forty minutes and were the best part of the day. This was something April had always understood about communal meals: the *after* is where the real conversation happens, freed from the formality of the table, the shared rhythm of work making honesty easier.

She and Dani washed and dried with the practiced coordination of people who discovered they worked the same way. Marcus had been recruited by Gerald for the football game in the living room. Renee sat at the kitchen table with her bourbon, supervising with the wisdom of someone who knew exactly when to step back.

"He hasn't brought anyone home since college," Dani said. It wasn't meant to shock—just to state a fact.

April paused, considering the weight of that. "What happened in college?"

"Her name was Simone. They were together two years. She wanted him to be more... open. He wasn't, then." Dani handed her a casserole dish. "He's better now. Noticeably."

April looked at her.

"I say that as someone who's watched him for thirty years," Dani said. "He texts me more. He called me last month just to talk, not because something was wrong. Those are not things he did before." She paused. "I don't know what you did. But whatever it is—keep doing it."

April stood with the dish in her hands, thinking about her promise at the coffee shop: *I want to do this right.* She thought about the mirror room, about staying in her own body and not managing the feeling away. She didn't know if she had done anything specific. She suspected they had done it together—two people committed, imperfectly and incrementally, to being honest about what they needed.

"We're doing it together," she said.

Dani nodded. "Good. That's the right answer."

Renee said nothing from the table, but April caught the small, satisfied expression she made over her bourbon glass and filed it away as something to revisit later with warmth.

They went to bed late, after the last guests had departed and the kitchen had been returned to order. The house had subsided into that particular post-holiday quiet—full, warm, and slightly exhausted, the way a home feels after it has performed its primary function.

Jason sat on the edge of the guest bed and set his watch on the nightstand. April sat beside him and leaned her head against his shoulder. They didn't speak for a long while. The quilt still smelled of cedar; the trees outside the window remained invisible silhouettes against the pale sky.

"Dani told me you haven't brought anyone home since college," April said.

"Dani should consider a career where she talks less."

"She was being complimentary."

"She's always complimentary when she's being an enormous intrusion."

April smiled against his shoulder. "Why haven't you?"

He was quiet for a moment—the long pause that signaled an actual answer rather than a pre-packaged retrieval. "Because it means something," he said. "This house, this family... bringing someone here means something specific. I didn't want to mean it until I meant it."

She lifted her head to look at him. "And you mean it?"

"Yes."

The word was simple, direct, and entirely devoid of theater. That was why it landed the way it did—not as a performance of significance, but as the plain, unvarnished fact of it. He meant it. He was telling her so.

She kissed him. He kissed her back. The lamp went off.

Outside, the Georgia coast did what it always did in the dark—the oaks held their leaves against the November wind, the salt air moved in from the unseen water, and the sky lightened and darkened in slow, ancient cycles that had nothing to do with any human timeline.

Inside the guest room with the cedar quilt, two people who had decided to mean something to each other lay in the kind of quiet that only exists when both people in a room have stopped holding anything back from each other—not all at once, not without effort, but enough. The particular quiet of *enough*.

April lay awake for a while after Jason's breathing slowed. She looked at the ceiling. She thought about Renee's laugh through the kitchen window last night. Gerald's bourbon. Dani's hands sure on the pie crust. The biscuits that disappeared in ten minutes.

She thought: *This is what I want.* Not this specific house, not this specific holiday. The texture of it. The being-inside-a-life rather than managing it from outside.

She thought: *I could build this.*

She did not know yet what it would cost. She did not know about the months ahead, the slow accumulation of small distances, the night Angel would be there when she needed not to be. She did not know the shape of what was coming.

She only knew what she was grateful for. And in the cedar-smelling dark, with the coastal November outside and Jason breathing beside her and the house quiet around her, *grateful* was the truest thing she had.

She closed her eyes. She slept.

Chapter 19: Unveiled Desires

They flew home on Saturday morning, the Georgia coast releasing them into a sky that was low and gray and moving fast—the kind of sky that is all business. April watched Savannah disappear through the oval window and felt the specific texture of leaving a place you've liked—not grief, not reluctance, but the mild wistfulness of someone who has been somewhere good and is carrying it back with her.

"What are you thinking?" Jason said beside her.

"I'm thinking I liked your family." She turned from the window. "More than I expected to. Which is not a criticism of the expectation—I expected to like them. I just didn't expect to feel—" She stopped, looking for the right word.

"At home?" he said.

She looked at him. "Yeah."

He nodded. The simplicity with which he received things—not making it more than it was, not underplaying it either, just acknowledging the weight of a thing and letting it sit at its actual size—was something she had come to rely on without noticing she'd started relying on it.

"Renee's going to text you," he said. "I want to prepare you for that. She texts."

"She can text me."

"She texts frequently. With opinions. About things that are not necessarily her business."

April smiled. "She can still text me."

Jason looked at her for a moment with an expression she had learned to read as the deepest version of his happiness—not the surface ease of his comfortable persona, but the interior kind, the kind that lived in the specific room where he kept the things that mattered. He turned back to his book.

She turned back to the disappearing Georgia landscape and thought: *This. Exactly this.* The ordinary Saturday morning of it all. The way the mundane was starting to feel extraordinary, which she understood now was how love worked—not as a grand gesture, but as the accumulated weight of ordinary mornings. This was the intimacy she had been too defended to allow before. She was letting it happen now.

Atlanta received them with the particular Saturday afternoon quality of a city in a good mood. The temperature was mild enough for shirtsleeves, the sky clearing as they drove in from the airport, the weekend spreading out around them with the unhurried generosity of unscheduled time.

"I need to move," April said as they pulled off the interstate. "I've been in transit since yesterday morning."

"Walk or drive somewhere?"

"Drive somewhere, then walk around."

"Atlantic Station?"

"That works."

They went home first to drop their bags and change. April swapped her travel clothes for jeans and a soft, camel-colored sweater; Jason emerged in something similar. It was the casual coordination of two people who hadn't discussed their outfits yet arrived at a complementary palette anyway. She noticed it, filing the detail away in her category of small evidence.

Atlantic Station on a November Saturday was busy without being oppressive. The outdoor spaces held enough mild afternoon air to make being outside the better option. Families, couples, and groups of friends moved through the retail corridors with the specific ease of people who had nowhere to be for a few hours and found that "nowhere" pleasant. April walked beside Jason, feeling herself fully inside the day—not monitoring herself, not managing her presentation, just present.

He found the bookstore first. It was small and independent, wedged between a restaurant with a long wait and a kitchen shop. He stopped in front of it with the arrested attention of a man who had identified something essential.

"Five minutes," April said.

"Fifteen," he negotiated.

"Ten."

"Done."

Inside, the air smelled of paper and that specific vanilla-dust scent where old books intermixed with new—a smell that served as its own argument for why physical bookstores needed to exist. Jason moved through the aisles with the purpose of a man who knew exactly how to navigate a collection—not browsing, but searching, checking spines against a mental list.

April followed at her own pace. She pulled volumes from the shelves without strategy, reading the first pages of three different novels before replacing them. She found a collection of essays on grief and held it for a long time, scanning the table of contents before deciding she wasn't ready for it. She set it down gently, as if the book had feelings about being returned.

Jason appeared at her elbow with two books under his arm and the look of someone who had located exactly what he'd come for. He glanced at the essay collection she'd just shelved. "You should get that."

"Not yet," she said.

He looked at her and didn't push, which was exactly right. "I found you something." He held out a novel with a simple cover and an unfamiliar author. "It's about a woman who builds a life in a city she arrived in for the wrong reasons and stays for the right ones. Renee sent me the recommendation two years ago. I've read it three times."

April took it, studying the cover. She thought about Atlanta—about the reasons she had arrived in her own life and the reasons she remained in it. She thought about the house on the hill, the mirror room, and following music down side streets. "Why didn't you give me this earlier?"

"Timing," he said. "It needed to be the right moment."

She looked at him over the top of the book. "You think in terms of timing a lot."

"I think most things have a right moment and a wrong one. Rushing the right moment usually turns it into the wrong one."

She considered everything he'd withheld and revealed in its correct sequence: Miami, Atlanta, the house, his mother, the guest room in Savannah. The patient architecture of his heart. "I'm starting to understand that about you," she said.

"Good," he said. He paid for both books. She bought the essay collection, too, despite what she'd told herself.

They found a table at a restaurant with outdoor seating and a menu that took its ingredients seriously without lecturing the diner. The afternoon had warmed enough that the heat lamp above them felt like company rather than a necessity. April ordered a glass of Pinot Gris and a salmon dish that arrived looking like someone had spent time on it. Jason ordered bourbon and a steak—the easy coexistence of two people who had stopped performing their food choices for each other.

"Tell me something I don't know about you," April said.

He considered this. "I was afraid of water until I was nine. Couldn't swim. My mother signed me up for lessons at the county pool and stood at the edge to watch every session. I hated it. Then I got good at it. Now, I swim every morning."

"Every morning?"

"When I'm home. Twenty minutes. It's the first thing I do."

April realized how many mornings she'd woken next to him without knowing this. "I don't even know where you swim."

"There's a pool in my building. Fifth floor." He looked at her. "You could come sometime."

"I don't swim."

"I could teach you."

She looked at him across the table. The November afternoon was fading; the heat lamp was warm on her shoulders, and the wine was cold in her hand. She thought about a nine-year-old boy afraid of the water, being put in the pool anyway by a woman who stood at the edge and watched. She thought about the version of that story that wasn't about swimming at all.

"Why were you afraid of the water?"

He was quiet for a moment. "My dad left around that time. I think I displaced the fear onto something concrete because the actual thing I was afraid of didn't have a shape I could learn to manage."

The honesty of it arrived with the particular quality of something he had worked out over time and was now able to offer without it costing him the way it used to. April received it carefully. "And the swimming lessons fixed it?"

"The swimming lessons gave me something I could master." He turned his bourbon glass slowly on the table. "My mother understood that. She always found me something I could get good at when the real problem was too large for a nine-year-old to solve."

April set down her wine glass. She reached across the table and placed her hand over his—not to comfort, but to witness. It was the specific gesture of someone saying: *I heard that. It mattered.*

"She was very wise," April said.

"Yes," he replied. Present tense.

The boutique was Dani's recommendation, sent via text that morning while they were still packing: a small shop off the main corridor, worth the detour. April found it easily—quiet, vanilla-scented, the kind of place that displayed beautiful things without making the observer feel inadequate for not yet owning them.

She moved through the racks with the ease of someone who had stopped shopping defensively. She wasn't acquiring armor or assembling a presentation for a specific person's gaze; she was just looking. The clothing possessed the quality she'd come to prefer: well-made, intentional, pieces that knew exactly what they were.

In the back of the store, she found a rack of lingerie—not the aggressive kind designed to make a point, but the kind that suggested the wearer had personal preferences and had found something to satisfy them. April pulled a set in deep burgundy silk and held it for a moment.

Jason waited near the front of the store, being patient in his specific way—genuinely present rather than performing endurance. He had picked up a small framed print near the register and was studying it with the quiet intensity characteristic of his focus.

She took the burgundy set to the fitting room without asking his opinion. The decision was hers. She was practicing making things hers—not performing for an audience or seeking a reaction, but choosing what she wanted because her preferences were valid.

She put it on and looked in the mirror.

The fitting room mirror was smaller than the one in the "mirror room" at the house; the light was practical rather than atmospheric, and she was alone in it. Yet she looked at herself with the same attention she had been learning to bring to her own reflection—not searching for flaws, not checking for approval. Just looking. The woman in the glass looked back with the quiet assurance of someone who had survived her history and found her own presence sufficient.

She liked what she saw. She bought it.

When she emerged, Jason was waiting with the framed print under his arm, looking like a man who hadn't even thought to watch the clock. "Ready?"

"I got something," she said.

"Good."

She didn't tell him what. He didn't ask. They left the boutique and continued down the corridor as the afternoon hummed around them—warm, ordinary, and entirely sufficient.

They cooked together that evening, another intimacy she hadn't expected to find so profound. The kitchen in Jason's apartment was well-organized, which didn't surprise her, and he moved through it with a quality of intention—nothing wasted, nothing careless, each step in its correct sequence. She had her own relationship with kitchens, distinct from his, and she was finding that the negotiation of a shared cooking space was a surprisingly reliable indicator of whether two people could actually share a life.

They negotiated well. She took the vegetables; he handled the protein. They arrived at a finished meal without it feeling orchestrated.

After dinner, they sat on his couch with the Saturday evening assembled around them. The city moved outside, the apartment was warm, and the books from the afternoon rested on the coffee table. The novel he'd given her sat at the top of the pile; she planned to start it tonight.

"Tell me something else I don't know," she said.

He thought for a moment. "I wanted to be a marine biologist until I was fourteen."

She turned to him, intrigued. "What happened at fourteen?"

"I read a book about financial systems and realized for the first time that money was a language—and that languages could be learned. It felt more urgent than the ocean." He paused. "I still think about the sea, though. Maybe that's why I swim."

April thought about the pelican in Miami, coasting past her hotel balcony with total indifference. She thought about Haulover Beach and about water as the thing that always returns to shore. "Tell me one more," she said.

"I've been in love once before. It didn't work because I held too much back. I've been thinking about that a lot lately." He looked at her with the directness she had come to rely on. "I don't want to do that again."

April looked at him. The evening light in the apartment, the books on the table, the lingering scent of the dinner they'd made together—everything was quiet. For once, everything was exactly what it appeared to be.

"Then don't," she said.

"I'm trying." He paused. "You make it easier."

She considered her response, thinking of the hotel room in Miami, the mirror room, Renee's kitchen, and every ordinary, extraordinary Saturday. She thought about the essay collection she'd bought despite telling herself she wasn't ready, and how the right things arrive in their own time. The best you can do is be available when they do.

"You make it easier, too," she said. "I want you to know that."

He reached over and tucked a strand of hair behind her ear with the unhurried care that characterized everything he did with his hands. She leaned into the touch. The gesture was small, but it was enough.

Outside, Atlanta finished its Saturday. The city went on—lit and moving and loud—while in the fifth-floor apartment, two people sat in the particular quiet of a life becoming something neither had entirely planned. Which was exactly why it felt real.

April picked up the novel. She read the first page. She kept going.

Chapter 20: A Lazy Day

She found him in the hammock at ten-fifteen, which was itself the beginning of something. Jason was not a "hammock person," or at least had not been in her experience. The sight of him horizontal in the backyard of the house they'd rented for the long December weekend—one foot dragging lightly on the ground, a book resting on his chest at the precise angle of a man who had paused mid-sentence and not yet decided what came next—made her linger in the back doorway just to look at him.

He had found the hammock strung between two live oaks and apparently decided it was a reasonable place to spend the morning. It was characteristic in the way his best qualities always were: not announced, just enacted. He did what seemed right without needing to justify the impulse.

The day was doing what December days did here when they were being generous: it was warm enough for shirtsleeves by mid-morning, the sky a particular, scoured blue that arrived only after a front had swept the air clear. The oaks held their leaves with the stubbornness of Southern evergreens, indifferent to the calendar's opinion of what winter was supposed to look like.

April stood in the doorway with her coffee, watching him. She felt something she recognized as happiness—but a precarious version, the kind that feels fragile when you aren't used to possessing it. Somewhere beneath the "having" was the awareness that it wasn't guaranteed. She was working on letting it be what it was without auditing it. She was still imperfect at this, but she was getting better.

"I can feel you staring," Jason said, his eyes still closed.

"I'm not staring. I'm observing."

"Same thing, just better vocabulary." He opened one eye. "Are you going to come out here or supervise from the doorway all morning?"

She stepped out, pulling a lawn chair to a spot adjacent to the hammock—close enough for conversation, far enough that she wasn't crowding his space. She sat with her coffee and the specific pleasure of having nowhere to be.

"What were you reading?" she asked.

"Organizational theory. I got distracted."

"By what?"

He looked up at the canopy of oak above him. "Thinking about Renee's house. About what it means to have a place that holds a family over time. The architecture of it." He paused. "What makes a place become the kind of home people always come back to."

April looked down at her coffee, thinking of the kitchen table, the cedar quilt, and the sound of Renee's laugh. "Consistency," she said. "Someone showing up. Over and over, without making a production of it."

"Yeah," he said. "That's what I think, too."

They sat in that quiet for a while as the oaks swayed above them and the December morning arranged itself with unhurried generosity. A mockingbird worked through its repertoire in a nearby tree, cycling through borrowed songs with the methodical confidence of a creature that had stopped worrying about its audience.

April was listening. She listened to the whole thing.

The car needed washing. It was a fact that had been pending for two weeks—the Nissan sat in the driveway coated in the fine red-clay dust of Atlanta roads, which April found aesthetically objectionable in a way she rarely felt about vehicles. She had mentioned it twice. Jason had agreed both times with the equanimity of a man who would get to it when he got to it, entirely unbothered by her sense of urgency.

"Today," she said, returning from her second trip to the kitchen.

Jason looked at the car from the comfort of the hammock. "Today what?"

"The car. You promised."

"I said I would. I didn't specify today."

"I'm specifying today."

He looked at her, then at the hammock, noting the quality of the morning light and the pleasant possibility of another hour spent within it. Finally, he looked back at her. "You're not going to let me stay in this hammock, are you?"

"Not while the car looks like that, no."

He climbed out with the good-natured resignation of a man who had chosen his battles and found this one wasn't worth the fight. April went inside and changed into clothes she didn't mind ruining—cutoff shorts and an old T-shirt from college—and brought out two glasses of rum and coke. If he was going to wash the car on a Saturday, she was at least going to make it festive.

She set his glass on the hood in a gesture that was technically helpful but primarily provocative. He picked it up with the expression of a man receiving fair terms for his labor.

She sat in the lawn chair and watched him work, telling herself she was supervising when she was actually just finding an excuse to watch him without pretense. He had taken his shirt off—practical, given the water—and moved around the car with the unhurried efficiency he brought to everything. Hose in one hand, sponge in the other, he worked in sections.

She supervised closely.

"You're not helping," he noted.

"I'm quality control."

"Quality control doesn't usually have a drink."

"Mine does."

He turned the hose on her. It was a short, deliberate burst, aimed with precision. The water hit her left shoulder and the front of her shirt; she gasped at the shock of the cold.

"That," she said, setting her glass down with the care of someone preserving the important thing before handling the crisis, "was a declaration of war."

"It was an accident."

"You looked directly at me before you did it."

"I was making eye contact. That's a separate thing."

She lunged from the lawn chair. He backed up, hose in hand, looking like a man who had started something and wasn't entirely sure how it would resolve. She reached the spigot before he could react, cranked it to full pressure, grabbed the second hose coiled against the house, and spun to face him.

What followed was approximately four minutes of the most undignified and thoroughly enjoyable behavior April had engaged in for years. They were both soaked within ninety seconds. The water was cold and their laughter was loud enough to set the neighbor's dog barking. The car was forgotten; the driveway became a lake. She caught him twice in the face, a significant tactical achievement. He eventually picked her up—she shrieked—and carried her toward the flower bed while she continued to blast the hose at close range.

They ended up on the grass in a mutual truce, breathing hard and dripping wet. The hose lay running on the driveway, and the car gleamed in a way that was less about a wash and more about collateral hosing.

April lay on her back and looked at the sky, laughing until it hurt. It was the real kind of laughter—the kind that starts deep in the chest, the kind you can't perform because performance requires a distance she no longer felt.

Jason lay beside her on the wet grass, laughing too. The mockingbird in the live oak seemed to regard them with the equanimity of a creature that had seen much stranger things.

"The car still needs washing," April said, once she found her voice.

"The car got washed," he countered. "Enthusiastically."

They dried out in the afternoon sun. April changed into dry clothes and returned to the garden beds along the south side of the house. She'd been intermittently tending them since they'd arrived—it wasn't her garden or her house, just a weekend rental, but she was drawn to it anyway. There was something useful in tending things, even borrowed things. The labor of it. The conversation it didn't require.

Jason sat on the porch steps with his organizational theory book, actually reading this time, occasionally looking up at her without comment. The afternoon organized itself around them with the slow, unhurried pace of a warm December. The light moved at a crawl. Nothing was urgent.

April pulled a weed she'd been eyeing since yesterday, sat back on her heels, and looked at the garden—the way it was growing, the patches that needed attention, the parts that were doing fine on their own. She thought about what Jason had said in the hammock about the architecture of places that hold families. About consistency. Someone showing up.

She had always been someone who showed up for other people's lives: for work, for Angel, for her parents, for anyone who needed managing. She had shown up reliably and competently, but at a cost to her interior life that she was only now beginning to calculate. The question she was working on was whether she could show up for her own life with that same reliability. Whether she could tend her own garden with the same devotion she gave to borrowed ones.

She was getting there. The evidence was present-tense and ongoing.

"What are you thinking?" Jason asked from the porch.

"About gardens."

"Specifically?"

"About how they require consistent attention. Not dramatic gestures—just the regular, ordinary act of showing up." She sat back on her heels, surveying the bed. "And how the things you neglect don't always die immediately. Sometimes they just get complicated."

He looked at her over the top of his book. "Are we still talking about the garden?"

"Partially," she said.

He set the book aside. "What's the part that isn't the garden?"

She looked at him on the porch steps in the waning afternoon light. The wet grass from their earlier battle was still visible in the tire tracks where the water had puddled and dried.

"I've been neglecting some things for a long time," she said. "In myself. I'm trying to figure out how much of that is recoverable and how much I just have to work around."

"What kind of things?"

She weighed the honest answer. "Knowing what I want and asking for it. Trusting my own judgment. Letting people in without immediately cataloging what it will cost me." She paused. "You know. The usual."

He watched her for a moment. Then, he stepped down from the porch, crossed the yard, and sat on the grass beside the garden bed. It wasn't something a man in clean clothes would do on damp ground unless he was choosing it—and he was. He sat beside her and looked at the soil.

"For what it's worth," he said, "you're better at all of those things than you think you are. At least from where I'm standing."

"You might be biased."

"Probably," he agreed. "Still true."

She leaned her head against his shoulder. He looped an arm around her. They sat together on the damp December grass, looking at the things that were growing and the things that needed tending, while the afternoon performed its slow, inevitable fade.

She had promised oysters.

The idea had surfaced during the weekend planning—a conversation about what to do with a Saturday evening in a coastal house with a well-equipped kitchen. April had insisted on oysters because she knew how to prepare them, and because they suited the occasion: the specific luxury of a thing done simply, a meal centered on quality rather than complexity.

She drove to the market while Jason showered. The fishmonger was a man in his sixties who took his stock seriously, possessing the quiet expertise of someone who had found everything there was to find interesting about a single trade. He helped her select two dozen, recognizing that a person who knew how to ask for the best was worth his time.

Back in the kitchen, she scrubbed them at the sink while Jason handled the drinks. He poured Champagne into wide-mouthed coupes he'd discovered in the back of a cabinet—glasses that had apparently been waiting for an occasion. The room filled with the scent of the sea: cold, sharp, and particular. The brine cut through the warm kitchen air the way ocean smells always cut through everything else.

She roasted half and left the rest raw, serving them with a mignonette of shallots, red wine vinegar, and cracked pepper. Jason set the table on the back porch; the evening remained mild, and the porch was the only right place to end a day spent mostly outdoors. A citronella candle in the center cast a flickering yellow glow over the floorboards, while the oak leaves caught the final bruised colors of the sunset beyond the yard.

They ate slowly. The oysters were perfect—the raw ones clean and briny, the roasted ones yielding to butter and herbs. Each was its own argument for paying attention. Jason had learned, in the months they had been building this, to eat the way she did: with focus, without hurry, as if the meal were an experience to inhabit rather than a task to complete.

She noticed this. She didn't comment on it; she simply let it mean what it meant.

"Best day we've had in a while," April said, once the shells were empty and the Champagne was nearly gone. The night had fully settled around the porch.

"Yeah," Jason said. He looked at her across the table with that interior version of happiness—the one that surfaced only when a moment was exactly right and he had allowed himself to notice. "It was a good one."

"The car incident," she said.

"Will not be mentioned in polite company."

"The mockingbird witnessed it."

"The mockingbird has no standing in court."

She smiled. The evening gathered around them. Above the yard, the oaks stood tall, their Spanish moss stirred by whatever breeze the night carried from the water. She held her glass, watching the candle flame, and thought about the day in its entirety: the hammock, the water fight, the garden, the honest conversation on the grass, and now this—the golden light of a December porch.

I want to remember this specific day, she thought. Not as a memorial of a time before things changed, but just as itself. A Saturday that was entirely what it was, without needing to be anything more.

She held the thought carefully.

"What are you thinking?" Jason asked.

"That I'm happy," she said. No qualifier. No audit. Just the plain fact, offered with the same directness she had been practicing. "I'm happy."

He looked at her, the candle flame dancing between them. "Me too," he said.

They sat on the porch until the candle burned low and the night turned generous. Inside, the house waited with its quiet rooms and cool sheets, but neither moved to go in until the last of the Champagne was finished and the oaks were merely shadows against the dark. There was nothing left to do with the day except carry it inside, set it down gently, and let it be what it had been.

A good one. One of the best.

The kind of day you only recognize for what it is once you are already inside it.

Chapter 21: Between Two Worlds

January in Atlanta had a specific quality April had never fully adjusted to—not cold in the way of cities that committed to winter, but unsettled. The temperature drifted between fifty and thirty-five degrees without the dignity of a consistent season. On this particular Tuesday evening, the sky was the color of old pewter, flat and low. The heavy overcast made the city lights below the balcony appear sharper by comparison, the buildings gleaming against the gray like something desperate to be seen.

April stood at the railing, her hands wrapped around a mug of tea she'd brewed twenty minutes ago. She hadn't drunk a drop; she held it now purely for the warmth. Behind her, through the glass door, she could hear Jason in the kitchen. He cooked with the same deliberate precision he brought to everything: the rhythmic strike of the knife on the cutting board, the low sizzle of something warming in a pan. He had promised dinner in forty-five minutes with the authority of a man who meant it.

She looked out at the city and thought about the house.

This wasn't a new fixation. The house had lingered in her peripheral vision for the better part of three months. It wasn't an urgent pull; she had been there, she had returned to Jason, and she had stood in the mirror room where she'd realized something vital about herself. She had carried that realization back into her life with him and used it as a foundation. It had been the right choice. She didn't doubt the rightness of it for a second.

But.

The house held something she had not yet fully accessed. She was aware of it the way one is aware of a room in a home they've been invited into but haven't entered—not haunting, not even a command, just a presence. The upper level, the floor she had looked at and deferred in October, still waited with the patience of something that understood it was not on a schedule.

She wasn't afraid of what lay up there. Over the past weeks, she had finally parsed the difference: she had been treating *not yet* as if it were the same as *not ready*. They were not the same. *Not yet* was timing. *Not ready* was fear. She was striving to be precise about that distinction.

She was ready. The timing simply needed to be hers.

The variable she hadn't yet sorted was what that timing looked like in the context of her relationship. She hadn't hidden the house from Jason; he knew it, had been there, and had stood beside her in the mirror room, being exactly what she needed him to be in that space. But the upper level felt different in ways she was still struggling to vocalize. The upper level was a journey she needed to take alone before she could share it with anyone else. She was trying to figure out how to explain that to a man who had asked her to be honest about what she needed.

The tea had turned lukewarm. She drank it anyway.

Jason appeared in the doorway with a second mug—fresh and steaming. He had evidently noticed from the kitchen that her drink had lost its heat. He handed it to her without commentary, then leaned against the railing beside her to watch the city.

This was one of the traits she had come to rely on: he didn't require a roadmap for every gesture. He saw a need, met it, and never turned the provision into a transaction that required her to account for herself.

They stood in the pewter evening in silence. The city moved below them, indifferent and ongoing. Someone in an apartment across the way was playing jazz—low and late, the kind of music that suited this specific hour, suspended after the day but before the night had fully settled.

"Are you happy?" Jason asked.

The question arrived with the gentleness of someone who had been carrying the weight of it for a while and had finally decided to set it down between them. It wasn't an accusation;

it was an honest inquiry, offered with the willingness to hear a difficult truth.

April looked back at the city. She thought about the porch, the oysters, the Champagne, and the words *I'm happy* spoken plain and true. She thought about the last three weeks since they'd returned from the rental—the specific quality of her own attention. She was present, yet periodically elsewhere. She went quiet in the middle of conversations; she sat on the balcony more than usual.

She thought about the honesty she had committed to. Not selective honesty—the kind that shares the easy parts and manages the rest—but actual honesty. The kind that had been required of her since Miami.

"I am," she said. "And I'm also..." She paused, searching for the word. "Restless. Both of those things are true at the same time."

He looked at her, not with the expression of a man who needed the restlessness to vanish, but with the expression of a man who wanted to understand its shape. "Tell me."

She turned to face him, leaning her back against the railing. The city was behind her now; Jason was in front of her, framed by the warm glow of the kitchen light.

"The house," she said. "There are parts of it I haven't gone to yet. I keep thinking about it. Not because what we have isn't enough—it is. But because there are things I need to understand about myself that I haven't fully reached, and I think some of those things are there."

He was quiet for a moment. She watched him process it— not defensively, not the way a man processes something that feels like a threat to what he's built. More the way a person processes information that requires them to update their model of a situation. "The upper level," he said.

"Yes."

"You said *not tonight* in October."

"I wasn't ready then. I think I am now." She looked at him. "But I need to go alone first. Before I share it with anyone. Even you."

She watched him sit with this. The specific quality of his silence—not hurt silence, not withdrawn silence, but thinking silence, the sound of a man doing the honest work of responding rather than reacting. "Why alone?" he said finally.

"Because what I'm looking for there is something about me. Not about us. And I'm afraid that if I bring you before I've found it, I'll end up looking at your face to understand what I'm experiencing instead of understanding it myself."

She held his gaze while he received this. She was aware of how it sounded and was not willing to soften it to make it easier to hear, because the thing she'd promised herself was precisely this: the actual version, not the managed one.

"That's honest," he said.

"You asked me to be."

"I did." He looked at the city for a moment, then back at her. "Go. Do what you need to do." A pause. "But come back and tell me. Don't make it a secret."

"I won't," she said. "I promise."

He nodded. He picked up her empty mug and carried it inside with his own. From the doorway he said, "Dinner's ready when you are."

She stood at the railing a moment longer. The city moved. The jazz from across the way continued its late work. She thought about what had just happened—the conversation she'd been circling for three weeks, had to herself in a dozen forms, and had just had out loud in its actual shape—and felt the specific relief of a thing that had been carried privately being set down in front of someone who had received it without flinching.

She went inside.

He had made pasta—something with roasted tomatoes and herbs, simple and exactly right for a January evening, the kind of meal that understood what it was supposed to do and did it without overreaching. He had set the table properly— not with the exaggerated precision of the Thanksgiving silverware joke, but with the ordinary care of someone who believed meals deserved to be treated as occasions even when they weren't.

They ate and talked about things that had nothing to do with the house or the balcony conversation or any of the heavy territory they'd just covered. They talked about his work—a project he'd been engaged with for six weeks that was nearing a decision point—and about her work, and about a text Renee had sent her that afternoon regarding a recipe she needed from the woman who'd brought the sweet potato casserole at Thanksgiving. Renee had indeed been texting her frequently. Always with opinions.

"I like her," April said.

"She likes you," Jason said. "She told me. In those exact words. Which she does not do."

"What did she say, exactly?"

He looked slightly pained. "She said, 'That woman sees things. Keep her.'"

April looked at him. "Keep her."

"Her word. Not a request, just—declarative. This is what you should do." He turned his wine glass slowly. "She's not wrong, usually."

April held the sentence in the warm kitchen air. *Keep her.* The confidence of it, the declarative certainty of a woman who had watched her nephew for thirty years and had decided in the course of a single Thanksgiving that this was the right call. She thought about what it meant to be kept—not in the diminishing sense, not as possession, but in the sense of someone choosing, repeatedly, to stay.

She thought about what she had said on the balcony: *Don't make it a secret.* She had promised, and she intended to keep it, and the keeping of it was the very thing that made the going alone possible—not a secret from him, just a thing she needed to do first, the same way you take certain steps alone before you can describe the view to someone else.

"I'll tell you when I'm going," she said, returning to it now as a confirmation rather than a negotiation. "And I'll tell you what I find."

"That's all I need," he said.

She dreamed about the house. This was not unusual—the house had been in her dreams intermittently since the first visit, appearing with the specific logic of dream geography, sometimes larger than it was and sometimes reduced to a single corridor, sometimes with people she knew in rooms she didn't recognize. The dreams were not frightening; they were the dreams of someone processing a mystery rather than someone being threatened by one.

In this one, she was on the lower level, in the main room with the fountain, and the fountain's rainbow was moving across the ceiling in slow arcs. The house was empty except for her. Not threatening—just waiting. She walked to the foot of the staircase and looked up.

From the upper level, there was light. Warm and specific, not the atmospheric dimness of the lower level but something more particular, more clarifying. She stood at the foot of the stairs and felt the pull of it—not a compulsion, just the specific gravity of something she had not yet reached that was ready for her now.

In the dream, she put her hand on the banister. She didn't go up, but she felt the wood under her palm—solid, warm, real in the way dream textures sometimes are—and she understood that the staircase was hers to climb whenever she decided to climb it. That it had always been hers. That the sign at the top had never been a prohibition, just a marker of distance still to be covered.

She woke in the gray January early morning. Jason was asleep beside her, breathing with the complete surrender of someone who had made peace with the night. She lay still for a moment and felt the dream settle, the way good dreams do— not fading but resolving, becoming part of the day's available information.

She was going to go. Soon. She knew the timing now the way she'd known in October that it *wasn't* tonight—that same interior knowing, simply the opposite reading.

She was going to go, and she was going to come back, and she was going to tell him what she found. The circuit of that—go, discover, return, tell—was not a betrayal of what they had. It was the practice of the thing she had promised at the coffee shop on that Saturday morning nine months ago when she'd said, *I want to do this right.*

This was doing it right.

She reached over and turned off the alarm before it could sound—she'd set it by habit, forgetting she didn't need it—and lay back in the January quiet. She thought about what it was to live in two worlds at once and have them both be fully hers.

Not split. Not divided. Hers.

The difference mattered. She was getting precise about it.

She found the photograph two days later while reorganizing the bookshelf in her apartment, where she'd been letting things accumulate since the fall. It was tucked inside a journal she'd stopped writing in—the journal that had been her attempt, in the months after the warehouse, to put language to things she hadn't been ready to say aloud.

The photograph was of the house. She had taken it on her phone during the second visit and printed it on a whim, slipping it into the journal and apparently not thinking about it since. She held it now and looked at it: the exterior of the house on the hill, the grand facade, and the light in the upper windows where she had never yet been.

She thought about what Jason had said: *Whatever it is, we'll get through it together. But you have to let me in.*

She thought about what she had said in return, on the balcony two days ago: *I need to go alone first.*

Both things were true. That was the thing she was learning about the interior life—it was not a problem to be solved or a loyalty to be assigned. It was a territory to be inhabited honestly, which meant sometimes alone, sometimes with someone else, and sometimes in the specific overlap of those two things that she was still learning to navigate.

She set the photograph on the nightstand, face up. Not hidden—she was done hiding things, even from herself. Just present. A reminder of where she was going and what she was going toward.

The house on the hill would be there when she was ready. She was almost ready.

That was enough for tonight.

Chapter 22: The First Door

The photograph was still on the nightstand when she woke the following Saturday morning. She had left it there deliberately—face up, not hidden, the small act of not hiding it a practice she was keeping. Jason had seen it, had not commented on it in the way he did not comment on things he understood were hers to bring up when she was ready. She was becoming fluent in his particular grammar of respect.

She picked it up now, bathed in the early morning light, and studied it: the house on the hill, its grand facade, the upper windows seemingly lit from within. She had taken this photograph approximately nine months ago, before she knew what the house was, before she had ever walked through its front door. She had been driving home from a long Saturday at work—the month after the warehouse, the month she'd spent with her face set and her interior life locked away, keeping the surface of her world perfectly managed. She had seen the house on the hill from the road and had simply pulled over.

She had taken the photograph and then sat in her car for ten minutes, just looking at it.

She hadn't known why. She didn't know now, not fully. But she was willing, finally, to sit with the not-knowing and examine its edges—the way one examines the ridge of a scar they've had long enough to stop being self-conscious about. She looked with the interest of someone who understands that the story of a wound is fundamentally part of the story of a person.

She lay back against the pillows with the photograph resting on her chest and let herself drift back.

She had been thirty-one years old, perfectly competent, and quietly coming apart. This was the season after Josh—not immediately after the breakup, which she had handled with the clinical efficiency she brought to things she could not let herself feel in real time, but during the six months that followed. It was the period in which she discovered that what she had "managed away" did not actually disappear; it simply moved deeper and continued its work there, out of sight.

She had been performing well-being for so long that she had lost track of where the performance ended. She went to work. She maintained her apartment with the immaculate attention she gave to everything she could control. She had dinner with her mother twice a month, listening to Cynthia's assessments of her casework, agreeing where Cynthia was right and pushing back where she was wrong. Then she went home, cooked the meals she'd planned at the start of the week, watched the television she'd selected in advance, and went to bed at eleven-fifteen to lie in the dark with her eyes open.

She had not told anyone about the warehouse. Not because she was ashamed—though she was, and that shame was its own burden she would eventually need to address—but because she had not yet found an accurate language for it. The words available to her were either too clinical or too dramatic, and the actual experience had been neither. It had been specific, quiet, and ongoing. It had left marks on her interior that clinical terms could not describe and dramatic language distorted into something unrecognizable.

She had been moving through her life with those marks and no language for them, which she now understood was the loneliest configuration a person could inhabit. It was worse than grief, which has its rituals, its timelines, and its social permissions. It was worse than fear, which has an object and a logic. This was neither. This was just *there*. Always just there, like a sound at the edge of hearing that she couldn't identify but couldn't stop listening for.

She had been driving home on a Saturday in March—the month she had decided she was fine, because deciding was something she could do regardless of whether it was true—and she had seen the house on the hill from the road.

It sat back from the pavement at the apex of a long drive: large, lit, and possessing the quality of a building with a specific purpose that wasn't any of the obvious ones. Not a venue—too private. Not a residence—too many cars. It was something else, something for which she had no category.

She had pulled over. She sat in her car and stared through the windshield with that particular arrested quality she sometimes felt in front of certain paintings—not knowing why she had stopped, only that the stopping felt obligatory.

She took the photograph. She sat for ten minutes. She drove home.

She looked the house up. This took longer than she'd expected. The house on the hill didn't have a website or a public listing; it wasn't the kind of establishment that appeared in search results for entertainment venues or private clubs. It appeared only in certain corners of the internet that required knowing what to look for—forums where people discussed it with that specific combination of discretion and enthusiasm that characterizes communities built around something operating at the edges of permission.

What she found was this: the house was a private membership establishment. It had been in its current location for eleven years. It required a referral from an existing member for access. It was a place where, within a framework of consent and confidentiality, adults explored dimensions of desire that the rest of their lives held no space for.

She read this and sat with it, feeling something she hadn't anticipated. It wasn't shock, nor was it the reflex of the "good girl" who had managed her interior life carefully since childhood. It was something quieter and more honest. It was recognition.

She hadn't sought the referral immediately. She lived with the knowledge of the house for six weeks before she acted. During those weeks, she was more deliberately honest with herself than she had been in years—sitting with the question of what she wanted from a place like that, what she expected to find, and whether she was running toward something or away from it.

The answer arrived slowly and without comfort: both. Running toward herself and away from the version of herself she'd been performing. These were not contradictory impulses; they were the same motion.

She mentioned the house to no one. There was no one she could tell in a way that would produce understanding rather than concern, and she didn't want concern. She wanted the thing itself, unmediated by anyone else's reaction.

The referral eventually came through a colleague—a woman she'd worked alongside for three years, a person capable, private, and possessed of the specific quality of someone who has organized her life exactly as she wants it and feels no need to explain that organization to anyone. April had noticed her over time, the way one notices people who aren't performing; her presence was different in quality from those who were. After the sixth week of living with the knowledge of the house, April mentioned it as briefly as possible during the ten minutes they spent together in the break room on a Wednesday afternoon.

The colleague looked at her with the level directness of someone who wasn't going to pretend the conversation wasn't happening. "How did you find out about it?"

April told her about the photograph. About pulling over. About the ten minutes in the car.

The colleague was quiet for a moment. Then she said, "I can make a call." She said it matter-of-factly, the way one offers to pass along a resume—without drama, without the suggestion that the favor was anything other than practical. "You'll need to go through their intake process. They're careful about who they admit. That's part of why it works."

April had said, "Yes. Please."

Three weeks later she had received an address and an appointment time and a brief document outlining the house's membership agreement, which she had read three times with the clinical thoroughness of someone who understood that consent began with comprehension.

She had worn the wrong thing. She understood this the moment the door opened and she stepped into the entrance hall—not wrong in the sense of socially incorrect, the house had no dress code in the conventional sense, but wrong in the sense of armor. She had dressed the way she dressed for anything unfamiliar: with the deliberate professionalism that communicated competence before anyone had the chance to form a different assessment. The clothes were beautiful and entirely beside the point.

The entrance hall had given her the time to understand this before she'd had to go any further. The space received her without judgment—neither the impersonal efficiency of a service establishment nor the studied warmth of a place trying to make you feel welcome. It simply was what it was, with the confidence of something that did not need to explain itself.

A woman had met her—older, composed, with the particular quality of a person who had seen many first visits and understood what they required. She had explained the house in the same matter-of-fact language of the membership agreement: the main floor, the corridor of rooms, the upper level for which additional access applied. The attendants. The protocols. The safeword that was always available and always honored without question.

April had listened with the part of her mind that processed information—thorough, precise, asking the clarifying questions of a seasoned clinician. But another part, running underneath, was doing something different: taking inventory of how she felt in this space, standing in this entrance hall, receiving this information. That part found, to its own mild surprise, that the primary sensation was not anxiety. It was not the adrenaline of transgression. It was something closer to— settling. It was the specific relief of a person who has been holding a rigid position for years and has finally been given permission to release it.

She had not ventured far on that first visit. She explored the main room, the fountain, and the corridor of doors with her hands at her sides—observing but not entering, much the way one walks through a museum on a first visit to understand the shape of the place before stopping at any particular exhibit. She stayed for two hours and left before midnight. On the drive home, she kept the windows down despite the cold; the sharp March air stung her face, and she welcomed it. She needed the bite of the wind to stay anchored in her own body.

She had sat in her apartment with her coat still on and thought: *There it is.* The thing she had been looking for without knowing its name. It wasn't the house itself—the house was merely the setting. It was the thing underneath: the permission. It was the idea that the parts of herself she had managed most carefully were not problems to be solved, but territory to be explored with the same rigor and honesty she brought to the rest of her life.

She had gone back the following week. And the week after that.

April set the photograph back on the nightstand, lying in the January morning light. She thought about the woman who had pulled over on that March Saturday and sat in her car for ten minutes. She thought about the six weeks of sitting with the knowledge before acting on it. She thought about the colleague who had made the call without drama, the entrance hall, and the settling.

Since the warehouse, she had been trying to quantify what had been taken from her. She struggled to understand the scope of the damage inflicted by Mr. Daley—not just the obvious violations of bodily sovereignty and trust, but the subtler erosions. The permission she had revoked from herself. The interior life she had reduced to its most manageable dimensions because the larger ones had been weaponized against her, used to reach her in places she hadn't known were reachable.

The house had given that permission back. Not all at once, but slowly, on her own timeline—the way things are restored when the restoration is real rather than performed. It had whispered: *These parts of you are not dangerous. They are not liabilities. They are yours, and they are worth knowing.*

She hadn't understood on that first night that this was what she was seeking. She understood it now.

She also understood something else—something she had been circling during the balcony conversation without quite landing on. The upper level was the last room she had not entered. The final door. And what lay behind it was not something the house would provide; the house gave permission, not content. What waited behind the door to the upper level was whatever she brought to it. It was her own truest self, in the configuration she had been working toward since that March, since the warehouse, since childhood's first realization that some parts of her required protection—and that protection had, over time, become a kind of confinement.

She was ready to stop being confined.

She picked up her phone and texted Jason: *I'm going to the house tonight.*

His reply arrived four minutes later: *Okay. Tell me what you find.*

She put the phone down and looked at the ceiling. The January light moved slowly across it as the morning progressed, the angle of the sun shifting with the patient, unhurried grace of a month doing the work of winter without drama.

She lay there for a while longer, inside the knowledge of what she was about to do, which felt neither frightening nor triumphant. It felt like the thing it was: a door she had always been going to open. She had simply needed to become the person who could walk through it.

She thought she was, finally, that person.

She got up.

Chapter 23: The Upper Level

She dressed alone in her apartment on a Saturday evening in late January with the particular deliberateness of someone who has decided something and is enacting the decision in sequence. Not armor this time; she knew better now. She chose things that were hers in the truest sense—soft leather trousers, a dark blouse that moved when she moved, boots with a heel that gave her height without the suggestion of performance. She looked at herself in the bathroom mirror with the attention she had been practicing and found the woman looking back ready in the way she had promised herself she would be before she came here.

The drive took twenty-two minutes. She had made the trip enough times now to navigate the route without conscious effort, leaving her mind free to drift as she drove. She thought about March—the first drive, the frantic energy, the wrong clothes. She thought about October, standing at the foot of the staircase with Jason beside her, saying *not tonight* with a newfound, accurate understanding of her own timing. She thought about that January morning, lying in bed with the photograph on her chest, and the text she'd sent: *I'm going to the house tonight.* And his four-minute reply.

She thought about the dream—her hand on the banister, the warm, solid wood, the light beckoning from above.

She thought: *I have been building toward this for a long time.* Not toward the house itself, but toward becoming the person who could walk through these doors and know exactly what she was looking for.

She pulled into the drive. The house received her as it always did—with the patient indifference of a place that did not require her to be anything other than herself. The parking attendant offered a brief nod. She went inside.

The main floor on a Saturday evening possessed its full, vibrant quality—the fountain performing its slow work with the light, and a hum that was part music, part conversation, and part the warm density of the air. She moved through the space without stopping. She wasn't dismissing it; she was grateful for everything she had discovered here—the mirror room, the corridors, and the slow education of her own desire across nine months of visits. But tonight, she was not here for the lower level.

She had spoken with the house's attendant earlier in the week—the same composed woman who had greeted her on that first night in March and provided the tour with a matter-of-fact precision April had admired. The conversation had been brief. April had stated she was ready for upper-level access. The attendant had simply said, "Come Saturday. I'll have someone meet you at the stairs."

April had not asked what the upper level contained. She had made this decision deliberately, applying the same reasoning she used for everything at the house: she wanted her experience to be her own, unmediated by anticipation. She couldn't stop herself from theorizing—the dominant room, the specific configuration she had been circling since October—but she kept her theories loose. She held them lightly, as hypotheses rather than blueprints.

The woman waiting at the foot of the staircase was not the head attendant. She was younger—April's age, perhaps slightly older—with the quiet composure of someone trusted with something vital. She greeted April with a nod.

"First time up," she said. It wasn't a question.

"Yes."

"There are three rooms. You'll be shown each. You choose what you engage with and how. Everything is consensual; the safeword is available at any time." She paused, her gaze steady. "The upper level is different from the lower in one specific way: down here, the house offers things to you. Up there, you decide what you bring. The rooms are responsive, but they don't lead. You do."

April absorbed this. It confirmed the conclusion she'd reached in the January quiet: whatever was behind the upper-level door was whatever she brought into it. "I understand," she said.

"Good." The woman gestured toward the stairs. "Take your time on the landing. The first room is to the left. Come find me when you're done, or sooner if you need anything."

April placed her hand on the banister. The wood was warm, solid, and real—exactly as the dream had promised. She had dreamed true. She began to climb.

The landing was smaller than she'd imagined. It was a narrow space with three doors and a window at the far end, through which the Atlanta night was visible—city lights, a low overcast, and the luminous quality of a cloudy urban sky. A single chair sat in the corner, unoccupied. The floor was old, well-maintained wood, and her boots made a sound against it that signaled her arrival.

She stood on the landing and breathed. The house seemed to breathe with her—responsive to her presence, the temperature, and the light, all calibrated in ways she couldn't entirely explain but had learned to trust. It wasn't magic; it was attention. The house had been built by people who understood that environment shapes experience—that the container matters, and the quality of attention a space offers its inhabitants affects the quality of attention they can offer themselves.

Three doors. She did not rush the choice.

She thought about what she knew of herself, a knowledge accumulated across thirty-two years and nine months of a very particular education. She thought about the warehouse—about what it felt like to have desire weaponized, to have the parts of herself that wanted and chose turned into instruments of someone else's power. She thought about Miami, about staying in her own body. About the mirror room, and the woman in the infinite reflection who was still figuring it out.

She thought about the *Dominari* room on the lower level—the room she had entered on her second visit and never returned to. She hadn't avoided it out of fear, but because she had realized, in the moment of being in it, that she had been in the wrong role. The role the room assigned her was not the one that fit. She had filed that away as information and carried it for months.

The door to the left. She opened it.

The room was not what she would have designed for herself, which meant it was right. She would have designed something too specific, too managed—her familiar failure mode. The room had its own logic, one she would have to meet rather than impose herself upon.

It was larger than the rooms on the lower level. The light was warm but not dim—it was a directed light that clarified rather than obscured. The walls were a deep, neutral hue, and the furniture was minimal and precise: a chair positioned centrally with the authority of its own function, and a table to one side with items arranged with deliberate care. A full-length mirror stood on the far wall, positioned so that anyone at the center of the room would see themselves completely.

And two people were already there. Not attendants, but participants—a couple who had been here before her and who looked up as she entered with the composed acknowledgment of those who understood that entry meant something specific. They had been waiting, she realized, for whoever came through that door. The house's Saturday offering. She was the *whoever*.

She had not known this would be the configuration, yet she found, standing in the doorway, that she was not unready for it. Her hypothesis—the dominant role—had been correct. She was here to be the person who set the terms. She was here to understand what it felt like to be the one who decided, who moved deliberately, who held the space.

Not because power was the point. But because she had spent so much of her life managing things from behind glass, keeping her own wanting at arm's length. Her choices had been taken, managed, or performed, but rarely actually made. She needed, in a way that was not at all abstract, to be in a room where the choosing was entirely and irrevocably hers.

She came fully through the door. She closed it behind her.

She looked at the two people in front of her and felt—and this was the thing she would remember, the thing she would come back to in the months ahead, the thing she would try to explain to Jason with the language she was still building—not power over them but clarity about herself. The room was not giving her something. It was showing her something that had always been there.

She said what she needed to say. She moved in the ways the room required. She was deliberate and unhurried and entirely present in her own body, and she kept her eyes open, and she was not performing anything for anyone, including herself.

An hour passed, or more. She did not track it.

She stood in front of the mirror afterward. The room had quieted around her—the couple gone, departed with the respectful discretion the house trained its members in, leaving her with the space and the particular silence of something that has been completed.

She looked at herself.

The woman in the mirror was not a stranger. She had been getting to know her for nine months, in increments—in the mirror room on the lower level, in her own bathroom the morning after the Dominari room, in the full-length glass of the boutique in Atlantic Station. The woman she had been building toward, slowly, the one who had come into focus in Miami and had continued resolving across the year.

This was the clearest she had ever seen her.

She thought about Mr. Daley. She thought about the warehouse. She thought about the specific damage those experiences had wrought—they hadn't destroyed her desire or rendered her incapable of it, but they had separated her from it. They had built a wall between the part of her that wanted and the part of her that chose. For years, she had wanted things she never fully chose and chosen things she never fully wanted, managing the gap between them so efficiently she had almost forgotten it existed.

The house had revealed the gap. The work of the past year had been closing it.

Standing before the mirror in the upper level, she felt that closure. It wasn't complete—she didn't believe in the "finished" version of a person, remembering Renee's words: *If you think you're finished, you've stopped being interesting.* But it was closed enough. The wall was thin enough now to see through.

She touched the mirror with the flat of her hand. Cool glass; her own warm reflection.

She thought: *I know who I am in here. Finally. I actually know.*

The realization possessed a specific quality: it wasn't triumphant. It was quiet. It was the silence of something that had been true all along and was only now being acknowledged— the way one recognizes a face seen before but never quite placed. It wasn't a revelation; it was simply the arrival of what was already there.

She stayed with that feeling for a long time.

She left the house at eleven-forty-seven. She sat in her car for a few minutes with the heater running and the windows fogging, the January night continuing its business outside. She felt the specific density of a post-arrival quiet—not an emptiness, but the opposite. She felt full, in the manner of someone who has found what they were looking for and is now beginning to understand what finding it actually means.

She drove home along her usual route, twenty-two minutes, the city going about its Saturday night around her, indifferent and ongoing. She kept the radio off; she wanted to remain in the silence.

She was in her apartment, sitting on the couch with her coat still on—just as she had been on that first night in March, nearly a year ago—when her phone lit up. Jason. Not a text, but a call.

She answered. "Hey."

"Hey." His voice had the quality of someone who had been awake—not quite waiting, but available. "How are you?"

She considered the honest answer. "Good," she said. "Really good. More than good."

A pause. "Yeah?"

"Yeah." She looked at the dark apartment around her, the familiar geometry of her own space, and felt herself fully inside it rather than arranged around it at a careful distance. "I found what I was looking for."

"Tell me," he said. It wasn't a demand or an urgent prompt; it was an invitation. It was the specific quality of a man who had been waiting for something important and understood that the way one receives a truth matters as much as the truth itself.

"Not tonight," she said. "In person. Tomorrow. I want to tell you properly."

"Okay," he said simply. "I'll come to you."

"Bring coffee."

"Done."

She sat in the dark apartment after the call ended, thinking about what she would say tomorrow. She thought about the mirror, the woman within it, and the closing of the gap. She thought about how to find the language for what had happened—not clinical, not dramatic, but the actual thing. She was going to need entirely new words for some of it.

She had been finding new words all year. She was getting good at it.

She took her coat off and hung it by the door. She looked at the apartment in the dark and found it sufficient, hers, and exactly what she needed it to be.

She went to bed and slept without dreaming.

For the first time in a very long time, there was nothing left to anticipate. The thing itself had arrived. She was inside it. She could rest.

Chapter 24: Angel's Reckoning

Angel called on a Tuesday evening in February, two weeks after the bar confrontation and six days after April had returned from the upper level. April sat at her kitchen table, where Jason's coffee cup from the morning still rested on the counter. He had come over Sunday as promised, bringing coffee and sitting on the couch while she finally found the language for what had happened at the house. He had listened with that specific gift of attention, asking three questions that were exactly the right ones. Since then, she had been settling into the aftermath of that conversation: the solid, good weight of having told the truth to the right person.

The phone rang. Angel.

April answered without hesitation—small evidence of how much had shifted. Six months ago, she might have let it go to voicemail, needing the buffer of a recorded message to gauge which version of a conversation she was being invited into. Now, she answered because they were in a different place, and because she genuinely wanted to know how Angel was.

"Hey, *chica*." Angel's voice had the specific texture of someone who is keeping it together and wants credit for the effort. "I was thinking—Thai food? Your place? There's a documentary I want to watch about deep-sea creatures, and I don't want to watch it alone."

April considered the logic of the request. Angel had spent the past two weeks doing the private work of her own reckoning, and now she was calling for pad thai and nature specials. It was a choice of a low-stakes format. The high-stakes conversation could wait for another night; Thai food and deep-sea creatures meant: *I need to be near someone safe tonight without it having to be a "thing."*

"I'll order," April said. "Come whenever."

Angel arrived at seven-fifteen with a bottle of Malbec she'd clearly plucked from the "good" shelf rather than the convenient one—a detail that told April how Angel was measuring the occasion. She was dressed simply in leggings and an oversized, deep rust sweater, her hair down and slightly undone. It was the look of someone who had stopped performing the day. She looked, April thought, like a person who had been doing real work on the inside and was showing the texture of it on the outside.

She also looked tired in a way that differed from exhaustion. She wasn't depleted; she was processed. It was the look of someone who had come far enough to the other side to be standing upright, but not so far that she had forgotten what the "going through" felt like.

"Hey," April said.

"Hey." Angel stepped in, set the wine on the counter, and scanned the apartment with her usual comprehensive glance. It was the way she always read a room—cataloging the energy in two seconds to assess if the person living there was okay. Whatever she found seemed to satisfy her.

"You look good," she said. "Different."

"Different how?"

Angel considered. "Settled. Like something landed."

April looked at her. "Something did."

"Tell me later," Angel said. "Food first. I'm starving and I've been in my own head all week and I need to eat actual food and watch something that has nothing to do with any of us."

"Deep-sea creatures," April confirmed.

"They found a squid last year that's basically transparent," Angel said, already moving toward the couch with the ease of someone who had been in this apartment enough times to know where she belonged in it. "You can see its organs. It's disgusting and incredible. I've been saving it."

"For the right occasion."

"For the right person," Angel said. She looked back at April over her shoulder. "You're the right person."

April opened the wine.

The food arrived at seven-forty-five—the usual order from the place they'd been going to since they were both newer to Atlanta. The restaurant had been new then, too; they'd found it together on a Thursday night after a bad week and had been going back ever since. April set the containers on the coffee table with the systematic efficiency she'd always brought to this specific domestic task, and Angel unpacked them with the comfortable familiarity of someone who knew which container was hers without checking.

They ate and talked about things that had nothing to do with Charles or the bar or Josh or the house. This was, April understood, the gift Angel was offering—the space of just being two people who knew each other well enough to be ordinary together. They talked about work. Angel had a client she was wrestling with, a woman who kept undercutting her own arguments in the middle of making them, and Angel found this both professionally frustrating and personally recognizable. "I want to hold up a mirror," Angel said. "But it's not my job to hold up the mirror. My job is to reflect back what she's already doing."

"You're doing the same thing yourself," April said.

Angel pointed at her with a dumpling. "I know. That's why it's frustrating. I recognize the pattern because I live it." She ate the dumpling. "My therapist and I have been having some conversations."

"Dr. Coleman?"

"Still Dr. Coleman. For six years now." Angel refilled her wine glass. "She said something last week that I keep turning over. She said, 'You've been waiting for permission your whole life. From your mother, from men, from your idea of who you're supposed to be.' She said, 'What if you just stopped waiting?'"

April set her fork down. She thought about the upper level. About the room where the choosing was entirely and irrevocably hers. About the wall between wanting and choosing—thin enough now to see through. "What did you say?"

"I said, 'I don't know what I'd do with the permission if I had it.'" Angel looked at her wine glass. "Which is apparently the whole problem."

April looked at her friend. She thought about the version of Angel she had known longest—vivid, magnetic, the woman who filled a room from the moment she entered it and seemed to require nothing from anyone. She thought about the Angel who had stood in the Monolith parking lot and deleted Charles's number, even though she knew it by heart. She thought about what Angel had said two weeks ago: *I always make the same choices. I just never saw it clearly before.*

"You're figuring it out," April said.

"Slowly." Angel looked up. "Very slowly. But yeah." She paused. "How about you?"

"Also slowly," April said. "But also yeah."

Angel nodded. This was the depth of the conversation they were having—not the full accounting, not the detailed exchange, just the mutual acknowledgment that both of them were in the middle of something real and were doing the work and were not alone in it. Sufficient. More than sufficient.

"Okay," Angel said. "Documentary."

The documentary was exactly what Angel had promised: both disgusting and incredible, the kind of nature filmmaking that justified the entire genre. Deep-sea creatures were rendered in extraordinary detail by cameras that had no business being at those depths—the transparent squid Angel had mentioned, its organs visible and pulsing, swimming through the black water with the unhurried certainty of something that had never needed to explain itself to anyone. A jellyfish the size of a car. Something that produced its own light in patterns that had no apparent purpose except beauty, which turned out—as the narration explained—to be sufficient purpose.

April watched the screen with the kind of attention she usually reserved for things she found genuinely interesting—the focus she was learning to apply to more of her life. It wasn't "managed" attention or the act of monitoring while appearing present, but actual, unvarnished engagement. The creatures were extraordinary; she found herself leaning forward at intervals, drawn toward the blue-white glow.

Angel was asleep forty minutes in.

It happened gradually and then all at once, the way sleep claims someone who has carried a heavy weight for weeks and finally put it down long enough for the body to notice. She had grown quiet during the last ten minutes of their conversation, her posture shifting from alert to settled, taking on the particular relaxed quality of someone whose defenses have dissolved in a space they trust. April had noticed the shift and said nothing. She simply reached over and turned off the lamp at Angel's end of the couch.

Now, Angel lay on her side, legs curled and hands tucked loosely under her cheek, her breathing slow and even. Her hair spread across the throw pillow at the arm of the couch, and her rust-colored sweater had ridden up slightly at the hem. In sleep, she looked like someone who had been running at high speed for a very long time and had finally been permitted to stop.

April turned the volume down to nearly nothing. She sat in the low television light and just looked.

She looked at Angel the way she rarely permitted herself to look at anyone—without the mediation of social management, without the monitoring of her own expression, and without the layer of professional scrutiny she brought to those she studied in a clinical context. It was just a look. It was the same way she had been learning to look at herself in mirrors.

Angel sleeping on her couch was a familiar sight, a recurring beat across eight years of various apartments, seasons, and configurations of their shared history. It wasn't new. Yet, as April sat there, she felt something move through her that she couldn't immediately name—not unfamiliar, exactly, but new in its specificity. It was like a note she had heard a thousand times finally finding the chord it belonged to.

She took a mental inventory of what she knew of Angel, a list built across a friendship that had survived because it was real rather than convenient. She knew Angel's laugh—the full, unguarded version, the performance, and the sharp one she made when she was genuinely surprised. She knew the particular way Angel moved through a room she had just entered, performing a quick, comprehensive read of the space. She knew that Angel played Missy Elliott when she was angry and kept a collection of oversized sweaters reserved exclusively for the moments she allowed herself to be undone.

The rust sweater was from that collection.

She knew that Angel had been waiting for permission her whole life and had not yet figured out what she'd do with it if she had it.

She knew, sitting in the blue television light watching Angel sleep on her couch, that what she felt for her friend was not entirely what she had always assumed it was.

This arrived not as a shock but as a clarification. It was the way things arrived, she had been finding, when you had done enough interior work to stop being afraid of what the honest accounting might show you. Not a bolt of lightning— the slow turn of a kaleidoscope, the pieces the same pieces but suddenly arranged so that the pattern was visible in a way it hadn't been before.

She sat with it. She did not manage it. She let it be what it was while she found out what it was.

What it was, she was beginning to understand, was something she did not yet have the complete language for. She had language for friendship—she and Angel were that, without question, and had been for eight years. She had language for the particular intimacy of two women who had known each other through the worst versions of the worst and had kept showing up anyway. That was all true, and all present.

This was something adjacent to those things, and also beyond them. It was something that had perhaps been there longer than tonight, and tonight—in the blue light with Angel asleep and the transparent squid moving silently across the television screen—she was finally available enough to see it.

She thought about the upper level. She thought about the room where the choosing was entirely hers, and about the wall between wanting and choosing that she had spent the year thinning.

She thought: *There is more wall to thin.*

She did not say anything to Angel's sleeping form. She did not touch her hair or her hand, or do any of the things that the moment might have invited if she were a person who acted before she understood. She was not that person. She sat in the blue light and felt the question beginning, and she understood that it was only the beginning—that it would require time, honesty, and the same slow, deliberate work she had been bringing to everything else. She was not going to rush it or manage it, or decide what it meant before she had lived with it long enough to know.

She thought about what Angel's therapist had said: *What if you just stopped waiting?*

She thought: *Not yet. But soon. And when I do, I'll know what to do with it.*

Angel woke at eleven-forty-three with the specific disorientation of someone who hadn't expected to sleep and surfaces in an unfamiliar darkness. April was still on the other end of the couch, the documentary long finished, reading the novel Jason had given her by the light of a small lamp she'd turned on at some point in the past two hours.

"Oh God," Angel said, her voice thick. "I fell asleep."

"You did."

"I'm sorry. I didn't mean—"

"Angel." April looked at her over the top of the book. "Stop. You needed to sleep. You slept. It's fine."

Angel sat up, pushing her hair back and looking at April with the unfocused warmth of someone still half-submerged in a dream. "Were you here the whole time?"

"I was reading."

"You could have woken me up. Made me go home."

"I could have," April said. "I didn't want to."

Angel looked at her for a moment—really looked, the way she looked at things when she was paying full attention rather than managing an interaction. April held her gaze with the steadiness she had been practicing. She did not look away. She did not offer an explanation. She simply let the look be what it was.

After a moment, Angel said, "Thank you. For tonight."

"For the Thai food?"

"For the Thai food. And the wine. And the squid." She paused. "And for letting me be a mess without making it a whole thing."

"You weren't a mess," April said. "You were tired. There's a difference."

Angel smiled—the real one, the unguarded one, the one April knew best. "You always knew the difference. Even when I didn't."

She stood, found her shoes and her bag, and refilled a glass of water from the kitchen tap, moving through April's apartment with the ease of someone who had always belonged there. At the door, she turned.

"Same time next week?" she asked. "There's a follow-up episode. They found something at six thousand meters that the scientists genuinely cannot explain."

"I'll order," April said.

Angel left. April listened to her footsteps in the hall, the hum of the elevator, and then the sound of the building resuming its nighttime quiet around her.

She sat in her apartment alone and looked at the couch where Angel had been sleeping—the indentation still visible in the throw pillow, the rust-colored sweater folded neatly on the arm. Angel always folded things before she left, regardless of whether she'd intended to sleep in them.

April picked up her novel, but she did not read. She sat in the silence with the question that was beginning and let it be what it was—nascent, honest, hers.

Not yet. But she was no longer running.

She was, for the first time in a long time, moving toward something she didn't have the full shape of yet, and finding that she was not afraid of the unknown. She was curious.

She had always been good at being curious. It had gotten her this far.

She turned off the lamp. She went to bed. She lay in the dark and thought about the beginning of a question and let it breathe.

Chapter 25: Shared Secrets

She sat with the question for a week before she told Jason. This was not a delay—it was the same principle she had applied to everything since Miami: understanding a thing herself before handing it to someone else. She had learned that she tended to discover her own feelings only in the telling of them, a kind of habitual dishonesty she was working to correct. She wanted to bring him the already-understood version, not the one she was figuring out in real time.

The week was useful. She sat with what had happened on Tuesday night—Angel asleep on the couch, the blue television light, the slow turn of the kaleidoscope—and examined it with the same clinical rigor she brought to everything she sought to understand accurately. She asked herself the hard questions, the ones that lacked flattering answers. Was this confusion born of the particular intimacy of two women who had navigated adjacent things in adjacent seasons? Was it the emotional openness of a year in which she had been, deliberately and at some cost, tearing down her own walls? Was it projection—finding in Angel a mirror of her own becoming?

She gave each possibility honest consideration. She dismissed none of them.

Ultimately, she found that the honest answer was this: all those things might be partly true, yet they did not change what she felt. What she felt was specific. It was not the feeling of a person confused by intimacy; it was the feeling of someone who had been looking at an object for a long time without the necessary light and had been given, suddenly, sufficient light to see by.

She texted Jason on Friday night: *Can you come over tomorrow? I want to tell you something.*

He replied in six minutes: *Yes. Morning or afternoon?*

She considered which time of day suited the conversation. Morning offered coffee and the clarity of early light, but carried the risk of feeling rushed by the day ahead. Afternoon meant they had time and nowhere to be.

Afternoon, she told him. *Two o'clock.*

He arrived at one fifty-eight.

He brought good coffee, as he always did when she asked—not the nearest adequate option, but the place three blocks out of his way that performed the pour-over correctly. She had come to recognize this as characteristic: he calibrated his effort to the occasion without making a performance of the calibration. He had known, from her text, that this was a two-o'clock-on-Saturday-with-good-coffee occasion, and he had come prepared.

They sat at the kitchen table rather than the couch. She had chosen this deliberately; the couch was where Angel had slept, and it carried that weight now. It was part of the story she was about to tell, and she needed the table's particular quality of being a place where things were said rather than where things were felt. She needed the slight formality of it.

Jason looked at her across the table with the level attention she had spent fifteen months coming to trust. He had not asked over text what she wanted to tell him. He would not ask now. He would wait for her to begin—one of his specific qualities. He wasn't being passive or withholding; it was the genuine patience of a man who understood that some things required their own timing and that preempting that timing was merely impatience dressed as helpfulness.

She held her coffee cup with both hands, looking at the table for a moment to find the start of it.

"I need to tell you something about Angel," she said.

She watched him receive this. His expression didn't change significantly, but she had learned to read the minor shifts—the small updates he made when incoming information required adjustment. He updated now. He waited.

"Last Tuesday, she came over. Thai food, a documentary. She fell asleep on the couch." April looked back at the table. "And I sat there for two hours watching her sleep and felt something I wasn't expecting."

A beat. Then: "Tell me."

She looked up at him. "I think I have feelings for her. Beyond friendship. I don't have the full shape of it yet—it's been a week, I've been sitting with it, and I'm not coming to you with a conclusion. But I'm coming to you with the truth of what I noticed, because I promised you I wouldn't keep secrets."

He was quiet for a long time. It wasn't the uncomfortable silence of a man managing unwanted information, but the genuine, thinking silence she had catalogued across fifteen months—the silence of a man doing the work of responding rather than the faster work of reacting.

She let him have the space. She did not fill it.

When he finally spoke, he asked, "How long do you think it's been there?"

She had not expected that. She had expected a question about their relationship, about what this meant for them, or whether she was telling him that something was ending. That he had gone instead to the timeline—to her, and to the understanding of her interior life—was characteristic. In this moment, it was exactly what she needed.

"I don't know," she said. "Longer than last Tuesday. I think I've been seeing things for a while that I wasn't ready to see clearly." She paused. "This year has been about getting my eyes open. This is part of that."

He nodded, turning his coffee cup in the slow rotation she associated with him processing something substantial. "How does it sit alongside what we have?"

"That's what I'm trying to understand," she said. "I'm not bringing this to you as a confession or an apology. I'm bringing it because it's true and you're the person I'm honest with. I don't think it contradicts what we have—but I don't know what it is yet, and I don't want to be the person who holds a thing and doesn't say it."

He looked at her steadily. "I'm glad you said it."

"Are you?"

"Yes." He meant it; she could read the difference by now between a performed affirmation and an actual one. "I'm not going to pretend I don't have things to sit with. I do. But I'd rather have the truth and sit with it than not have the truth at all." A pause. "That's what we said we were doing."

"That's what we said," she agreed.

"Does Angel know?"

"No. I needed to tell you first."

He absorbed this. She could see him working through the implications—not jealously, nor with the specific anxiety of a man threatened by the landscape of his partner's interior life, but with the rigor of someone trying to understand a situation accurately. This was what she had loved about him from the beginning: he did not require her to be simpler than she was.

"What do you need from me?" he asked.

The question landed exactly where it was meant to. Not *what are you going to do*, or *what does this mean for us*, but *what do you need*. He placed the center of gravity on her, because she was the one navigating something new.

"I need you to know," she said. "And I need you to not make it something I have to manage. I'll figure out what it is and what to do with it on my own timeline. But I can't do that well if I'm also managing your response to it."

He looked at her. Something moved through his expression that she recognized as the internal version of something difficult being received and accepted.

"Okay," he said. "I can do that."

"Thank you."

"I'm going to ask you one thing in return."

"Ask."

"Keep telling me the truth. Even when it's—" He stopped. Found the word. "Even when it's this."

"I will," she said. "That's why I'm here."

They sat at the kitchen table for another twenty minutes with the good coffee and the particular quality of two people who have just said something real and are letting the saying of it settle. Not awkward—the opposite. The specific ease of a conversation that has gone where it needed to go and has left both people more accurately located than before.

April told him about the documentary. The transparent squid. Angel folding the sweater before she left even though she'd fallen asleep in it. He listened with the quality of attention that had always been his specific gift.

"She folds things before she leaves?" he said.

"Every time. Even when she didn't intend to stay long enough to unfold anything."

He smiled—the interior version. "That's very Angel."

"It is," April agreed. Something about the ease of the exchange—the way Jason could hold what she had just told him alongside the small, affectionate detail of a folded sweater, without requiring the two to be in conflict—made her feel his specific rightness. The foundation she had been building with him for fifteen months was real and hers, and it was not at risk from the new territory she was beginning to navigate. Both things could be true. She was learning to live in that.

They spent the rest of the afternoon quietly. She read while he worked at the other end of the table, the apartment settling into its Saturday rhythm around them. At five-thirty, he made dinner from whatever was in her refrigerator, displaying another of his core qualities: an easy competence in domestic spaces. They ate at the kitchen table where their serious conversation had unfolded, discovering that the space could comfortably hold both.

Before he left, standing at the door, he held her face in his hands for a moment. He looked at her with an expression she had learned was the outward sign of his deepest certainty.

"I trust you," he said. It wasn't a performance; it was information.

"I know," she said. "I trust you, too."

He kissed her, then he left.

She stood in her apartment in the February evening and reflected on what had just happened. She had told him the hardest truth she'd ever had to share, and he had received it with the integrity she had come to expect. He had asked the right questions, given her exactly what she needed, made dinner, and told her he trusted her.

Standing there, she did not know that the very integrity with which he had received the truth in this kitchen would make what came next harder, not easier. She did not know that the trust she had placed in him would be the specific factor that made the coming breach feel like a betrayal rather than a mere failure. The honesty she had brought to this table was the very thing that would give the coming months their particular quality of tragedy—not one born of accident or weakness, but the specific loss of something that had been profoundly real.

She did not know that Angel would call Jason in three weeks, asking to talk, in the way Angel called people when she was trying to locate herself by finding someone safe. She did not know that Jason would agree, because he was kind and because he understood that Angel was April's person—that this was an extension of the grace he had offered this afternoon. She did not know that the wine and the conversation would loosen something in him he hadn't realized was slack—the room he kept closed, the "Vanessa lesson" imperfectly learned—or that what would happen between him and Angel would be neither planned nor wanted nor understood until after it had already occurred and could not be undone.

She did not know any of this. She knew only what she stood in: the February evening, the good coffee still on the table, the truth told and received, the trust intact.

She cleaned up the kitchen. She washed the cups. She thought about Angel and let the question breathe and found it still there: patient and honest and hers.

She thought: *I have everything I need right now to navigate this well.*

She thought: *I am in good hands. Mine and his.*

She was right. She would be wrong. The distance between those two things was three weeks and one evening she had no way to anticipate, and it would be the most expensive thing she had paid for in a long time.

But tonight she cleaned the kitchen and was grateful and went to bed early and slept without the kind of weight that comes from secrets.

The weight would come. It always did, eventually. But not tonight.

Tonight she was only honest, and honest was enough.

Chapter 26: Crossroads

Jason had always understood himself as a man who knew his own edges. This was one of the things he had worked on in the years since Vanessa—the specific self-knowledge of someone who has made a significant mistake and has tried, in good faith, to understand what produced it. He had not held too much back with April. He had named the pattern. He had told her about it at her kitchen table on a Saturday afternoon with good coffee and the particular February light. He had been honest. He had thought that was the work.

He had not understood that naming a pattern was not the same as dismantling it.

Angel called on a Tuesday evening in early March, three weeks after the kitchen-table conversation and two weeks after April had told him the documentary follow-up was scheduled and that Angel would be coming over again. He had received both pieces of information with the equanimity he had genuinely felt. He was not a man who required April to have a narrower interior life than she did, and what she had told him about Angel had not threatened him in the way he had been watching himself for signs of threat.

It had made sense. In some ways, it had made the architecture of who April was clearer to him. He had sat with it and found it manageable and had felt—if he was being honest—a certain quiet respect for the specificity of her honesty.

So when Angel called, he answered because he was kind, and because Angel was April's person. He answered because April had told him the truth about the full complexity of that, and he had said he could hold it. He answered because not answering would have been the kind of small cowardice he had been working to eliminate from himself.

"Jason," Angel said.

Her voice carried the particular texture he had come to associate with her over the months of knowing her through April—vivid, self-possessed, but with an undertow tonight that was different. Something held together effortfully.

"I'm sorry to call. I wasn't sure who else—" She stopped. "Can I come over? Just to talk. I won't stay long."

He thought about April. He thought about what April had told him and what he had agreed to and what being the person he said he was required of him in this specific moment. He thought: *This is April's person, in some kind of difficulty, and April is not available tonight, and I am.*

"Yes," he said. "Come over."

She arrived at seven-forty looking like someone who had been in her own head for too long—the particular quality of a person who had been running a loop without resolution and needed the loop interrupted by something external. She was dressed simply, nothing like the Angel he had met at the bar over the summer—no performance in it, just clothes, a dark coat, the kind of presence that arrived before the presentation.

He made tea because she had not asked for wine and he was not going to offer it without being asked. They sat at his kitchen table—he noted, not without awareness, that this was the same configuration as April's disclosure three weeks ago: same table, different person—and he let her talk.

She spoke of Charles. Not the infidelity—that was settled territory, months behind her—but the longer accounting. Together with Dr. Coleman, she had been excavating a pattern: her habit of choosing men who required her to be a specific version of herself. These men found the "performance" of her useful, and for a long time, she hadn't even recognized it as an act.

She used Dr. Coleman's phrase, "waiting for permission," noting how differently it landed when told to a man versus when she had shared it with April over Thai food.

"I keep looking for someone to give me permission to just be what I actually am," she said. "And I keep choosing people who can't give me that, because what I actually am would be inconvenient for them."

Jason listened with the focused intensity he reserved for things that mattered. He asked three questions—the kind asked when someone wants to understand the core of a thing rather than just reacting to the surface. She answered with a bluntness he had come to expect, a directness that lacked any performance at all. Watching her, Jason realized that this—the way she said exactly what she meant—was what he found so genuinely interesting about her.

April said she had feelings for this woman, he thought. *I understand why.* He set the thought aside, though he didn't let it go completely.

Two hours in, she sighed. "Is there wine? I think I need a glass. I've been in my own head all week and tea isn't cutting it."

A man with full access to his better judgment would have suggested an Uber or mentioned an early morning. He should have said any of the things that maintained a safe distance.

Instead, he poured the wine.

He poured a glass for himself, too. That was his first real mistake—not because of the alcohol, but because of what the gesture communicated. The frame of the evening had shifted. He was no longer just a man being kind to his partner's friend in a moment of need; he was in a different frame entirely. He knew it, yet he refused to name it. It was the same failure of self-knowledge he'd carried since Vanessa: the ability to identify his patterns in the abstract while remaining powerless to catch them in real time.

They moved to the couch. This, too, was a choice he did not interrogate in the moment but would interrogate extensively afterward. The kitchen table was the place for the conversation they had been having. The couch was a different room, with different implications, and he had made the transition without being asked.

Angel sat at the far end of the couch, her legs tucked under her the way April sometimes sat, and held her wine glass and looked at him with the particular look she had when she was about to say something true. "Can I ask you something?"

"Yes."

"What do you do with the parts of yourself you don't want to show April? The parts that are inconvenient."

He looked at her. The question arrived in the place questions arrive when they are the right question asked by the right person at the wrong time. He thought about the room he kept closed. He thought about what he had told April about Vanessa—*I held too much back*. He thought about the private vow he had made in the quiet: he would let her in, door by door.

He had been doing that. He had been doing it well, he thought. But the question Angel had just asked identified something he had not yet looked at directly: what he had been showing April was the improved version of himself. The version that had done the work. He had not shown her the room that still contained the unfinished work—the part of him that could still be reached by proximity and wine and a woman who asked the right question and looked at him like he was worth looking at.

"I'm still working on some of those," he said. Honest. Also insufficient.

"Me too," Angel said. She looked at her wine glass. "I think that's what I'm most afraid of. That I'll be working on them forever and still not be done."

"Renee says if you think you're finished, you've stopped being interesting," he said.

Angel looked at him. "I like Renee."

"She'd like you," he said.

The space between them on the couch had a quality he was aware of and not addressing. He was aware that he was aware of it. He was also aware that awareness was not the same as action, and that he had been here before—caught in the specific gravity of a moment pulling in a direction he had never intended to go. The last time he had been here, he had done the right thing, lost the woman, and spent six months in Miami building the fortress of himself that April had only just begun to dismantle.

He thought: *I am not going to do this.* He thought: *I am going to say something that closes this.*

He held both thoughts and did not act on either immediately, which was the specific failure—the specific, irreversible, inexcusable failure.

She reached over and placed her hand on his arm. It wasn't a calculated move, or at least not with the deliberateness of someone who had planned a gesture. It was the movement of someone who had been talking for two hours with a person she trusted and had crossed a small distance without accounting for it.

He did not move away. This was the moment. This was the specific, small, irrevocable moment.

He said her name. He said, "Angel."

She looked at him. Her eyes held that quality he'd noticed from the start—direct, yet layered with a submerged sadness. It was the look of someone who had spent a lifetime reaching for things, only to learn they would never quite arrive.

We should stop here, he thought. But he didn't say it in time.

What followed over the next hour wasn't violent, coerced, or even premeditated. It was the collision of two people operating from "unfinished rooms." His was the room that still swung open when someone looked at him a certain way after enough wine and talk; hers was the very pattern she and Dr. Coleman had identified but hadn't yet broken. It wasn't nothing. It was the exact shape of a mistake made by people who are "working on themselves" but aren't there yet—caught in the wrong configuration at the wrong hour.

The worst part was that he knew it while it was happening. He wasn't swept away or unconscious. He was present, making choices—the wrong ones—and refusing to stop.

Afterward, Angel found her coat. She looked at him with an expression that carried the full weight of the night: not just the two of them, but April, Charles, and every cycle she had been trying to escape.

"I'm sorry," she said. Then, "I don't know if that's the right thing to say."

"It's not," he replied. "There isn't a right thing."

She left.

Jason sat on the couch for a long time. He didn't lean on the usual crutches—no bargaining, no rationalizations, no mitigating narratives. He had always dealt in accurate information, and the facts were these: April had trusted him with the most difficult truth she possessed, and three weeks later, he had proven exactly why she was right to fear his unfinished rooms.

He remembered the kitchen table. The good coffee. Her hands around the mug. *I need you to not make it something I have to manage,* she'd said. *I can do that,* he'd promised.

He had not done that.

He thought of his mother, who understood a truth he was only just beginning to grasp: you cannot master something through theory alone. You have to get in the pool. You have to stay in the water even when it's hard, never substituting the *knowledge* of swimming for the act itself.

He had substituted. He had told April about Vanessa and believed the telling was the learning. He hadn't understood that the learning was a lifetime of being in the water.

He picked up his phone, looked at April's name, and set it back down. He couldn't tell her tonight—not to delay the inevitable, but because he owed her an accounting that had been lived-in. He owed her a version of the truth that had been fully examined, not just the raw, shocked aftermath. She had given him that same grace when she waited a week to tell him about Angel.

He would tell her. He had promised to *keep telling the truth even when it's this,* and he would keep that promise, even though it would cost him everything.

In the dark apartment, he pictured April on the staircase, her hand on the warm, solid wood of the banister. He thought of the choice of which door to open and how to open it. He had chosen the wrong door. He hadn't been ready, yet he had chosen anyway—the same mistake the pool had been trying to teach him to stop making since he was nine years old.

He turned off the light but didn't go to bed. In the morning, he would be the man he had always been: careful, deliberate, capable of the right thing. But tonight, he was the man who had failed the person who trusted him most, in the exact way he had sworn he never would again.

He sat in that.

He did not look away from it.

That, at least, was something.

Chapter 27: Entangled Passions

She drove home in the specific silence of someone who is not ready to think and knows it. The radio stayed off. The city moved past her windows with its indifferent, ongoing quality—lit storefronts, late pedestrians, the red and white of traffic signals cycling through their patient sequences. She gripped the wheel with both hands and kept her eyes on the road, refusing to enter the interior accounting yet; the reckoning was going to cost her everything, and she needed to be stationary before she paid it.

She parked in her building's garage and sat in the car for seven minutes.

Then she went upstairs and stood in her apartment with her coat still on, looking at the space around her—her things, her order, the specific arrangement of a life she had been deliberately reassembling since January. The therapy. The rust-sweater evenings with April. The documentary and the Thai food and the beginning of something she had been calling friendship—something she had understood, lately, might be more, and had been examining carefully, waiting to name until she was sure she was naming it accurately rather than performing a name for it.

She sat down on her couch.

She thought: *I just did the thing.*

Not the thing she had identified in therapy. Not Charles's thing—the habit of being chosen by someone who needed her performance and mistaking that need for love. This was a different thing. A new thing. It was the thing Dr. Coleman had warned her to watch for: the pattern running faster than the awareness of it. The choosing that happened before she had finished choosing.

She put her face in her hands.

She did not sleep well. This was not guilt-induced insomnia; she did not romanticize her own suffering that way.

She was not a woman who lay awake feeling dramatically terrible as a substitute for reckoning with her actions. She lay awake because her mind was doing the honest work of accounting, and the accounting was thorough and could not be rushed.

What she reached, by three in the morning, was this:

She had gone to Jason's apartment because she needed someone safe. She had identified him as safe because he was April's person and April trusted him—and April's judgment, she had learned over eight years, was reliable in the specific areas where her own had historically failed. She had not gone there with a plan. She had not—she was being accurate with herself now—wanted him in the particular way she had wanted Charles or the men before him: that specific wanting that was really a hunger to be chosen, to be needed, to have someone find her indispensable enough to reorganize their life around her.

What she had wanted, in the honest accounting, was to be seen by someone who knew April. To be in the proximity of April's world when she could not be with April herself. She wanted to be held, in the loose sense, by the network of people who had come to know and choose April, because something in her believed that the people April chose were the people who would not require her performance.

And what had happened was not that. Or not only that. She had been in a room with a man who had the room he kept closed slightly ajar—she could feel it the way one feels a draft from a door that isn't fully shut—and her own pattern had reached toward it in the way her patterns always reached toward openings they could fill. She had not planned the reaching. She had reached anyway.

Dr. Coleman's phrase: *The pattern running faster than the awareness.*

She was aware of it now. She had been aware of it approximately forty-five minutes too late.

She called Dr. Coleman's answering service at eight in the morning and left a message asking for an emergency appointment. This was the first decision she made that she was fully confident in. Whatever came next, she was not going to try to navigate it without the specific mirror of that particular relationship, which had been showing her things she did not want to see for six years and which she trusted precisely because it had never told her what she wanted to hear.

Then she sat with the question of April.

She had been sitting with April in a different way since January—since the night she had shown up with Thai food and the documentary and had fallen asleep on the couch and woken to find April still there, reading, having let her sleep without making it a thing. She had been sitting with what that meant. With what she felt in the rooms where April was and in the rooms where April wasn't. With the specific quality of April's attention—the way she looked at things she was trying to understand accurately, and the way she had started, over the past year, to look at Angel with that same attention.

She had been doing the slow, honest work of figuring out what was there. She had not finished the work. She had last night effectively detonated the conditions under which the work could continue.

She thought: *April is going to find out.*

She thought: *Jason is going to tell her.*

She thought this not as a fear but as a fact—she knew enough about who Jason was, from what April had told her across fifteen months of building something with him, to know that he was not a man who sat on things. He was a man who told the truth even when it was *this*, to use April's phrase. He had been trusted with April's truth. He would be unable to hold his own untruth for long.

The question was not whether April would find out. The question was what Angel was going to do before she did.

She picked up her phone six times that morning. She put it down six times.

The impulse she fought—to call April, tell her immediately, and get ahead of it—was the version that served Angel rather than April. It would transfer the weight from Angel's conscience to April's day before April was ready to carry it, before there was context or processing or the particular care that a truth of this magnitude required. It would be Angel doing what she had always done: finding relief in the telling rather than taking the responsibility of the delivery.

She had spent six years learning to distinguish between what she needed and what the situation required. This situation required something she did not need.

It required Jason to tell April first, because Jason was the person who had made the choice that mattered most in that room. He had known what he was doing—she was increasingly certain of this—and the failure to stop was his in a way it was not equally hers. She had reached in the way her pattern reached; he had possessed the awareness of what was happening and continued anyway. That asymmetry mattered. April needed to hear from him first.

What the situation required from Angel was availability. She had to be there when April was ready to come to her. She had to not disappear. She had to refrain from managing the fallout with the efficiency she usually brought to the things she feared. She had to sit in what she had done and let it be what it was, without reaching for relief.

She put the phone down for the seventh time.

She made coffee and stood at her kitchen window, looking out at the March morning—gray and still, the city doing its Wednesday thing below her, indifferent to her particular wreckage. She had always found the city's indifference useful on bad mornings. It reminded her that her interior weather was hers alone, and that the world was not organized around her difficulty.

She thought about the documentary. The transparent squid, organs visible, swimming with the unhurried certainty of a creature that never needed to explain itself. She thought about April's face in the blue television light, the specific quality of attention she had felt but hadn't been able to name—had not named, careful not to until she was sure.

She thought: *I think I am in love with my best friend.* She thought: *I think I have been for a while.* She thought: *I just made it extraordinarily complicated to do anything about it.*

Dr. Coleman had a cancellation at eleven. Angel arrived in the specific state of someone who had been in her own head since midnight, carrying something that needed to be set down in a supervised space.

Dr. Coleman was a woman in her late fifties who possessed the quality Angel had been drawn to since their first session six years ago: she did not flinch. Whatever you brought into that room, she received with the level attention of someone who had done this long enough to lose the reflex of shock. Her face was not unkind, but it wasn't performing kindness, either. It was the face of a person who was paying attention.

Angel told her what had happened. All of it—the call to Jason, the tea, the conversation, the wine she had requested, the couch, the moment she had not interrupted. She told it with the same directness she maintained in this room, without the softening she reached for everywhere else.

Dr. Coleman listened without interrupting. When Angel finished, she remained quiet for a moment, deciding where to begin.

"You said you went there because you needed someone safe," she said.

"Yes."

"And you identified him as safe because he was April's person."

"Yes."

"Tell me about that logic."

Angel looked at her hands. She had been aware of the logic since three in the morning, but saying it aloud was different. "I think I've been trying to get to April," she said slowly. "And I keep going through things adjacent to her instead of—straight at the thing."

Dr. Coleman waited.

"I think I'm in love with her," Angel said. "I think I have been. And I don't know how to go straight at that because 'straight at it' is terrifying, and I have a very efficient pattern of finding complicated ways around terrifying things."

"How long have you known?" Dr. Coleman asked.

"I've been knowing for months. I've been calling it something else. Friendship. Closeness. Two women who went through adjacent things." She paused. "I think I stopped being able to call it something else the night I fell asleep on her couch."

"And last night?"

Angel looked at the window. The March sky was still gray, still indifferent. "Last night was the pattern. Reaching for what was adjacent because the actual thing was too much. Finding an opening and moving toward it before I'd finished thinking." She turned back. "I know. I know that's what it was."

"What do you do with that?"

"I sit in it," Angel said. "I don't reach for relief. I let April find out from Jason and I wait. I don't disappear, and when she comes to me, I tell her the truth about all of it." She paused. "And I accept whatever she decides."

Dr. Coleman looked at her with an expression that wasn't pride, but was something adjacent to it—the look she gave when Angel arrived at the right answer on her own. "That's the work," she said.

"I know," Angel said. "I know it's the work. I'm just—I'm tired of the work being this hard."

"It gets easier," Dr. Coleman said. "Not easy. Easier."

Angel nodded. She sat in the session for the remaining forty minutes and let herself exist within it without trying to resolve it, which was the skill Dr. Coleman had been teaching her for six years. She was, finally, getting better at it.

She went home and put on the rust sweater. Not the armor version of herself. Just herself, in the sweater she wore when she was allowing herself to be undone, which was what the situation called for.

She sat on her couch—her own couch, in her own apartment, the one she had been painstakingly reassembling since January—and she let herself feel the full weight of what she was waiting for. April's call. April's voice doing whatever it did when something had happened to it. The conversation she had no way to prepare for, because there was no version of preparation that was not also a performance.

She thought about the door scene from Chapter 15—the moment she had closed the door on Charles and felt the specific relief of no longer carrying something that was not hers. She thought about what she had said to April afterward: *I'm tired of accepting love that only wants the performance of me.*

She was not tired of April. She had never been tired of April. April had always wanted the actual version—had always looked at the parts of Angel that the performance covered and been interested in them rather than threatened by them.

That was the thing. That was what she had been calling something else for eight years.

She sat with it. She did not reach for her phone. She did not plan what she would say. She waited.

Outside, the March city was doing its thing—gray and ongoing and entirely indifferent to the particular quality of this specific Wednesday in one specific woman's specific apartment. The city had been there before she arrived in it and would be there after. It did not need her interior weather to be anything other than what it was.

She found this, as she always had on bad mornings, oddly comforting.

She would wait. She would be honest. She would not disappear.

Whatever April decided, she would accept.

That was all she had. She was going to make it be enough.

Chapter 28: Discovery

She had a good Thursday. This was the specific cruelty of it—the goodness of the day she did not know was happening inside a "before." She ran in the morning, the March air still carrying winter's edge but with the quality of something loosening; the light was arriving a few minutes earlier than it had the week before. She showered, dressed, and went to work with the particular clarity of someone who had been sleeping well—which she had been, since January's resolution. Her caseload was manageable. She had a productive session with a client who had been circling a decision for three months and finally made it. She ate lunch at her desk and read six pages of the novel Jason had given her, thinking: *This is a good book; I am going to tell him tonight.*

She texted him at four-fifteen: *Dinner tonight? I'll cook.*

He replied in eleven minutes—longer than his usual four to six, but not long enough to register as anything other than a man who had been in the middle of a task. *Yes. Six-thirty?*

She went home. She cooked chicken thighs braised with olives and tomatoes, a recipe she had developed across a winter of Saturdays—the kind that smelled like something tended carefully. She opened a bottle of the Malbec she kept for evenings that warranted it. She set the table with the attention she gave to things she wanted to be good.

At six-twenty-eight, she heard the door.

She knew something was wrong before he spoke. This was the specific education of fifteen months of paying attention to a person—she could read the minor shifts, the small interior updates he made when incoming information required adjustment. She had learned this about him and had been proud of the knowledge, filing it away as evidence of the specific intimacy they had built. It was the way you file things that confirm you are doing it right.

He came through the door and looked at her, and she saw it. Not guilt, exactly, but something more precise: the expression of a man who has been carrying something heavy for a specific number of hours and has arrived at the place where he must set it down.

She placed the wooden spoon on the rest beside the stove. She looked at him.

"What happened?" she said. It wasn't a question, but a statement issued to someone she trusted to fill it accurately.

He sat down at the kitchen table—the same table where she had told him about Angel three weeks ago. The table where he had asked the right questions, said, "Keep telling me the truth even when it's this," and looked at her with that look of deepest certainty, saying, "I trust you."

She remained standing at the stove. She did not move toward the table, aware of this as a choice her body was making before her mind had caught up.

"Angel called Tuesday night," he said. "She asked if she could come over. To talk."

April waited.

"I said yes because she's your person and she sounded like she needed someone. I made tea. We talked for a while. And then—" He stopped. He looked at the table, then back at her. "I poured wine when she asked for it and we moved to the couch. I had a moment where I knew what was happening and I didn't—I didn't close it in time."

The kitchen was very quiet. The braise was doing its slow work on the stove; the Malbec stood open on the counter. She could smell the olives, the tomato, the particular warmth of a meal that had been tended for an hour.

"Nothing happened that she initiated that I didn't allow," he said. "That's not an excuse. It's just the accurate version."

April looked at him for a long time. She was aware of many things simultaneously—the specific sensation in her chest that was not the sharp, stabbing variety, but the slow-pressurizing kind that builds rather than strikes. She was aware of the kitchen table and what it held. She was aware that her hands were very still at her sides. She was aware of the novel on the counter, the one she had been planning to tell him about tonight.

"Okay," she said.

He looked at her. "April—"

"I need you to go," she said. She was still quiet, still speaking with the specific steadiness of a person who has not yet let the full weight arrive because allowing it to land in front of someone else was not what she needed. "Not forever. I don't know. But tonight. I need you to go."

He stood. He did not argue. He did not reach for her. He understood, she realized, that the reaching would be for his benefit, not hers, and he refrained. He picked up his coat from the hook by the door. He paused with his hand on the handle.

"I'm sorry," he said. "I know that's not the right thing. There isn't one. But I am."

She did not answer. She listened to his footsteps in the hall, then the elevator, then the building resuming its evening quiet around her.

She stood at the stove for a long time.

Then, she turned off the burner. She did not eat the dinner she had cooked. She sat at the kitchen table—that specific table—and put her hands flat on its surface. She looked at the grain of the wood and let the full weight arrive.

It arrived in stages, which was how it always came for her—not a sudden flood, but the systematic filling of a space that had been holding something too large for it. She sat with each stage and did not try to organize or manage it into something she could process efficiently. She was doing this deliberately; she had been practicing "not managing" for a year, and this was the test of that practice.

The first stage was the specific image of the two of them on Jason's couch. She did not linger there. She let the image arrive and pass, knowing that lingering would be a form of self-harm she had been working to outgrow.

The second stage was the kitchen table conversation, three weeks ago. His questions. His agreement. *Keep telling me the truth even when it's this.* She had held that sentence across the past three weeks the way you hold something you have been given that you intend to keep. She felt the loss of it now in the specific way you feel the loss of something you had been certain was going to be yours permanently.

The third stage—and this was the one she had not expected—was Angel.

She sat with this one longest. She thought about Angel's rust sweater and the documentary and the folded sweater on the couch arm. She thought about the question beginning. About the kaleidoscope. About sitting in the blue television light and feeling the pattern resolve into something she had not yet had language for but had been building toward, carefully and deliberately, the way she built toward everything that mattered.

She thought: *Angel was in Jason's apartment on Tuesday.*

She thought: *Angel knew, when she called me about next week's documentary, what had happened two nights before.*

She thought about the specific quality of Angel's voice on that call—the warmth in it, the ease that had not quite been ease, the fraction of something held. She had registered it and filed it as Angel still processing her own week. She had not known it was this.

She sat with the double loss of it. Not simultaneously—she was careful to let each one have its own space. Jason, who had been given the truth and had not been able to hold it for three weeks. Angel, who had been the truth herself and had reached for something that was not hers to reach for.

She did not cry. This was not suppression—it was the specific quality of a grief that was too large for the immediate hour. It would find its form. She knew herself well enough to trust that. It was not tonight.

At nine o'clock she called Tasha.

Tasha answered on the second ring with the voice of someone who had not been asleep, which meant she had been reading or watching something she was not going to admit was a reality show. "Hey. What's going on?"

"Something happened," April said. "Can I come over?"

A beat. "How fast can you get here?"

Twenty minutes. She brought the bottle of Malbec because she had opened it and it deserved to be finished in the company of someone who would understand its selection. She drove with the windows up and the heat on and no music—she needed the quiet the way she had needed it on the drive home from the upper level, for different reasons, the same principle. She needed to be inside her own processing rather than surrounded by someone else's.

Tasha met her at the door in the specific state of a woman who had arranged herself quickly—the good candles lit, two glasses on the coffee table, the television off. She looked at April the way she always did when something had happened: with a full attention that did not immediately attempt to fix anything.

"Sit," Tasha said.

April sat. She poured two glasses. She told Tasha what Jason had told her, using the same direct language he had used—because the direct language was the accurate language, and because managing the telling for Tasha's comfort was not the priority tonight. Tasha listened with the stillness she brought to things that required it. She did not interrupt. She did not make the sound April had always disliked in people receiving difficult news—that performative intake of breath that was really about the receiver's discomfort.

When April finished, Tasha was quiet for a moment. Then she asked, "How are you?"

"I don't know yet," April said. "I'll know better by morning."

"That's honest."

"I've been practicing."

Tasha looked at her with the expression April had come to associate with her across the years of their particular friendship—one that contained both affection and the specific respect of someone watching a person do hard things well. "What do you need tonight?"

"To not be alone with it," April said. "I don't need advice. I don't need you to tell me what to do. I just need to be in a room with someone who knows me."

"Done," Tasha said. She refilled both glasses. "We can watch something stupid if you want. Or we can just sit."

"Sit," April said.

They sat. The candles did their slow work. The Malbec was good—the good-shelf version, opened for a dinner that had not happened, finding its proper occasion here instead. Outside, the March night was doing its thing, indifferent and ongoing. April sat in her friend's living room and let the evening be what it was, without trying to manufacture it into anything else.

She did not call Angel. She did not call Jason back. She made no decisions about what came next, because what came next required the version of herself who had slept and eaten and possessed the morning's particular clarity—and that version was not available tonight.

Instead, she let herself exist in the specific grief of having lost two things she had not known she was going to lose on a Thursday she had thought was a good Thursday. She did not organize the grief into its component parts. She did not audit it for lessons or seek the version of events that was most efficient to process. She sat in Tasha's living room until eleven, when Tasha mentioned the guest room was made up if she wanted it.

She wanted it.

She lay in the dark with the March night outside the window and thought about her kitchen table. About the braise cooling on the stove she had turned off. About the novel she had been going to tell him about.

She thought about the upper level—the closing of the wall between wanting and choosing. She thought about the specific quality of the knowing she had found there: not triumphant, just quiet. It was the quiet of a truth finally being recognized.

She thought: *I did not lose that. They cannot take that. Whatever happens next, I am still the person who climbed those stairs.*

She thought about Angel. About the question that had been beginning in the blue television light—patient and honest and hers. She thought about what it meant that Angel had been in that room on Tuesday and had not called her until Thursday, as if the room had not happened.

She thought: *I am going to need to understand what Angel's version of this is.* She thought: *Not tonight. Not until I am the version of myself who can hear it accurately.*

She closed her eyes. Sleep did not come immediately, but it came. She had always been able to sleep when she was in a place that was safe, with a person who knew her, even in the middle of the hardest things. This was one of the things she had learned about herself in the past year—the specific interior conditions under which she could rest.

She rested.

In the morning, there would be decisions. There would be conversations she did not yet know how to have. There would be the full accounting of what she had built with Jason, what Angel's version of the truth looked like, and what she wanted her own life to look like once the wreckage had been cleared.

In the morning she would begin.

Tonight she slept.

Chapter 29: The Reckoning

She woke at six-fifteen in Tasha's guest room with the particular clarity of someone who has slept through genuine grief and arrived on the other side of it as the morning version of themselves. Not healed—she was not interested in performing recovery on a timeline that served other people—but clear. This was the specific clarity she had been building toward for a year: the version of herself who could exist within the hardest things without being managed by them.

She lay in the borrowed dark and took inventory. The grief was still present—a double loss, with Jason and Angel each in their own compartment, each requiring its own attention. She did not try to resolve either one. She let them be what they were while she decided what the day required.

The day required two conversations. Not simultaneously; she was not going to conduct a confrontation with two people in the same room, refusing to allow the particular diffusion of responsibility that happens when those who have failed you can look at each other instead of at you. Two separate conversations. Jason first, because Jason had possessed the full knowledge of what he was doing and had done it anyway. Then Angel.

She texted Jason at seven: *Can you come to my apartment at ten?* She texted Angel at seven-oh-three: *I need to see you this afternoon. Two o'clock. My place.*

Both replied within ten minutes. Both said yes. This told her something she already knew: neither of them was going to run from what they had done. That was something, at least. Not sufficient—but something.

She thanked Tasha for the guest room, the candles, and the sitting. She drove home. She made coffee, ate toast, showered, and dressed with the deliberateness she brought to things that mattered. It wasn't armor; she had learned the difference. These were the clothes that were hers in the truest sense, the ones that let her be the size she actually was rather than a managed version.

She sat at the kitchen table and waited.

He arrived at nine fifty-eight. He looked like a man who had not slept—not disheveled, but possessed of the specific quality of someone who had been awake inside a difficult truth for many hours and was carrying it without pretense. She noted this and did not soften. His difficulty was not her responsibility to manage; it was the result of his choices.

She did not offer coffee. She gestured to the chair across from her, and he sat, looking at her with an expression that contained no defense—just the full weight of someone who had decided to be present for whatever came next.

"I need to understand something," she said. "I heard what you told me last night. The accurate version. Now I need you to tell me the part that came before it—the part where you had the moment of knowing what was happening and you didn't close it. I need to understand that part."

He looked at the table, then back at her. He did not look away to organize his answer; he found it while looking directly at her, which was the specific quality of honesty she had come to expect from him—and which made this conversation simultaneously easier and harder.

"I've been telling myself I learned from Vanessa," he said. "That holding back was the failure and I wasn't going to do it again. But I was only accounting for one kind of holding back—the kind where you don't let someone in. I wasn't accounting for the other kind." A pause. "The room I kept closed wasn't the one I thought it was. It wasn't the room I was being careful about."

"Explain that."

"The room I showed you," he said slowly, working through it as he spoke, "was the room I'd cleaned up. The version of myself that had done the work. I gave you that version and thought that was openness." He stopped. "But there was another room. The one that still opens when the conditions are right—when someone is close and it's late and I've had wine and she looks at me a certain way. I knew that room was there. I named the pattern in the abstract. I just didn't—I didn't understand that naming it in the abstract was not the same as being in the water."

She heard the swimming reference. She heard it and felt its weight—the origin story he had told her at Atlantic Station, the one she had received with both hands. She had given his vulnerability the full attention it deserved, and he had taken that same vulnerability and left a room in himself he did not fully inventory.

"Did you want her?" she asked. "Or did you want the opening?"

He was quiet for a long time. Long enough that she understood he was giving the question honest consideration rather than reaching for an answer that served him. When he spoke, he said, "I wanted the room to be open. I don't think it was about Angel."

"That's worse," April said quietly.

"I know."

She looked at him. She thought about what she had told him about Angel three weeks ago, the care with which he had received it, the promise he had made, and the eleven minutes it had taken him to reply to her text last night—slightly longer than usual, just long enough, she now understood, for him to decide what he was going to do.

"You decided to tell me," she said. "On Thursday. You decided before you came over."

"Yes."

"Why?"

"Because you told me the hardest true thing you had and I promised I would do the same. And because—" He stopped, then started again. "Because the version of this where I didn't tell you was not a version I was willing to live in. I've lived in that version before. It costs more than the telling."

She sat with this. She thought about the six months in Miami—the fortress, the distance, the specific quality of a man who had not been in the water long enough. She thought about the swimming origin: afraid of the water at nine, the father who had just left, the mother who signed him up anyway.

"What do you want to happen?" she said.

"I want to know if there's a version of this where I can earn back what I broke." His voice did not waver, but it was carrying a heavy burden. "I'm not asking you to decide that now. I'm asking if the conversation is still possible."

She looked at the table. She looked back at him.

"I don't know yet," she said. "That's the honest answer and I'm not going to give you a different one."

He nodded. He received this the way he received things—without bargaining, without attempting to convert her uncertainty into something that served him. "Okay," he said.

"I need time," she said. "And I need you to not fill the time with things designed to change my mind. No gestures. No calls. Let me come to it at my own speed."

"I can do that."

"You said that before," she said. "Three weeks ago at this table."

The accuracy of it landed in the room between them. He did not defend against it. "I know," he said. "I did. And I failed it. I'm asking for the chance to be the version of me that doesn't."

She stood. The conversation was complete—not resolved, not finished in the sense of being over, but complete in the sense of having said everything it needed to say for today. He stood. He did not reach for her at the door.

"Thank you for telling me," she said. "That part mattered. It doesn't fix it. But it mattered."

He left.

She had four hours between Jason's departure and Angel's arrival. She used them with the deliberate economy of a woman who understood she had a second difficult conversation ahead and needed to be her best self for it. That meant eating, which she had not done adequately; walking, which she did for forty-five minutes in the March afternoon air, still cold enough to be useful; and sitting in quiet long enough to locate her own center before she had to engage with Angel's.

On her walk, she thought about what Angel's version of Tuesday night looked like. She had heard Jason's version—the tea, the conversation, the wine requested, the movement to the couch. She had heard how he described his own failure: the moment of knowing and the not-closing. She had not yet heard Angel's version, and she knew she needed it before she could understand the full shape of what had occurred.

She was also aware—and this required its own sitting-with—that Angel was the person she had been examining her own feelings for across the past two months. The question that had begun in the blue television light was still there, patient and honest and now extraordinarily complicated. She did not know what to do with this yet. She set it aside for after the conversation.

She walked back, made fresh coffee, and sat at the table to breathe.

At one fifty-nine, her buzzer sounded.

Angel arrived looking like someone who had been doing the interior work since Wednesday morning without pause— the specific quality of a person who has been in their own honest accounting for forty-eight hours without relief. The rust sweater was absent. She wore dark clothes, nothing performative, just herself in the configuration of a person who was not going to try to look like anything other than what she was.

She came in and did not speak immediately. She sat across from April at the kitchen table—the same table, the same configuration—put her hands in her lap, and looked at April with the full directness she was capable of when she wasn't protecting herself.

"Tell me your version," April said.

Angel told it. Not the version that served her—April could tell the difference after eight years, identifying the shape of Angel's self-protective stories versus the Angel who was trying to tell the accurate thing. This was the accurate thing. The call to Jason because she needed someone safe. The tea. The conversation about Dr. Coleman and "waiting for permission." The wine she had asked for. The couch. The reaching that had happened before she finished thinking.

"I knew what I was doing before it was done," Angel said. "Not before I started. But before it was finished. And I finished it anyway."

April looked at her. "Why?"

"The pattern," Angel said. "Going toward the adjacent thing instead of the actual thing because the actual thing is terrifying. That's what Dr. Coleman and I have been working on for six years, and I ran it anyway."

"What's the actual thing?"

A long pause followed. Angel looked at the table, then back up at April with the expression that appeared when she was about to say something she had not yet said aloud to another person.

"You," Angel said. Quietly. Without drama. It was the specific flatness of something true that has been held for a long time finally finding air. "The actual thing is you. It's been you for a while. I've been calling it something else, and I stopped being able to call it something else the night I fell asleep on your couch."

April sat very still. She let the sentence exist in the room. She did not react immediately—not out of suppression, but the deliberate practice of letting things arrive fully before responding.

"How long?" she asked.

"I don't know exactly. Long enough that I can't point to a beginning."

"Were you going to tell me?"

"Yes." There was no hesitation. "I've been working out how. I needed to be sure I wasn't calling it something it wasn't. That I was naming it accurately rather than—" She stopped. "Rather than performing a name for it."

April heard her own language in that: the accuracy, the not-performing. The principles she had been building toward all year were reflected back from Angel's mouth.

"And Tuesday night," April said. "Was that part of figuring out how?"

Angel did not look away. "No. Tuesday night was the pattern. Going sideways instead of straight. It was not—it was not about Jason. Not really. And that makes it worse, I know. Using someone that way."

"It does make it worse," April said.

"I know."

The room was quiet. The coffee was cooling on the counter. Outside, the March afternoon was doing its patient thing. April looked at Angel—the woman she had known for eight years, the woman who had been in the adjacent rooms of her life through the warehouse and Josh, the house on the hill, the beginning of Jason, the upper level, and the question beginning in the blue television light. The woman who had, apparently, been navigating her own parallel interior work toward the same territory from a different direction.

She thought about what she felt, giving it an honest examination without the reflex of managing it into something more acceptable. What she felt was multiple things, each real, none canceling the others.

Hurt—specific and legitimate, the hurt of someone whose trust had been taken to a place she had not given permission for it to go.

Anger—clean and clear, the anger of someone who had done the honest work of telling the truth and had not been extended the same honesty in return.

And underneath both of those, still present, the specific thing she had been sitting with since January. Still there. Still hers. Not resolved. Not simple. Hers.

"I need time," she said. "With this. With all of it."

"I know," Angel said.

"I'm not telling you we're done," April said carefully. "I'm telling you I don't know yet what we are. And I need you to let me find out at my own speed without trying to fill the space."

Angel nodded. "I can do that."

"Don't disappear," April said. "But don't reach, either. Let me come to it."

"Okay," Angel said. She stood. She looked at April with the expression that contained the full weight of eight years of genuine friendship and the specific grief of someone who has complicated something that mattered to them. "I'm sorry. Not just for Tuesday. For not coming straight at the actual thing sooner."

"I know," April said. "I'm not ready to say it's okay. But I know."

Angel left.

She sat at the kitchen table for a long time after Angel left. The afternoon light moved across the floor in the patient way it moved in March, the sun's angle shifting as the season slowly turned. She did not try to resolve anything. She had done what the day required—two conversations, both honest, both complete in the sense of having said what needed saying. That was enough for today.

She thought about what she had. Not what she had lost— she would come to that in its own time—but what she possessed. She had herself. She had the work of the past year: the mirror and the upper level, the thinned wall and the choosing that was irrevocably hers. She had Tasha and the guest room and the candles. She had the clinical precision of a woman who could exist within the hardest things without being managed by them.

She still had the question that had begun in the blue television light. It was more complicated now—complicated in the way honest things often become when they are fully seen. But it was still there. Still hers. Still waiting for the version of herself who would know what to do with it.

She was not that version yet. She would be.

She got up and opened the refrigerator. She had not eaten since Tasha's toast at seven that morning. She made eggs—scrambled, with the herbs she kept because she had learned to cook for herself this year rather than for the performance of it. Eggs with herbs was what she wanted at five-thirty on a Friday, having completed the hardest day's work she had done in a long time.

She ate at the kitchen table. She did not look at her phone.

Outside, the March evening was beginning—the light softening toward the particular blue of early spring dusk, the city doing its Friday thing, indifferent and ongoing. She ate her eggs and looked at the light and thought: *I am still here. I am still myself. That is not nothing.*

That is, in fact, everything.

Chapter 30: Healing Begins

The first week was the hardest because it was the week of not knowing what anything was yet. She went to work and performed her job with the clinical precision that had always been available to her, regardless of her interior weather. She came home. She cooked. She read the novel Jason had given her—not because she had decided anything about him, but because the book was good. Stopping because of him would have been a form of letting him take something else from her, and she was not prepared to do that.

She did not contact Jason. She did not contact Angel. She had asked for time and she was using it, which meant sitting with what she actually felt rather than reaching for the resolution that would relieve the discomfort of not-knowing.

What she actually felt, across that first week, was a rotation of truths. Anger on Monday and Tuesday—the clean, specific anger of someone whose trust had been deployed against them; not the hot variety, but the cold, precise kind she had learned to sit with until it had told her everything it knew. Grief on Wednesday and Thursday—the particular grief of losing something she had been building carefully for fifteen months, the cost of having her honesty received with integrity only to watch that integrity fail at its first serious test. Something closer to sadness on Friday—quieter than grief, less specific—the sadness of being reminded that the people you love are capable of the very things they most fear being capable of, regardless of how much work they have done.

She let each emotion have its day. She did not try to resolve them into a single feeling she could act on. She had been practicing this for a year; it did not make the rotation comfortable, but it made it honest.

***

She ran every morning. This was not new—she had run the same route at the same early hour for years—but the running had a different quality now. She was more present in her body, aware of the specific sensation of her feet on the pavement, the cold air moving through her, and the way her lungs adjusted to the effort. She had been learning to inhabit her body for a year, at the house and the mirror and the upper level; the running was simply another room in that same building.

On the eighth day, she ran a different route. It wasn't planned; she had simply taken a left where she usually went right and found herself on an unfamiliar street with buildings and rhythms she had not yet learned. She found it interesting. She noted a coffee shop she hadn't known existed, a small park tucked behind an apartment complex, and a bakery whose exhaust vent produced the specific scent of something being made at six in the morning.

She thought: *I have been in this city for four years and there are still streets I don't know.* She thought: *That is not a failure. That is just the size of a city.*

She ran home on the new route and stood in her kitchen drinking water, thinking about the size of a city, which was also the size of a life—always more rooms than you had opened, always territory you had not yet walked. This had been terrifying to her once: the not-having-seen-everything, the incompleteness of her own map. It was less terrifying now. In certain moments, it was interesting.

Her mother called on the ninth day. Cynthia, who had always possessed the specific antenna of a woman who had spent decades reading rooms professionally, called on a Tuesday evening without any indication that something had happened.

"You sound different," Cynthia said, approximately four minutes into a conversation that had ostensibly been about a conference she had attended.

"I'm fine," April said.

"I know you're fine. You sound different than fine. You sound—settled. And sad. At the same time."

April looked at the ceiling, considering how to answer. She and her mother shared a complex relationship—the professional respect was real, but so was the dynamic of two women who were both good at the same things and had never quite figured out how to exist around each other's goodness without it becoming a competition. She had been working on this, too, quietly, across the year.

"Some things happened," April said. "I'm processing them."

"Do you want to tell me?"

A pause. April thought about the version of her mother who would receive this information—not the Cynthia who gave assessments and corrections and the particular brand of care that arrived as instruction, but the other version. The one who had sat with April in the hospital after the warehouse and said nothing for two hours because she understood, that one time, that nothing was the right thing to say.

"Not everything," April said. "But someone I trusted failed a promise they made to me. And someone else I care about was involved. I have a lot of feelings about both things, and I'm trying to let them be what they are before I decide what to do with them."

Cynthia was quiet for a moment. "Are you safe?"

"Yes."

"Are you sleeping?"

"Mostly."

"Are you eating?"

April thought about the eggs with herbs on Friday. The toast at Tasha's. The pasta she had made on Sunday because she wanted it and had prepared it carefully, with the attention she gave things she wanted to be good. "Yes," she said. "I'm eating."

"Good," Cynthia said. A pause. "You know what I'm going to say."

"That I should talk to someone."

"You should talk to someone."

"I know," April said. "I'm going to." She had been thinking about it—not as a crisis intervention, but as the natural next step of a year of interior work that had reached a point where an external mirror would be useful. She had been doing this mostly alone, with the house and the reflection it offered. She was ready for a different kind of mirror.

"Good," Cynthia said again. Then, more quietly: "I'm proud of you. The way you handle things. It's different than it used to be."

April held the phone. This was not the kind of thing her mother said often. She received it without deflecting, which was something she had been practicing. "Thank you," she said. "That means something."

They talked for another twenty minutes about nothing difficult. When she hung up, April sat in her apartment and thought about her mother and the specific quality of being known by a person who had also been a problem to be navigated. Both things could be true. She was getting better at holding both things.

She found a therapist on a Thursday—a woman named Dr. Osei whose practice was three miles from her apartment. Her intake questionnaire possessed the specific quality of someone who had thought carefully about which questions revealed the most accurate truths about a new client. April filled it out with the same thoroughness she brought to clinical instruments and felt, in the process, something she recognized from the house's entrance hall: the specific settling of a person being received without judgment by a space built to do exactly that.

The first session was typical—the establishing of the container, the history, the presenting concerns. April told Dr. Osei what had happened with the accuracy she had been developing all year. It was not the softened version; it was not a version that protected either Jason or Angel from their full responsibility. Dr. Osei listened with the focus of someone intent on understanding the situation fully before offering a word.

At the end of the session, Dr. Osei said, "You've done a significant amount of work on yourself in the past year. I can hear it in the way you describe things. What brings you here now, rather than six months ago?"

April considered this. "Six months ago, I was still figuring out who I was inside the work," she said. "I think I needed to know that before I could use a room like this well."

Dr. Osei looked at her with an expression April associated with the specific quality of being accurately seen. "That's a good answer," she said. "Let's use it well."

April drove home from that first session with the particular aura of someone who has found the right room for the work they need to do. It wasn't relief—the work had not truly begun yet—it was something more like readiness.

She went to the house on a Saturday in the third week. She bypassed the upper level for the main floor, the fountain, and the corridor of rooms she had walked through on her first visit nine months ago with her hands at her sides, looking but not entering.

She sat by the fountain for an hour.

The house received her the way it always had—with the patient indifference of a place that did not require her to be anything other than what she was. She thought about March of the year before: the wrong clothes, the entrance hall, the settling. She thought about everything the house had shown her across nine months—the permission, the mirror room, the upper level, the closing of the wall. She thought about what she had come for, what she had found, and what she was carrying back out with her.

She thought: *The house gave me permission. What I did with it was mine.*

She thought about the warehouse. About the years she had spent managing the parts of herself that had been made dangerous by someone else's cruelty. She thought about how the house had said: *Those parts are not dangerous. They are yours, and they are worth knowing.* She had spent a year learning to believe this, and she believed it now. What Jason and Angel had done did not change it.

She put her hand in the fountain. The water was cool, moving steadily in its small circuit. She watched the light play on the surface.

She thought: *I am the same person who walked up those stairs. I am the same person who looked in that mirror and knew herself. No one can take that. It is not available to be taken.*

She stayed until the space had done what she had come for—not providing consolation or easy answers, but offering the reminder of her own ground. The reminder that the ground was hers and solid, not contingent on what other people did with the trust she gave them.

She drove home. She made dinner. She ate at the kitchen table, read another chapter of the novel, and went to bed at a reasonable hour.

At the end of the third week, she found herself thinking, for the first time since the reckoning, about what she wanted. Not about what had happened—she had thought about that thoroughly and was not finished—but about the future shape of things.

She thought about Jason. She wondered if there was a version of what they had that could survive this and emerge stronger rather than merely repaired. She did not know yet. She was not going to pretend to know. But she could think about it now without the cold anger and grief arriving simultaneously, which meant she was closer to the version of herself who could examine it accurately.

She thought about Angel. About the "actual thing" Angel had named at the kitchen table—the flatness of it, the long-held quality, the parallel interior work they had been doing from different directions. She thought about the question that had begun in the blue television light, which was now both more complicated and more named than it had ever been. Both things at once. Both real.

She thought: *I have time. I am not on anyone's timeline. The decisions will be ready when I am ready for them.*

This was not resignation. It was the specific patience of a woman who had learned that the truest things arrived in their own time, and that rushing them produced the performed version rather than the real one.

She had the real one in reach. She was going to wait for it.

She picked up her phone. She looked at Jason's name. She looked at Angel's name. She put the phone down.

Not yet. But soon.

She opened the novel. She read until the light changed, then she made tea and kept reading, letting the evening be exactly what it was—quiet, hers, and full of the specific potential of someone who has done the hard work and is finally approaching the place where she can begin to build.

Chapter 31: Rebuilding Trust

She called Tasha on a Sunday morning in the fourth week. "I think I'm ready to talk about what I want," she said. "Not what happened. What I want."

Tasha didn't hesitate. "Come over. I'll make brunch."

April arrived at eleven with the particular quality of someone who had completed a phase of interior work—not finished, but arrived at a point where the processing had produced enough clarity to be spoken aloud. She needed the specific mirror of someone who knew her well enough to distinguish between the honest version and the managed one.

Tasha had made shakshuka—a meal that required attention and produced something worth the effort. The eggs were exactly right. April ate with the appetite of someone who had been eating adequately but not well, finding that the right meal at the right table was its own form of restoration.

They ate in the comfortable quiet of people who did not require constant conversation. When the plates were clear and the coffee was poured, Tasha looked at her. "Okay. What do you want?"

"I want to tell you what I've figured out about Jason first," April said. "Because that one is clearer."

She had spent three weeks sitting with the image of him at the kitchen table; the promise and the room he hadn't inventoried. She thought of his origin story—the father who left, the mother who put him in the water anyway, the nine-year-old who was afraid of the wrong thing because the right thing didn't have a shape he could manage. She thought of his words: *I wanted the room to be open. I don't think it was about Angel.*

"I believe him," she said. "That it wasn't about Angel specifically. I think he has a room that still opens under certain conditions, and he was in those conditions, and it opened. That's not an excuse. But I think it's the accurate version."

"Does the accurate version change what you want?" Tasha asked.

"It changes what I think is possible," April said carefully. "Not whether I'm hurt. I'm still hurt. The hurt is legitimate, and I'm not going to manage it into something more acceptable just to make a decision faster." She held her coffee cup, feeling its warmth. "But I think there might be a version of what we had that could be built on what happened, rather than destroyed by it. If he does the actual work. Not the naming-the-pattern work. The being-in-the-water work."

"Can you tell the difference?" Tasha asked. "Between him doing the actual work and him performing it for you?"

April looked at her. This was the question she had been sitting with since the fourth day. "I think so," she said. "I've been learning to read the difference between the performed version and the real one in myself for a year. I think I can apply it to him." She paused. "And I think I need to give him the chance to try. Not for his sake. For the sake of what we actually had, which was real and worth something. It deserves the chance to still be worth something."

Tasha was quiet for a moment. "Is that what you want? Or is that what the fair thing looks like?"

The distinction landed with precision. April sat with it, giving the question an honest examination rather than a quick answer.

"Both," she said finally. "I think what's fair and what I want happen to be the same thing here, which is why I trust it." She looked at the table. "I'm not going back to what we had. I don't want to rebuild the exact same thing. I want to find out if there's something different we can build from what we both know now—including how he fails, what I need when he fails, and whether he has the capacity to be in the water instead of just knowing how to swim."

Tasha nodded slowly. Not agreement—consideration. The specific quality of someone processing what they've heard with the full attention it deserved. "When are you going to tell him that?"

"Soon," April said. "Not today. But soon."

She refilled her coffee. She looked at the window. The April morning was doing its thing outside—the season fully turned now, the city in the specific quality of early spring, trees with the first suggestion of green, the light different in its angle and its color from the March light she had been living in.

"Angel is harder," she said.

"I know," Tasha said.

"Tell me what you actually think," April said. "Not the supportive version. The honest one. You've been watching me think about Angel for two months."

Tasha looked at her with an expression that combined deep affection with the specific willingness to say the true thing. "I think you've been in love with your best friend for longer than you know," she said. "And I think you've been calling it something else because the 'something else' was safer. I think Tuesday night—what Angel did—scared you more than it hurt you, because it showed you the feeling was visible. Other people could see it from the outside even if you hadn't named it on the inside."

April looked at the table. "That's the honest version."

"You asked for it."

"I know." April thought about the blue television light. The kaleidoscope. The pieces—the same pieces arranged suddenly so the pattern was visible. She thought about Angel at the kitchen table: *The actual thing is you.* The long-held flatness of it. The parallel interior work from different directions. "I think you're right," she said. "About the fear. What Angel did—it was wrong, and I'm still hurt by it. The hurt is legitimate. But the part that sits most heavily isn't the betrayal itself. It's that she went sideways to get to something she could have come straight at. She went through Jason instead of through me. And that—" She stopped, searching for the words. "That tells me she didn't trust that what she felt would be received. I need to sit with what that means. What I communicated to her, or didn't, that made 'straight' feel less possible than 'sideways.'"

Tasha studied her. "You're not responsible for her pattern."

"I know. I'm not taking on her failure. But I'm also asking: what's the version where I'm honest about what I felt and how I communicated it? Because I was working up to it. I had the question beginning. I was waiting until I was sure." A pause. "And maybe I waited past the point where she needed to know I was waiting."

"That's a lot of grace for someone who hurt you."

"It's not grace," April said. "It's accuracy. I'm trying to understand what actually happened. I can be hurt by what she did and also understand the conditions that produced it. Both things are true."

Tasha was quiet for a moment. Then: "What do you want? With Angel. Not what's fair or accurate. What do you *want?*"

April looked at the window. The April morning. The green suggestion in the trees. She thought about eight years— the warehouse and Josh, the house and the beginning of Jason, the upper level, the documentary, and the blue television light. She thought about the quality of Angel's attention, the way she filled a room, the rust-sweater evenings, and the question that had been beginning.

"I want to find out what it is," she said. "What we are when everything is named and nobody is performing. When she's not going sideways and I'm not calling it something else." She looked back at Tasha. "I don't know what that looks like yet. I don't know if it's friendship or something past it, or both at the same time. But I want the actual thing. Whatever it is. Properly."

"Are you going to tell her that?"

"Yes," April said. "When I'm ready. And when she's done her own work on what happened. I don't want the version of that conversation where she's still in the aftermath. I want the version where we're both standing up."

Tasha nodded. She looked at April with the expression April valued most—not the warmth, but the respect underneath it. The specific respect of someone watching a person navigate something difficult with the full use of their faculties. "You know what you want," Tasha said. "Both of them. You know exactly what you want."

"I know," April said. "I've been learning to."

They stayed at Tasha's through the afternoon, the conversation moving off the difficult things and onto others—Tasha's work, the neighborhood, the shakshuka recipe Tasha would not entirely divulge on principle, and a film they had both seen separately. They argued about the movie with the specific pleasure of people who could disagree without it meaning anything other than that they were different people. Across the afternoon, April felt the restoration of being known by someone who did not require her to be any particular version of herself.

She drove home in the early evening with the windows down despite the chill—the same instinct she'd had on the drive from the house's upper level months ago, needing the sharpness of the air. She was in her own processing, the path ahead was clear, and she wanted to be present in it.

Arriving home, she stood in her apartment and felt the space differently than she had over the past four weeks. This was no longer the home of someone sitting in wreckage. It was the space of someone who had cleared the debris, who was beginning to see the ground beneath it and consider what could be built on earth that had been cleared rather than covered over.

She picked up her phone. She looked at Jason's name. She thought about what she had said to Tasha: *Not the exact thing they'd had. Something different.*

She texted him: *I'm ready to talk. This week. You choose when.*

She set the phone down before he could reply. She was not in a hurry. She had said the thing, and the thing was in motion; the motion could take the time it needed.

She looked at Angel's name for a longer moment. She thought about the "actual thing." The long-held quality of it. The parallel work from different directions. She thought: *Not yet.* But the "not yet" was different from before. Before, it was "not yet" because she was still figuring out what it was. Now, it was "not yet" because she was waiting for the right conditions. That was a different "not yet" entirely.

She put the phone face-down on the counter and opened the refrigerator. She made dinner with the attention she brought to things she wanted to be good, ate at the kitchen table, and read the last chapter of the novel Jason had given her. She had been saving it without quite knowing it, and tonight felt like the right night to finish.

It was a good ending. She sat with it for a moment after she closed the book—not rushing on, just being inside it before putting it down.

Then she put it down. She went to bed. She lay in the dark and felt the specific quality of someone who had located themselves—not fully arrived, not finished, but located. She knew where she was. She knew what she wanted. She was beginning to see how to get there.

That was enough. For tonight, that was more than enough.

Chapter 32: New Beginnings

She texted Angel on a Wednesday in the fifth week: *I'm ready. Sunday, if you are.*

Angel replied in three minutes: *Yes. Where?*

April thought about this. Not her apartment—the kitchen table carried too much from the reckoning, and she wanted neutral ground, or at least different ground, space that had not been shaped by the previous conversations. Not a restaurant—too many people, too much ambient noise requiring them to manage their expressions for a room. She thought about the third option.

My place, she wrote back. *But the balcony. I want to be outside.*

Understood, Angel said.

April spent the days between Wednesday and Sunday not preparing for the conversation—she had been doing that for five weeks without knowing it. It was prepared. Further rehearsal would only result in the managed version rather than the honest one. Instead, she spent those days existing in the final week of April, a month that possessed the specific quality of a season fully arrived. She ran the new route she had discovered during her first week of healing—the one with the bakery and the small park. She had her second session with Dr. Osei, which was better than the first; the first had been about establishing the container, but the second was the actual beginning of the work. She had dinner with Tasha on Friday and did not mention Sunday.

She slept well on Saturday night. She woke Sunday with the clarity she had been finding each morning since the healing began—not certainty, but locatedness. She knew where she was. She knew what she was going to say.

Angel arrived at two o'clock. She was not wearing the rust sweater; she was in clothes that were simply hers—nothing performing ease or undone-ness. She was simply Angel in the specific configuration of someone who had been doing interior work for five weeks and was not trying to communicate anything about it, except that it had happened.

She looked, April thought, like someone who had been through something and had not come out the other side yet, but had traveled far enough in to be standing upright. It was the specific quality April had seen in her the night of the Thai food and the documentary—the night she had arrived with the good Malbec and the rust sweater. Processed. Not finished. Standing.

"Hey," April said.

"Hey."

April had made tea—not coffee, which carried the ghost of the kitchen table and Jason's Saturday visits. Tea was its own thing: neutral and warm. She handed Angel a mug and led her to the balcony, where she had placed two chairs facing the April afternoon. The city was doing its thing below them—Sunday easy, that particular quality of two o'clock when most people are somewhere comfortable and the pace has slowed to something voluntary.

They sat. They held their mugs. The silence had the specific quality of two people who had things to say and were not avoiding them, just finding the right beginning.

Angel found it first.

"I've been in therapy twice a week since that Tuesday," she said. "Not crisis therapy. Work therapy. The kind where you go because you've identified something you need to understand better, and you need help understanding it accurately."

"I know the kind," April said.

"Dr. Coleman and I have been talking about the pattern," Angel said. "The full version of it. Not just the going-sideways-instead-of-straight. The whole thing. Where it starts." She looked at her mug. "It starts with believing the 'actual thing' isn't available. That what I actually want—who I actually want—is too much, or too specific, or too—I don't know. Too real to survive being asked for."

April looked at her. "So you reach for the adjacent thing because losing the adjacent thing is survivable."

"Yes," Angel said. "That's the exact shape of it." A pause. "I've been running that pattern my whole life and I never named it that clearly until now."

"Dr. Coleman?"

"Me," Angel said. "She asked me a question last week and I answered it. When I heard myself say it, I understood. She asked: *What is it you're most afraid of asking for?* And I said your name."

The April afternoon did its patient thing around them. The city below. The late-season light hit at an angle that made everything look slightly more real than usual—the specific quality of Sunday afternoon light in spring.

April looked at Angel for a long time.

"I need to tell you something," April said. "About what I was doing before Tuesday. Before everything."

Angel waited with the specific stillness she held when she was paying full attention.

"I had been sitting with something since January," April said. "The night you fell asleep on my couch. I sat in the blue television light and watched you sleeping and felt something I wasn't expecting. And I spent the next weeks—the weeks before Tuesday—trying to understand it accurately. Trying to make sure I wasn't calling it something it wasn't." She looked at the city below. "I was close to ready. I was almost at the place where I could come straight at it. And then Tuesday happened, and I didn't know anymore if what I was feeling was real or just the architecture of what had just been broken."

Angel absorbed this in silence. April could see her doing it—the specific processing that was not reactive, not reaching for relief, just receiving.

"So you were—before Tuesday, you were—"

"I was working up to it," April said. "Yes."

The weight of that settled between them. The parallel timelines. Both of them moving toward the same thing from different directions, both waiting for the right conditions, and the Tuesday that had made a collision of what should have been a meeting.

"I'm sorry," Angel said. It wasn't the rote version; it was the one that carried a full understanding of what she was sorry for. "Not just for what happened. For not trusting that straight was possible. For going around instead of to."

"I know," April said. "I've been sitting with my part of it too. Whether I communicated—whether there was something I did or didn't do that made sideways feel safer than straight."

"That's not yours to carry," Angel said immediately.

"I know it's not mine to carry," April said. "But I can examine it anyway. Because it's part of understanding what we are and how we got here and what I want to do about it."

Angel looked at her. "What do you want to do about it?"

April set her mug on the balcony railing. She turned in her chair to face Angel fully—offering the same attention she had been practicing all year: the full-body version, the one that refused to maintain a managed distance.

"I want to find out what this is," she said. "What we are when neither of us is calling it something else. When you're not going sideways and I'm not waiting until I'm completely sure." She paused. "I'm not completely sure. I've been working toward 'sure' for five weeks and I'm not there yet. But I'm far enough that I don't want to wait anymore for a certainty that might just be another form of management."

Angel looked at her with a raw directness—the version of her with no performance in it, which April had recognized since the first year of their friendship as Angel at her most entirely herself.

"I've been in love with you for a long time," Angel said. Her voice was quiet, possessed of the same flatness as their kitchen table conversation—the long-held thing finally finding air. "I don't know when it started. I know it was before I knew what to call it. It survived Charles and Josh and the house and

Jason—not despite any of those things, but alongside them. I've been loving you in the margins of everything else."

April heard this. She let the weight of it arrive fully before she answered.

"I don't know if what I feel is the same thing," she said. "I'm not going to say it is just to match you. I know something began in January that I haven't been able to call anything else since. I know it's specific to you—it's not the intimacy of friendship confused for something more; I've checked that. It's its own thing." She looked at Angel. "I want to find out what 'its own thing' is. Properly. Not in the margins. Not sideways."

"What does 'properly' look like?" Angel asked.

"Slowly," April replied. "Not because I'm hedging, but because I want to do it in the full light. I want to see what it actually is rather than what I want it to be. I've been learning all year to wait for the real version instead of the performed one. I want the real version of this."

"Slowly," Angel repeated. "I can do slowly."

"And I need you to know—this is separate from what's happening with Jason. I'm not choosing. I'm not replacing one thing with another. I'm—" She searched for the words. "I'm figuring out what I have and what I want. I need both of those conversations to happen in their own spaces without them being about each other."

Angel looked at her steadily. "I understand that. I don't need you to choose."

"Good," April said. "Because I'm not ready to."

"Okay," Angel said.

"Okay," April said.

They sat on the balcony for another two hours. The conversation drifted away from the difficult things and onto others: the fifth week of documentary episodes, which Angel had been saving to discuss; the research trip Dr. Coleman had mentioned regarding therapeutic approaches; the book April had finished and was now going to lend to Angel.

The afternoon light moved across the balcony with the patient grace of a Sunday in April. The city below maintained its easy pace. They refilled their mugs and let the ordinary quality of their long-standing bond settle over the hour—not replacing the difficult truths, but coexisting with them.

At four-thirty, Angel stood to leave. She looked at April, and there was a moment of specific not-knowing—the threshold of something named but not yet acted upon. It was the productive uncertainty of two people who had told the truth and were beginning to discover what it meant in practice.

April looked back at her. She thought about the "not yet" and the "when ready," about all the thresholds she had stood at over the past year, and what she had learned about the difference between right timing and a managed delay.

She stepped forward. She put her arms around Angel with the deliberate intent of a choice, not a reaction. Angel went still for a moment—from surprise, perhaps, or the sheer disbelief of receiving something long-awaited—and then her arms came up. They stood on the balcony in the April afternoon and held each other with the particular quality of a beginning.

Not a kiss. Not yet. Something prior to that: the acknowledgment of what was there, the permission for it to exist, the start of finding out what it was when allowed to be fully itself.

April stepped back and looked at Angel.

"Sunday next week?" Angel asked. Her voice held the quality April had known for eight years—the real one, under the performance, the one she had been learning to recognize.

"Sunday next week," April confirmed.

Angel left. April stood on the balcony, looking out at the city, feeling the specific quality of a start—not certain, not complete, but begun. It was the beginning that follows hard work, an honest accounting, and a long wait for the right conditions. It was the beginning that is earned rather than stumbled into.

She thought about Renee's line: *If you think you're finished, you've stopped being interesting.*

She was not finished. She was beginning. Both things were true and both were good.

She went inside. She put on music—Missy Elliott, the album she played when she needed to remember that joy was available, that her body was her own, that the future was something she moved toward rather than something that arrived without her consent.

She danced alone in her apartment in the April evening and thought: *I am the most myself I have ever been.*

And that was not the end. It was the beginning of what the ending was going to be.

Chapter 33: The Letter

The conversation she had told him to initiate happened on a Friday evening in the fifth week, two days after the Angel Sunday. She had chosen the order deliberately—Angel first, because that conversation needed to be complete before she walked into the Jason one, needed to be its own thing that didn't bleed into the assessment of what she was going to do about him. She arrived at Jason's apartment with the specific quality of someone who had done the interior preparation and was ready to be present rather than managed.

He made dinner. It wasn't a gesture—she had told him not to make gestures, and he had understood the instruction accurately enough to know that making dinner was the ordinary thing people did when someone came to their home in the evening. He had prepared the braised chicken she'd taught him in the fall, which was a different kind of thing entirely: a marker of the specific intimacy of having taught someone something that was yours and watching it become theirs, too.

They ate. They talked for three hours. She told him what she had told Tasha—not the same words, but words reshaped for him—that she was not interested in rebuilding the exact thing they'd had. What she wanted was something different, built from what they both knew now. She told him what that difference looked like from where she was standing: the actual water, not the knowledge of swimming. The room he had not inventoried, opened and examined and closed properly, rather than just named in the abstract.

He listened with the full attention that had always been his specific quality. He did not defend. He did not bargain. He asked one question: "What does being in the actual water look like to you, in concrete terms?"

She had thought about this. She told him: a therapist, which he had already started; honesty about the room when he felt it opening, rather than after it had already opened; and time. Not a timeline she was giving him, but the acknowledgment that the rebuild would take as long as it took, and she was not going to pretend otherwise. Finally, the understanding that what she was navigating with Angel was its own thing in its own space, and he did not get to bring his feelings about it to her.

He received all of this. He said, "I can work with that."

"I know you can," she said. "That's not the question. The question is whether you will."

"I know," he said. "I'm asking for the chance to show you the difference."

She drove home thinking about the swimming—about the nine-year-old who had been afraid of the wrong thing because the actual fear didn't have a shape. She thought: *He is in the pool now. Whether he gets good at it is the open question.*

It was a real question. She did not know the answer. She was willing to find out.

The letter arrived on a Saturday morning, eleven days after their Friday conversation. It was a physical letter, handwritten, her name on the envelope in his specific handwriting—the compressed architectural print of someone who had learned to write carefully and had never unlearned it. She recognized it from the grocery lists he left on her counter, from the inscription in the book he had given her.

She set it on the kitchen table and looked at it for ten minutes before she opened it.

She thought about the Friday conversation and the ask for the chance to show her the difference. She thought about a note he had left on her counter once in October, when he had been at her apartment before she was home: *Back by seven. Made coffee.* The specific economy of it—three words that contained the entire agreement of two people who had learned each other's rhythms.

She opened the envelope.

April—

I've been trying to write this for ten days. The first four versions were apologies, and I kept deleting them because you already have the apology and I don't think that's what this is for.

What I want to say is this: I understand now what I didn't understand before, and I want to try to say it accurately rather than in a way that sounds like it's serving me.

The room I thought I had closed was the room where I held things back from people I loved. I had been working on that room since Vanessa, and I thought I had the work done. I gave you access to it. I told you about the room and what it had cost, and I believed that was the work. What happened with Angel showed me that I had been accounting for only one direction of failure.

The other room—the one that opened when the conditions were right, when someone was close and the evening was late and I had had enough wine to stop interrogating my own choices—that room I had not inventoried. I knew it was there. I had felt it open before, in the years between Vanessa and Miami and Atlanta, and I had always managed to close it before anything happened. I believed the managing was the same as having closed it. I was wrong about that.

What I understand now, that I did not understand before: naming a room is not the same as clearing it. You can know the exact shape of a failure and still fail in exactly that shape if you have not done the work of being in it—actually in it—and finding out what you do when you are.

You said: the actual water, not the knowledge of swimming. That is the most accurate thing anyone has ever said about what I have been doing wrong. I have been very good at swimming in theory. I need to get good at swimming in practice. I am working on it. I started working on it before you told me I needed to, which I want you to know not as a point in my favor, but as evidence that the naming finally became real rather than abstract.

I am not telling you this to change anything you've decided or are deciding. I am telling you because you told me to keep telling you the truth even when it was this, and this is the truth: I understand what I did and why and what it cost, and I am in the water now. I am not going to substitute the knowing for the doing again.

The other thing I want to say: whatever you are figuring out with Angel is yours to figure out. I mean that without reservation and without the kind of saying-it-while-meaning-the-opposite that I know you can read. I know what you told me about what you felt, and I know what it meant that you told me. I am not going to make that something you have to manage alongside whatever you are building with her. Both things are real. You do not have to choose between them on my account.

I want to earn back what I broke. I don't know if I can. I know that whether I can is entirely contingent on whether I do the work and not on whether I want to and not on how clearly I can describe wanting to. I know the difference. I am in the water.

—Jason

She read the letter twice. The first time with the speed of someone following the sense of it. The second time slowly, with the specific attention she brought to things she needed to understand accurately rather than quickly.

She set it on the kitchen table and looked at the April morning coming through her window and thought about what she had.

She had a letter from a man who had understood precisely what she had told him. He had been honest about the shape of his failure without using that honesty as an argument for forgiveness. She considered the swimming reference; it told her he was in the pool—not merely performing the analogy she had given him, but inside it, working from it. She returned to the line about Angel: *Both things are real. You do not have to choose on my account.* She read it three times. It was a line that could not be convincingly performed by someone who did not mean it. She had been learning for a year to distinguish the performance from the reality. This was the real one.

She thought about what she had told Tasha: *I want to find out if there's something different we can build from what we both know*

now. I want to give him the chance to show me the difference between the knowing and the doing.

She thought: *He is showing me.*

Then: *This is the beginning of the showing, not the proof of it. The letter is not the work; it is the accurate description of the work. The work will take as long as it takes.*

She was willing to wait. She had spent the year learning to wait for the real version of things.

She sat at the kitchen table for a long time. It was a May morning now—the month after her own namesake, a time of unambiguous spring with the trees fully arrived. The light moved across the floor with the patient grace it possessed when she wasn't trying to rush anything.

She considered the full shape of what she possessed. Not the losses—she had spent five weeks with those and knew their dimensions—but the architecture of what she had built and where it had brought her.

She had herself, in the clearest configuration she had ever inhabited. The wall was thinned. The choosing was irrevocably hers. She had the mirror room, the upper level, and the year of deliberate work that had produced a woman capable of existing within the hardest things without being managed by them.

She had Tasha, the guest room, the candles, and the specific friendship of someone who offered the truth when the truth was exactly what was required.

She had Dr. Osei and a room built for the work she was finally ready to use well.

She had Angel—the beginning on the balcony, the Missy Elliott evening, and the "slow-and-in-the-full-light" version of discovering what their "own thing" actually was.

And she had this letter. It was from a man in the pool for the first time in his life—in the actual water, possessed of the awareness of his failure and a commitment to something beyond merely naming it.

She picked up her phone and called Jason.

He answered on the second ring. "Hey."

"I read your letter," she said.

A pause. "Okay."

"You understood what I told you," she said. "And you told me the truth about what you understood. That matters."

"I know it's not the work," he said. "The letter isn't the work."

"I know you know that," she said. "That's partly why I'm calling." She looked out at the May morning. "I'm not giving you a 'yes.' I'm telling you the door is open. Whatever we build from here—if we build something—it's going to take time, and it's going to look different from what we had. But I'm willing to find out what it looks like. If you're actually in the water."

"I'm in the water," he said.

"Then we'll see," she said. "That's what I have right now. We'll see."

"That's enough," he said. "That's more than I had this morning. Thank you."

She ended the call. She set the phone on the table beside the letter. She looked at both of them—the phone with its small domestic history, the letter with his compressed architectural print.

She thought: *I am not the same person who pulled over on a March Saturday and sat in her car for ten minutes looking at a house she didn't have a category for. I am not the person who sat in her coat in her apartment and thought: there it is. I am not the person who stood at the foot of that staircase in October and said "not tonight."*

I am the person who climbed the stairs. I am the person who stood in front of the mirror and knew herself. I am the person who told the hardest truth and held the permission and did not let anyone take the ground.

I am the most myself I have ever been.

She folded the letter. She put it in the drawer of the table where she kept things she was going to keep. She picked up her phone. She opened a new message to Angel: *Documentary tonight? I'll order.*

Angel replied in two minutes: *Yes. Bring the good wine this time. I'm tired of being the one who brings the Malbec.*

April smiled—the real one. She put the phone down and looked at the May morning and thought about what was beginning and let it be what it was: unfinished, honest, entirely hers.

Epilogue

Eighteen Months Later

The September light entered April's apartment at the specific angle unique to early fall—lower than summer, sharper, with the quality of something that had decided to be precise after months of being generous. She had come to associate this light with clarity. She had many such associations now. That was what happened when you paid attention to a life for long enough; it accumulated meaning the way a good kitchen accumulated tools—each one specific, each one earned.

She sat at the kitchen table with her coffee, the Saturday morning, and her own company, which she had learned over the past eighteen months to inhabit without her former restlessness—that constant, low-frequency need to be doing, managing, or preparing. This table had held a great deal during those months: the conversations, the reckonings, and the slow accumulation of ordinary Saturdays that formed the actual architecture of a life. She had come to understand that these Saturdays were not the space between the important things. They *were* the important things.

Her phone buzzed. She looked at it without urgency.

Jason: *Pool at noon? Bring the good sunscreen.*

She smiled—the real one, the interior version that reached the surface without being summoned. She typed back: *Already bought it. See you at noon.*

She set the phone down, picked up her coffee, and looked at the September light, thinking about how different the same table could feel from one year to the next.

What they had built from the wreckage was not what they had possessed before. This was the fact she had been most honest about from the beginning: there was no restoration, only construction. The thing they were building was new, set on ground cleared by the hardest year either of them had navigated.

That clearing was in the foundation now, part of what made the structure solid rather than a hurdle it had to overcome.

He had stayed in the water. This was not a metaphor she used lightly; she had spent eighteen months watching for the difference between the knowing and the doing with the clinical attention of a woman who had earned the ability to read it. He had seen a therapist consistently since that March—work she recognized not because she tracked his appointments, but because she saw it in how he navigated his own failures. He had called her twice in the past year when "the room" had begun to open—not after it happened, but before. He had told her, she had received the truth with accuracy, and they had navigated it together. That was the new thing. The actual water.

It had not been easy. There were months in the fall and winter when the distance between their current state and the original relationship felt like a loss rather than a foundation. There were conversations that failed and needed to be revisited. There was the specific difficulty of building trust that had been broken—not the performed version, but the real kind, which grew slowly and could not be rushed. She had refused to pretend it had arrived before it truly had.

But it had arrived. Or the beginning of it had.

She had told Tasha in the spring, "I think we're actually building something. Not the old thing. Something I didn't have a name for before."

"What does it feel like?" Tasha asked.

April thought about it. "Like the new running route," she said finally. "The one I found after the reckoning. The street I didn't know was there. It's different from the old route—better in ways I couldn't have anticipated, because I couldn't see the bakery from the old path."

Tasha had laughed. "You're going to make me use that metaphor forever."

"Good. It's the right one."

The thing with Angel had taken the time it needed, a lesson in the patience April had been cultivating. She had said "slowly" and meant it. "Slow" had been the right pace—not because of uncertainty, but because the real version of something built deliberately was superior to a performed version built in haste.

Across eighteen months of Sunday documentaries, honest conversations, and the gradual dissolution of every managed distance, it had become the most specific bond April had ever shared. It didn't fit the conventional architecture of romance; they had found the standard vocabulary insufficient, deciding that the lack of a label was not a problem to be solved, but a feature of something truly unique.

Angel was the person who understood the full map. She had been present for the warehouse, the house, the upper level, the reckoning, and the healing—not just as an observer, but as someone inside them, navigating her own adjacent versions of each. She was the one who sat in April's apartment on Sunday evenings and folded her sweater before she left, even if she'd fallen asleep in it. She was the one who saw Dr. Coleman twice a week and had stopped running the pattern toward the "adjacent thing," learning instead to go straight at what she actually wanted.

And then there was the question that had begun in the blue television light, now fully arrived and fully answered. April had taken the time to know it accurately. She was not performing a certainty; she had arrived at it slowly, in the full light, and it was real.

She had said as much to Angel on a Sunday in February— the second February, eight months into their deliberate, illuminated version of "us"—sitting on the balcony with the cold air doing its sharp, useful thing.

She had said, "I know what this is now. I'm not calling it something else anymore."

Angel had been quiet for a long time. Then she had said, "Tell me."

And April had. In the specific language she had been building across three years of deliberate work—not the performed version, not the vocabulary that was insufficient, but the true thing in the truest words she had.

Angel had said, "I've been waiting for that for longer than you know."

April had said, "I know. I'm sorry it took so long."

Angel had said, "It took exactly as long as it needed to. That's not an accident."

It was not an accident.

She still went to the house. This surprised some people—and would have surprised more if she felt the need to explain it—but she had found no reason to justify herself to anyone who didn't already understand. The house was not a phase she had passed through on the way to the rest of her life; it was part of the architecture of it. It was no longer the urgent need for permission that had brought her to the entrance hall three years ago, but something that had evolved alongside her.

She returned now the way one returns to a place that has given them something vital: with gratitude and without urgency. She moved with the specific ease of someone who knows what she is looking for, how to find it, and what to do with what she finds. The house had given her the permission, and she carried it with her now—inside her own body, internalized rather than borrowed. She did not need the house to know who she was, but she went because it was where she had become herself. Returning was its own form of honoring that becoming.

She had brought Angel once, in the spring, to the main floor and the fountain. She had not brought Jason. This was not a decision made against him, but a decision about what the house represented. It was hers—specifically and fundamentally hers—in the way a small number of things in a life must remain a person's own to stay real.

She had not returned to the upper level. It wasn't because she was unready, but because she had found what she needed there and carried it out. The carrying was sufficient. There was a version of herself who might return someday, in a different configuration, for something she could not yet name. She held that version as a possibility rather than a plan. She had learned the difference between the two.

She had made a change at work in the spring of the second year that she had been building toward without knowing it across the entire eighteen months. She had applied for a clinical supervisor position that her director had mentioned in passing—the kind of position she would have quietly decided was not hers three years ago, would have filed under other people's ambitions without examining whether it could be hers. She had examined it. She had applied. She had gotten it.

The work was harder and more interesting and required of her the specific combination of clinical precision and genuine presence that she had been developing all along, that the year of interior work had produced as a professional outcome she had not anticipated when she started. She supervised six clinicians now, each at a different stage of their own development, each requiring the specific kind of attention that was hers to give— the attention that saw the gap between where someone was and where they were working to be, and met them in that gap without judgment and without the performed warmth that was really just discomfort with difficulty.

Her mother had said, at dinner in July, "You're different at work. I can hear it when you talk about it."

April had said, "I'm more myself at work. I think that's what you're hearing."

Cynthia had looked at her across the dinner table with the expression that contained both the assessment and the thing under the assessment—the woman who had sat for two hours without speaking in a hospital waiting room, who had said *I'm proud of you* on a Tuesday phone call when it mattered. "Yes," she said. "That's it exactly."

Jason picked her up at noon with the specific efficiency of someone who had learned her rhythms and honored them—on time, not early, devoid of the performance of punctuality. They drove to the community pool they had discovered in June on an afternoon when neither of them had a plan, finding themselves driving with the windows down in the particular, aimless pleasure of a summer Saturday.

The pool was not extraordinary. It was a public space with adequate lanes and the specific scent of chlorine and summer that April now associated with the pleasure of being in the water—a sensation she had not expected, eighteen months ago, to ever enjoy. Jason had taught her throughout the summer with the patient attention of someone who understood that the teaching was also a way of being in the water himself. He was a good teacher; he had learned how to inhabit the pool by helping her navigate it.

She swam ten laps without stopping—something that would have been impossible in June, but which she could do now without drama, simply the steady application of a learned skill. She pulled herself up at the end and sat on the pool's edge, the sun on her shoulders and the smell of chlorine around her, and watched Jason finish his own laps with the smooth, unhurried efficiency of someone who had been in this water since he was nine years old.

He pulled up beside her. They sat together on the edge in the September sun.

"Good," he said. She had come to love the economy of it—not *good job*, not *you did it*, just *good*. It said: *I see you, and what I see is sufficient.*

"Getting there," she said.

He nodded. They sat in the sun and let the afternoon be exactly what it was.

The Sunday before the pool, Angel had come over with Thai food and the newest documentary—bioluminescent plankton, the ocean still producing its extraordinary inventory of things that made their own light. She had stayed until ten and hadn't fallen asleep this time, a small piece of evidence of where they stood. She folded her sweater before she left, as she always did, and paused at the door in the particular way that had become their own private language across eighteen months.

April said, "Next Sunday."

Angel said, "Next Sunday."

And then—because they were in the full light now, because the vocabulary had been built and the slow, deliberate version of them had produced something real enough to be acted on without performance—April stepped forward. She moved in the way she had learned to move when she had decided something and was enacting that decision. Angel was there to meet her. What happened in the doorway of April's apartment on that Sunday evening in September was both entirely its own thing and the logical culmination of everything the year before had been.

April stood in her doorway afterward and watched the elevator take Angel down. She thought: *There it is.* It was not the echo of the first time she had thought those words—standing in her apartment in her coat after her first visit to the house, three years ago. This was the full version. The arrived version.

The first time she had thought: *There is the permission.*

This time she thought: *There is the thing itself.*

The difference between those two thoughts was the distance the novel had traveled.

On the drive home from the pool, Jason put Tupac on the stereo without asking, which he did now because he knew—not the full story, not the warehouse, not the specific architecture of what the music meant. But enough. The *enough* that came from eighteen months of paying attention to a person you were building something with.

She sat in the passenger seat with her damp hair and the September light and Tupac's voice doing what it always did— finding her in the specific place the music had always found her, the place where her mother was and the girl she had been and the woman she was becoming simultaneously—and she felt the specific quality of an arrival.

Not the finished version. She was clear-eyed enough to know she was not finished, that finishing was not the point, that Renee had been right: *If you think you're finished, you've stopped being interesting.* She had not stopped being interesting to herself. She did not intend to.

She had arrived at the clearest configuration of herself she had ever inhabited. Her life was no longer managed around the edges of who she was, but built from the interior outward—constructed from the ground she had cleared, the permission she had found, the wall she had thinned, and the choosing that was now irrevocably hers.

She thought about the photograph on her nightstand: the house on the hill, its upper windows lit from within. She had taken it on a March Saturday from the side of the road, sitting in her car for ten minutes without knowing why she had stopped. She had gone home, sat with that knowledge for six weeks, and then finally walked through the door.

Everything that followed had begun at that threshold.

She thought of the other doors: the mirror room, the corridor, the staircase to the upper level, the balcony conversation, the kitchen table, the reckoning, the healing, and the apartment doorway last Sunday. She viewed them all as doors, each opened in her own time and at her own speed. Each led to the next—not because the future was visible from the threshold, but because she was the kind of person who, once she opened a door, walked through it.

She thought: *There are still doors I haven't seen yet.*

She thought: *Good. That is the point.*

Jason turned off the highway. The September afternoon was doing its precise, beautiful thing. She looked at the city approaching—Atlanta in early fall, specific and hers, a place she had chosen that had given back more than she had ever come looking for.

She thought about Angel's text from that morning, which she had yet to answer: *Brought you something back from the farmers market. Leave it outside your door?*

She thought about Dr. Osei's question from Tuesday's session—the best one yet, and one April was still sitting with: *What would you do next, if you trusted yourself completely?*

She thought about her caseload. She thought about the clinician she was supervising who was three months from her own breakthrough and didn't know it yet. She thought about the work that was hers and was good, made better by everything she had become.

She thought about the pool. About swimming ten laps without stopping. About the year before, when she could not have done it, and this year, when she could—and the year ahead, when she would do more.

She thought: *I am not the woman who pulled over on that March Saturday. I am the woman that woman was becoming. And I am not finished becoming.*

Jason parked. He looked at her.

"Still thinking?" he asked.

"Always," she said.

"Good," he replied. The economy of it. The sufficiency.

She got out of the car. She stood on the sidewalk in the September afternoon with the faint scent of chlorine on her skin and the rhythm of the music still moving through her. Her life was arranged around her—not perfect, not finished, and certainly not simple. It was real. It was hers. It was built from the interior outward.

She thought: *I want to see what comes next.*

She walked toward the door.

— END —

EPIC TALES BOOKS

Finding Joy: My Life Began
When I Pawned The Ring

Joy Elise Fox was born in Scotland in 1935 and lived in England until 1958, when her family emigrated to Vancouver, BC, Canada. She was educated in England and continued her self-education in Canada by taking courses at colleges and universities related to her fields of interest during her working life.

Throughout her career, Joy has earned multiple certifications and diplomas, including a B.Sc. in International Relations. Her dedication and achievements have earned her several awards and media recognition.

Joy's professional experience spans both government and private sectors in Canada and England, where she held various roles in commercial real estate, research, engineering, automotive, hospitality, and tourism – each involving liaison and communication functions.

In 1990, she founded Conference Management Services, specializing in meeting planning. She also utilized her certification from The Protocol School of Washington to offer protocol and etiquette training for adults and children.

A pivotal milestone was the founding of the Canadian Association of Independent Meeting Planners (now CanSPEP) in 1996, where Joy served as the first president. The organization celebrated its 30th anniversary in Regina in 2026, and in 2006, Joy received the Joy Fox Award for Innovation, Vision, and Leadership, which was named in her honour.

Joy's community involvement has been extensive, volunteering in every community she has called home. Her activities include work within the meetings industry, community organizations, and participation in choirs and dance groups. Notably, she sang with the band Remember When for 20 years, managing their banking and website design, and appeared on several of their CDs.

Currently, Joy is a member of the JourneyWoman Advisory Council, an organization dedicated to supporting women over 50 in travel. In 2024, she was honoured with the inaugural Evelyn Hannon Award for Solo Travel. She continues to enjoy solo travel and celebrates each birthday with enthusiasm.

Her media presence has been consistent throughout her life, including TV, radio, newspapers, and magazines. The viral article by the BBC following her JourneyWoman Award further increased her recognition.

Now residing in Parksville, BC, on Vancouver Island, Joy relishes her beautiful garden. She is working on another memoir. Her hobbies include painting, knitting, writing,